Text Classics

PETER CORRIS was born in Victoria in 1942, and did his undergraduate degree at the University of Melbourne. He took a doctorate in history from the ANU, but in the mid-1970s he left academia for journalism. From 1980 to 1981 he was literary editor of the *National Times*.

Corris's first Cliff Hardy novel, *The Dying Trade*, was published in 1980. It not only introduced a sleuth who was to become an enduring legend, but was also a long love letter to the seamy side of Sydney itself. Over more than three decades Corris has now written thirty-seven Cliff Hardy books, and the city of Sydney is as significant a presence in the books as the figure of Hardy. The third in the series, *The Empty Beach*, was in 1985 made into a film starring Bryan Brown. In 1999 Corris was presented with a Ned Kelly Lifetime Achievement Award.

Peter Corris is the author of more than sixty titles in all. He has written both historical fiction and other crime series. He has also worked extensively in non-fiction, including an as-told-to autobiography of the Australian eye surgeon Fred Hollows, and books on sport and history. He lives in New South Wales with his family.

CHARLES WATERSTREET is author of the memoirs *Precious Bodily Fluids* and *Repeating the Leaving*. He was co-creator of *Rake*, the award-winning ABC series. He is currently writing the third volume of his memoirs.

ALSO BY PETER CORRIS

Recent titles from the Cliff Hardy Series
Comeback
Follow the Money
Torn Apart
Deep Water

Selected non-fiction
Heart Matters: Personal stories about that heart-stopping moment
  (ed. with Michael Wilding)
Fred Hollows: an autobiography (with Fred Hollows)
Fighting for Fraser Island: the autobiography of John Sinclair
  (with John Sinclair)
Ray Barrett (with Ray Barrett)
Best on Ground: Great writers on the great game (ed. with John Dale)
Lords of the Ring: A social history of prize fighting in Australia

The Dying Trade
Peter Corris

Text Publishing Melbourne Australia

The Text Publishing Company acknowledges the Traditional Owners of the country on which we work, the Wurundjeri people of the Kulin Nation, and pays respect to their Elders past and present.

Proudly supported by Copyright Agency's Cultural Fund.

petercorris.net
textclassics.com.au
textpublishing.com.au

The Text Publishing Company
Wurundjeri Country, Level 6, Royal Bank Chambers, 287 Collins Street, Melbourne, Victoria 3000 Australia

First published by McGraw Hill Australia 1980
This edition published by The Text Publishing Company 2012
Reprinted 2021

Cover design by WH Chong
Page design by WH Chong & Susan Miller
Typeset by Midland Typesetters

Printed in Australia by Griffin Press, an Accredited ISO AS/NZS 14001:2004 Environmental Management System printer

Primary print ISBN: 9781921922176
Ebook ISBN: 9781921981339
Author: Corris, Peter, 1942-
Title: The dying trade / by Peter Corris ; introduction by Charles Waterstreet.
Series: Text classics.
Other Authors/Contributors: Waterstreet, Charles.
Dewey Number: A823.3

CONTENTS

Brick by Brick
by Charles Waterstreet

AUSTRALIA started its white life at a distinct advantage in the telling of criminal stories. Everyone was a criminal. But until Peter Corris invented Cliff Hardy and introduced him in *The Dying Trade* in 1980, we had, as with many of our natural resources, left great seams of these stories in the ground for others to find. Corris may have forged the international reputation of Australian crime fiction almost single-handedly, but I could be wrong, as he uses two hands to type. The waters of the Mississippi and the Potomac might flow through his novels, but his work tastes definitely and defiantly of the Murray Darling, or rather the big beautiful bowl of salty blue water contained in Sydney Harbour. Hardy patrols the city shoreline as if it were his own private verandah. He knows that crime infects all levels of society, under every rock is a paedophile spider, money is always in the wrong hands, the rich abuse their privileges and the poor, physically, sexually and socially. Hardy must work in a conspiracy of one to carve the rot from the good fruit. He does not solve cases so much as create a chaos within the frenzy of plot until secrets fall out of the characters' pockets when he turns their worlds upside down.

The *Atlantic* recently published a song of praise to the brilliant strangeness of Australian crime fiction. Corris was identified as one who gives 'no special thought to the foreign reader'. This accounts for the celebration of his work in literary circles. He writes in Australia, about Australia and about Australians, and by being specific he communicates something that can be read internationally. Australian films have flopped, year after year, by following and imitating American trends. The *Atlantic* identified the mateship tradition in the fierce 'joshing camaraderie' that exists in Australia generally but not in America, save occasionally in frat houses. In our country there is a subterranean reflexive prickliness between everyone. Stephen Knight talks of 'dryly aggressive wit'. Our verbal blows often fall on deaf ears in foreign countries. We are a nation of smart-arses, ready to joust with anyone.

All this gives Corris another colour to add to the mix. He brings a quick-drying cement to his sentences, where his genius for metaphor lays the words down, brick by brick. We read with a constant suppressed smile, admiring every simile, aghast such serious detective work could be so funny and deadly at the same time. His writing is as arresting and as easy on the eyes as a blonde tanning on Bondi Beach. He captures the permanent smirk on Australian faces and puts it into short bursts of language like rapid fire from a machine-gun. Everyone is in on the joke, all coppers are crooked. It's just a matter of degree.

In *The Dying Trade* Corris's hero travels in traffic 'which was thick and moving as slow as a senile snail'. His women clients are *femmes fatales*: one of them has her 'eyes shut tight as if she wanted to blind herself'. Detail is king in crime fiction. On arriving at a small coastal town, Hardy discovers that 'the streets were as quiet as a Trappist prayer meeting'. Corris is even-handed in dispensing the best lines to his characters. He is a democratic author; his hero is often outwitted, out-wisecracked and out-thought. He has ethical standards and like Adlai Stevenson he is a man of principle but his first principle is flexibility. Corris gives Hardy's client Ailsa, with whom he has more conflicts of interest than a bookie taking his own bets, this exchange:

> I rolled two cigarettes, gave one to Ailsa and lit them. After a few puffs she butted it out.
> 'I'm going to stop smoking, really! Stop tempting me!'
> 'You never know how strong you are till you know how weak you are.'

'Bullshit!'

'Yes, yes it is.'

I sat down on the bed and ran my fingertips down her arm.

'I'm getting better,' she said, 'I won't break.'

I leaned down and kissed her. After a minute she pushed me back. She smoothed down her cap of hair and gave me a look that reminded me that she was paying my hire.

'Well, you certainly broke her up,' she said.

'I didn't mean to, but it was bound to happen.'

'I suppose so, I've never had any children, you?'

'No.'

'They make you vulnerable.'

'You're vulnerable anyway.'

'Oh, profound.'

'That's me.'

I meant it though and I was considering how to face her with her own little piece of vulnerability right then. I couldn't think of any subtle way and it probably wasn't necessary.

'Do you want to know who Susan's son is?'

'Yes of course, you've been detecting?'

His characters couldn't be played by foreign stars. Bryan Brown, who portrayed him in *The Empty Beach*, even smells like Cliff Hardy. When we read Corris, we see ourselves, we laugh at ourselves, we cringe at ourselves, and finally we understand ourselves a little better. He reflects the way in which the Australian psyche is imprisoned by its past, the way we walk as if in invisible shackles, our arms handcuffed by our sides instead of raised in outrage. He holds the mirror up to Australian society at a very funny angle that seems about right, a slight angle to the universe. Try this:

> Ailsa was sitting up in bed wearing a white cheese-cloth nightgown. She had no make-up on and had lost a lot of colour in her face, her eyes were shadowed and huge so that she looked pale and fragile like a French mime. The bronze hair was newly washed and a bit curly and she had a scrubbed clean look as if she was about to be delivered somewhere. Her face and lips were still puffy and bruised, but when she looked up from her book she managed to work her features into a smile.
>
> 'Hardy,' she said, 'the great protector.'

Corris has won a Ned Kelly Lifetime Achievement Award for Crime Writing. He has been called the 'godfather of Australian crime writing'. He has written thirty-seven crime novels and has made more out of crime than any barrister I know. What is remarkable is the consistency of excellence in tone and in his impeccable ear for the peculiarities of dialogue between strangers, friends, lovers and enemies. Without Corris, there would be no *Underbelly* series, or dare I say *Rake*, no Australian accent in our crime fighters, criminals, victims, coppers; no Australian point of view in the very stuff of our own restless history.

Cliff Hardy represents the true Australian male at his best: a larrikin, despising greed and conservatism, living hand-to-mouth while cursing the affluence around him. He treats every client as if he or she were a potential hostile witness who will be giving evidence against him one dark day in the future. He has the perfect CV for a PI: ex-army (Malaya), law school drop-out, a real Bra Boy in Maroubra before they had to gang up to make an impression, an ex-insurance investigator who asked too many questions; and finally, like his creator, he comes equipped with an inbuilt bullshit detector.

Corris has outstanding academic qualifications in history and journalism that he does not allow to infect his writing at all. He writes with no hint of self-importance or showing off. He hides his many bright lights under many bushels. He draws chalk lines around victims while they are still walking and talking. In *The Dying Trade* we experience foreboding, dread, prickly anticipation and a real sense of satisfaction that we are in the hands of a master storyteller, a true magician who could pull a rabbit out of a hat at any time—and shoot it dead.

The Dying Trade

For Jean

BOOK ONE

BOOK ONE

CHAPTER 1

I was feeling fresh as a rose that Monday at 9.30 a.m. My booze supply had run out on Saturday night. I had no way of replenishing it on the Sabbath because we still had Sunday prohibition in Sydney then. I didn't have a club; that'd gone a while before, along with my job as an insurance investigator. I also didn't have a wife—not any more—or friends with well-filled refrigerators. Unless I could be bothered driving twenty-five miles to become a bona fide traveller, Sunday could be as dry as a Mormon meeting hall. I didn't travel. I spent the day on Bondi beach and the evening with tonic water and Le Carré, so I was clear-headed and clean-shaven, doodling on the desk blotter, when the phone rang.

"Hardy Investigations?"

"Yes, Cliff Hardy speaking."

"Good. Mr Hardy, I need your help. You've been recommended."

I could think of perhaps ten people who'd mildly recommend me. None of them would know the owner of this voice—eight hundred dollars a term, plenty of ordering people about and international travel.

"Yeah, who by?"

He named a name and I heard a faint bell ring. An insurance area boss or something, a hundred years ago. Still, it was a better start than the faded wives whose husbands had taken a walk or the small businessmen with payroll panic.

"Who am I talking to?"

"My name is Gutteridge, Bryn Gutteridge."

That didn't mean anything to me. There are three million people in Sydney, maybe a hundred are named Gutteridge and I didn't know any of them.

"What can I do for you, Mr Gutteridge?"

Mr Gutteridge didn't want to say too much on the phone. The matter was delicate, urgent and not for the police. He said he wanted advice and possibly action and asked if I could come out to see him that morning. Maybe he wanted to see if I was the advising or the active type. I felt active.

"I ask for a retainer of two hundred dollars, my fees are sixty dollars a day and expenses. The retainer's returnable if nothing works out, the daily rate starts now."

He spoke as if he hadn't heard me.

"I'm glad you're free. The address is 10 Peninsula Road, Vaucluse. I'll expect you in an hour."

"The money's OK then?"

"Oh yes, fine."

He hung up. I leaned back in my chair and dropped the receiver onto the handset. I traced a dollar sign with my little finger in the dust beside the dial. Money would be no object to that voice; it came from a world of Bible-fat cheque books and credit cards that would get you anything, anytime.

I left the office, went down two flights of stairs and out into St Peters Street. It was hot already, and a dry wind was pushing the exhaust fumes and chemical particles down the throats of the people in the street. I went round the corner, down a lane and into the backyard behind the tattoo parlour. The tattooist lets me park my car there for ten bucks a week. I backed the Falcon out into the lane and headed north.

Gutteridge's address fitted his voice. Vaucluse is several million tons of sandstone sticking out into Port Jackson. The sun always shines on it and the residents think it vulgar to talk about the view. I permitted myself a few vulgar thoughts as I pushed my old Falcon along the sculptured divided highway which wound up to the tasteful mansions and shaven lawns. Mercs and Jags slipped out of driveways. The only other under-ten-thousand-dollar drivers I saw were in a police Holden

9

and they were probably there to see that the white lines on the road weren't getting dirty.

Bryn Gutteridge's house was a steel, glass and timber fantasy poised on the very point of a Vaucluse headland. It stretched its sundeck out over the sandstone cliff as if rebuking Nature for lack of imagination. The Falcon coughed its way through the twenty-foot high iron gates which were standing open and I stopped in front of the house wondering what they'd think about the oil on the drive after I'd gone.

I walked up a long wood-block path to the house. A gardener working on a rose bed looked at me as if I was spoiling the landscaping. I went up fifty or sixty oregon timber steps to the porch. You could have subdivided the porch for house lots and marched six wide-shouldered men abreast through the front door. I stabbed the bell with a finger and a wide-shouldered man opened the door while the soft chimes were still echoing about in the house. He was about six feet two, which gave him an inch on me, and he looked like he'd been the stroke of the first rowing eight maybe ten years before when the school had won the Head of the River. His suit had cost five times as much as my lightweight grey model, but he still wasn't the real money.

"Mr Gutteridge is expecting me." I passed a card across into his perfectly manicured hand and waited. He opened the door with a piece of body language which stamped him as a man of breeding but a servant nonetheless. His voice was a deep, musical throb, like a finely played bass.

"Mr Gutteridge is on the east balcony." He handed the card back. "If you wouldn't mind following me?"

"I'd never find it on my own."

He let go a smile as thin as a surgeon's glove and we set off to discover the east balcony. The rich always have lots of mirrors in their houses because they like what they see in them. We passed at least six full-length jobs on the trek which put expensive frames around a thinnish man with dark wiry hair, scuffed suede shoes and an air of not much money being spent on upkeep.

The rowing Blue led me into the library cum billiard room cum bar. He stepped behind the bar and did neat, fast things with bottles, ice and glasses. He handed me two tall glasses filled with tinkling amber liquid and nodded towards a green tinted glass door. "Mr Gutteridge is through there sir," he said. "The door will open automatically."

That was nice. Perhaps I could have both drinks and take the glasses home with me if I asked. The oarsman shot his cuffs and went off somewhere, no doubt to fold up some untidy money. The door slid apart and I went out into the harsh sun. The balcony was got up like the deck of a ship with railings and ropes and bits of canvas draped about. I started to walk towards a man sitting by the railing in a deck-chair about twenty feet away. Abruptly I stopped. He was a picture of concentration, resting his arm on the railing and taking careful sight along it and the barrel of an air pistol. His target was a seagull, fat and white, sitting on a coil of rope ten yards from his chair. He squeezed the trigger, there was a sound like a knuckle cracking and the seagull's black-rimmed eye exploded into a scarlet blotch. The bird flopped down onto the deck and the man got up quickly from his chair. He took a dozen long, gliding strides and kicked the corpse under the rail out into the bushes below.

I felt sick and nearly spilled the drinks as I moved forward.

"That's a shitty thing to do," I said. "You Gutteridge?"

"Yes. Do you think so, why?"

Despite myself I handed him the drink—there didn't seem to be anything else to do with it.

"They're harmless, attractive, too easy to hit. There's no sport in it."

"I don't do it for sport. I hate them. They all look the same and they intrude on me."

I had no answer to that. I look like a lot of other people myself, and I've been known to be intrusive. I took a pull on the drink—Scotch, the best. Mr Gutteridge didn't look as if he'd be nice to work for, but I felt sure I could reach an understanding with his money.

Gutteridge stabbed a block of ice in his glass with a long finger and sent it bubbling to the bottom. "Sit

12

down Mr Hardy and don't look so disapproving." He pointed to a deck-chair, folded up and propped against the railing. "A seagull or two more or less can't matter to a sensible man and I'm told you are sensible."

I thought about that while I set down my drink and unfolded the deck-chair. It could mean a lot of things, including dishonest. I tried to look at ease in a deck-chair, which I wasn't, and intelligent.

"What's your trouble, Mr Gutteridge?"

He put the pistol down and sipped his drink. He was one of those people you describe as painfully thin. He had a small, pointed blonde-thatched head on top of shoulders so narrow they scarcely deserved the name. His bony torso and limbs swum about inside his beautifully cut linen clothes. He was deeply suntanned but didn't look healthy. Under the tan there was something wrong with his skin and his eyes were muddy. He didn't seem particularly interested in his drink so the cause of his poor condition might not be that. He was somewhere in his late thirties and he looked sick of life.

"My sister is being harassed and threatened," he said. "She's being goaded into killing herself—in strange ways."

"What ways?"

"Phone calls and letters. The caller and the writer seem to know a lot about her. Everything about her."

"Like what?"

13

"People she knows, things she does or has done, the perfume she wears. That sort of thing."

"Has she done anything special with anyone in particular?"

"I resent that Hardy, the implication . . ."

I cut in on him, "Resent away. You're being vague. Is this private information coming through damaging to your sister's reputation?"

He clenched his teeth and the skin stretched tight over the fine bones of his face. Letting my roughness pass exasperated him. He gave a thin sniff and took a tiny sip of his Scotch. "No, it's quite innocent—innocent meetings, conversations reported back to her. Very upsetting, almost eerie, but not what you're getting at. Why do you take this line?"

"She might be a blackmail prospect, the harassment could be a softening up process."

He thought about it. The outward signs were that he had good thinking equipment. He didn't ape the appearance of a mind at work by scratching things or screwing up his eyes. I rolled a cigarette and put my own tired brain into gear. I find that people are very reluctant to tell you the nub of their worries. Perhaps they think the detecting should start early, as early as detecting what they really have on their minds. The trick was to hit them with the right question, the one to open them up, but Bryn Gutteridge looked like a man who could keep his guard up and slip punches indefinitely.

14

"How's your drink, Hardy?"

"Like yours, barely touched."

"You're direct, that's good. I'll be direct too. My father committed suicide four years ago. He shot himself. We don't know why. He was prosperous, healthy, the original sound mind in the sound body." He looked down at his cadaverous frame. He was saying he wasn't sound himself, underlining the verbal picture of his father. There was something disembodied about him, fragile almost. I thought I had my question.

"How was his love life?"

He paid serious attention to his drink for the first time before he answered. He looked like Tony Perkins playing a suffering Christ.

"You mean how's mine," he said. "Or you mean that as well. You're an uncomfortable man, Hardy."

"I have to be. If I'm comfortable for you I'm comfortable all round and nothing gets done."

"That sounds right, glib perhaps, but right. Very well. *His* love life was fine so far as I know. He'd married Ailsa only about two years before he died. They seemed happy."

"Ailsa?"

"My stepmother. Ridiculous concept for grown people—my father's second wife. My mother and Susan's died when we were children. We're twins by the way, although we're not alike. Susan's dark like our father." I nodded to show that I was following him.

15

"My father was fifty-nine when he remarried. Ailsa was in her mid-thirties I suppose. As I say, they seemed happy." He jerked a thumb at the house. "He bought this to live in after he was married and he bought another place down there for Susan and me." He pointed down into the expensive air over the balcony. "He wanted us all to be close but independent."

It sounded about as independent to me as the pubs and breweries but Gutteridge didn't need telling. He finished his drink in a gulp and set the glass down. A real drinker, even if he paced himself, likes to have them end to end, gets nervous in the gaps. I knew the signs from personal experience and it was comforting to observe that Gutteridge wasn't a drunk. He ignored the glass and went on with his story without the support of liquor, another sign. He crossed his skinny ankles which were bare and black haired above long, narrow feet in leather sandals.

"Mark made a lot of money. He was a millionaire a few times over. Death duties took a lot of it, but there was still plenty left over for Susan and me. And Ailsa. I don't know why I'm telling you all this, we seem to be getting away from the matter at hand."

"I don't agree," I said. My drink was finished now and the tobacco between my fingers wasn't burning. I felt fidgety and ill at ease. Gutteridge's personality had had a strange effect on me, his words were hard and economical. He'd be a terror in the boardroom when he was trying to get his way. He made me feel flabby and self-indulgent, this in spite of what I'd seen of his failings and the fact that it was he who had the million dollars. Or more. I felt about for the words.

"Things are connected," I said. "It sounds obvious but sometimes the connections are extraordinary. I don't mean to sound Freudian, but I've known men who've beaten the life out of other people because of what happened to them when they were ten years old. There's a background, a connection to something else always. This trouble of your sister's, you can't expect to cut it out of your life, clean and simple. I'll have to look around, look back . . ."

"You're a voyeur," he snapped.

We were way back. He was feeling intruded upon and that, with him, was dangerous as I'd seen already. I tried to slip sideways.

"Tell me how your father made his money," I said. "And you could try thinking how it might link up with what's happening to your sister."

"Mark's was real estate money, of course," he said, sounding a bit too pat, as if he'd rehearsed the answer. "This place should tell you that. It's the ultimate development, the ultimate spiel. He sold people on this sort of thing and he believed in it himself."

"He was a developer then. Did he build houses himself?"

"Yes, hundreds, thousands."

"Good ones?"

"Fair, they didn't wash away in the first rain."

"He sounds like par for the course. What else did you know about his business?"

"I can't see what you're driving at."

"Enemies, people with grudges, visiting the sins of the father and all that."

"I see. Well, I don't think Mark had enemies. He didn't have many friends come to that, mostly business acquaintances, lawyers, a couple of politicians, senior administrative people, you know."

"I get the idea. Pocket friends, just as good as enemies any day."

"I don't think you do get the idea." He emphasised the words snakily. "My father was a warm and eloquent man, he won people to his point of view. He almost invariably got what he wanted. He pulled off some remarkable deals, some colossal gambles."

"You liked him?"

He looked down at the deck, the first evasive gesture he'd made.

"Yes," he said softly.

It was beginning to look to me as if Mark Gutteridge and his manner of departing this life were more interesting than his children's problems, but that wouldn't pay the bills, so I just nodded, rolled another cigarette and snuck a look at my glass.

"Would you like another drink?"

"After you tell me some more about your sister's problem. When it began and your ideas on it."

"About a month ago Susan got a phone call. It was from a woman with a foreign accent—French possibly. She talked to Susan about her underwear, what brands she bought and how much it cost."

"No heavy breathing?" I asked.

"Nothing like that at all. She said things that upset Susan very much. Mostly about the money Susan spends on clothes and things. It's rather a lot I suppose. Susan likes nice things, nice things cost money."

His silver spoon was shining; some nice things don't cost money and some things that cost money aren't nice.

"It doesn't sound particularly sinister to me," I said. "It could almost be funny. Why was your sister so upset?" I could guess at what was coming next, but I wanted to hear how he put it.

"Susan has a strong social conscience. She's involved on Community Aid Abroad, Amnesty International, Freedom from Hunger. She's very busy and devoted to these causes."

I could just bet she was. The sweat from all that devotion and business was probably running down into her crepe-de-chine knickers so fast that she had to change them three times a day. I was having trouble getting interested in Susan Gutteridge's troubles and beginning to suspect that this investigation wasn't going to bring out the best in me.

"There was more than one phone call? And you mentioned letters?"

"Yes, calls have come at all hours of the day and night. The Voice—that's what Susan calls it—goes on and on about her private life, tells her how useless and parasitic she is, how meaningless her life is. It . . . she . . . refers to our father and tells Susan to do the same thing, tells her that she's cursed and her suicide is ordained."

I felt more interested and asked again about the letters.

"I only have one to show you," he said. "Susan tore up another five or six, she's not sure how many." He stood up, six feet of bony, moribund elegance and took a folded sheet of paper from his hip pocket. He handed it to me and reached down for his air pistol.

"Please don't do that," I said.

He sneered at me. "You mentioned your fee and your terms on the telephone. You didn't say anything about your sensibilities." He slid back a lever on the pistol and checked a pencil-thin magazine of lead pellets. "Have another drink, Mr Hardy, and turn your attention to what you'll be paid for." He rammed home the lever. "Or piss off!"

I shrugged. Big men were raping little girls, fanatics were torturing each other and people were going mad in cells all over the world. A protest here and now seemed a vain and futile thing,

"I'll take the drink," I said.

"I thought you might." He moved along the deck to where it took a right-angle bend into what I supposed was the south balcony. His hand came up sharply and he squeezed the trigger six times. Fifty yards away the pellets rattled like hailstones against metal and glass.

"The drink's on its way." He weighed the pistol in his hand.

"This is the most fun I have," he said. He waved the thing at me like a conductor's baton, signalling me on. "Get on with it!"

I got on. The paper could have been hand-rolled or beaten out with steam hammers for all I knew. It was a bit smaller all round than quarto and the words on it were in red ballpoint ink, printed in capitals like things of this kind usually are:

SUSAN GUTTERIDGE
YOU DESERVE TO DIE

Gutteridge hadn't fired his pistol while I was studying the note. He moved back to where I was sitting. He was tense, stretched tight.

"What do you think?"

"I don't know. I wish she'd kept the other notes. Did any of them mention money?"

He put the pistol down on the deck again and slumped down into the canvas chair. He was about to speak when the rower came out onto the deck carrying a tray with the drinks aboard. Gutteridge nodded at him in the first friendly gesture I'd seen him produce. He took one of the glasses and sipped it. "Just right, Giles," he said. Giles looked pleased in a well bred way and extended the tray to me. I took the glass and put it down beside me. I thought Giles was all right but Gutteridge seemed to think he was something more than that. He picked up the threads.

"Money, no I don't think so. Susan didn't say and I think she would have. I think the other notes were in the same vein as this, getting more savage."

"In what way more savage?"

He spread his hands and took a deep, tired breath. "I didn't see them all. One I did see said that Susan was sick. Another one said she was rotten. That's what I meant, sickness, rottenness, death."

"I see, yes. I still think this could be connected with your father's death in some way. But I suppose you've thought of that too?"

"No, I hadn't, but you've had experience of this sort of thing I presume, and I can see why the thought suggests itself. I don't think it's likely though."

This was better. He was beginning to afford me some field of expertise and it looked as if I might get enough cooperation from him to allow me to do the job. The sister was an unknown quantity at this point and my prejudiced snap judgment about her on the basis of the little I'd been told might be inaccurate.

"What do you think is likely then?" I asked.

"A crank I suppose, someone who gets kicks from baiting the rich."

"Maybe. Any political angle?"

"I shouldn't think so, we're not at all politically-minded, Susan and I."

Of course not, with their money you don't have to be. You win with heads and you win with tails, one way or another. But it would be easy enough to check whether or not Susan's actions had offended some part of the lunatic fringe.

"I have to know more about your sister, obviously," I said, "I'll have to talk to her. Where is she now?"

"She's in a clinic at Longueville. I suppose I could arrange for you to see her if you think it's essential."

"I do. She took all this so badly that she had to go into a clinic?"

"Partly this business," he said slowly. "Partly that, but there are other things involved. My sister is a diabetic and as I said she keeps very busy. She neglects her diet and regimen and her health suffers. She spends a week or so in Dr Brave's clinic a few times a year to recover her balance."

I nodded. I was thinking that my mother was a diabetic and she often went off the rails, but she didn't go into clinics, just ate apples and drank milk instead of beer for a while. But then, she died at forty-five. Money helps. "A diabetic clinic doesn't sound too

23

formidable," I said. "No reason why I shouldn't see her if they had some notice."

He looked uneasy. "Dr Brave's clinic isn't exclusively for diabetics. It's for people who need care in different ways. Some of them need mental care. I'm not wholly in favour of the place but Susan won't hear a word against the doctor. She always seems rested and secure when she comes out so I go along with it."

He didn't like going along with anything that wasn't his idea, but his sister was his weak spot apparently. She was responsible for my being here talking to him and he didn't altogether like it. He seemed anxious for our talk to end.

"I'll give you the address of the clinic and telephone to let them know you're coming. When will I say?"

"This evening, about seven or eight."

"Why not this afternoon? What will you be doing then?"

They're all the same, rich or not rich, when they're paying for your time they want to see you running. Perhaps he thought I'd spend the day knocking down his retainer in a pub and doctoring the odometer on my car. I had a feeling that there was more to learn from him, perhaps just a point or two but they could be important. To get them I had to sting him.

"I'll be checking on things," I told him, "including you. It's standard procedure. Perhaps you could save me time and your money by telling me some more."

He bristled. "Like what?"

"Like how do you keep this going? Like what share in it does your sister have? Like where can I find your . . . stepmother?"

"Her? Why in hell do you want to know?"

"The connections, that's where they might lead."

He looked straight at me with all the hardness back in his face. He was a capricious bird, intelligent, resentful of something and charming in a grim way, and these qualities washed across him alternately like intermittent rainstorms across a desert. He held up three skeletal fingers. "I'll answer your questions. One," he touched the tip of the first finger to his mouth and pulled it away, "Mark left his money well invested, it brings in now much more than he ever had. I sit on some boards, I own a couple of concerns outright and have interests in quite a few others. Two," he made the same gesture with the next finger, "Susan's interests are quite separate from mine. She *has* business dealings of course, here and in New Zealand and the Pacific. She did a tour of some of the places where her firms operated a couple of years ago. She's got a good business head, like me. Three," the finger flicked, "Ailsa lives in Mosman. She sold this house to me and bought one over there. I can give you the address."

He did and I clinched the arrangement by accepting his cheque for the retainer and three days at the rate I'd quoted. I was convinced that he had the money

25

in the bank to cover the cheque, but even if I hadn't been, I'd still have taken the cheque because it's nice to have your client's name on a piece of paper if you have to yell for help. I agreed to keep him regularly informed and not to worry Susan unduly. The only thing he said about his father's second wife was that I was on no account to bring her to his house. I agreed. Giles showed me out through the corridors and ball-rooms saying just what he'd said on the trip in, which was nothing.

I'd been in the house for over an hour so the gardener looked at me with new respect. I tried to look as if I always spent my Monday mornings with million-aires but I didn't quite bring it off. My car betrayed me by refusing to start. It caught just as the gardener was sauntering over with a supercilious smile on his face to give me a push. I sprayed a little gravel over him and took off on the long drive to the front gate. I didn't have to move over an inch to allow a white Bentley to go through the gate in the opposite direction at the same time as I did. The car was driven by a guy in a cap and through the grey tinted glass I caught a glimpse of a man whose face must have been paper-white in the sunlight, if he ever went out in it.

CHAPTER 2

My first stop was the Public Library. I parked the car over near Mrs Macquarie's Chair and walked through the Gardens. There were people in shorts, shirt sleeves and light cotton dresses sprawling on the grass and eating lunches. Flights of gulls came wheeling down when they spotted bits of thrown and discarded bread. I felt like telling them to stick to the public parks, they were safer there than at millionaires' mansions although the pickings mightn't be so good.

Who's Who and *Who Was Who* confirmed the outlines of the Gutteridge family picture as Bryn had given it to me. His father had been self-made, no old school ties and titled antecedents to back him up. He had remained a very private individual; there were few entries under the categories of clubs and interests. Horse-racing was his only spotlight activity. The only thing to cross-reference him under was "money". My researches turned up only two points of interest. One, Ailsa Gutteridge, nee Sleeman, had been married previously to James Bercer (deceased) who had been a tycoon on much the same scale and in much the same area of business as Gutteridge. Two, no Dr Brave was listed in the medical directory.

I walked back through the park. The rubbish of scores of lunches was being picked over by the birds and made me feel hungry. I drove home to Glebe, stopping only to pick up a flagon of white wine. I was thinking about Ailsa Gutteridge. I had a feeling that she might be a key to it all. If I was wrong I was prepared to try a new tack, but it's nice to get off on the right foot once in a while.

My place in Glebe is a small, two-storey sandstone terrace close to the dog track. I put most of the severance money I got from the insurance company down on it and in good months I can make the payments. The dog track is a convenient meeting-place for some transactions in my trade and, as they say, Glebe is one of those places where if you can't see a pub by looking both ways down the street then you must be standing outside one. The Falcon just squeezes into the back courtyard of the house which has two rooms up and three down. I cook, after a fashion, and listen to music on the bottom floor and sleep and read on the top.

I showered in the outhouse two feet away from the toilet and wolfed down a curried egg sandwich and several glasses of the wine. I put Nina Simone on the stereo partly for pleasure and partly to annoy my neighbour on the left. She sings the songs other people write better than they do, but for Dr Harry Soames, my neighbour, Dylan is king and Mitchell is queen so that Nina's versions of their stuff drives him beserk. Soames is an economist and when he isn't on sabbatical he spends his time under earphones or bitching about my not repairing the iron lace on the front of my house. Word is that he wants to buy me out to raise the tone of the street.

Three o'clock seemed as good a time as any to call on Ailsa Gutteridge. There wasn't anything useful I could say over the phone and if she wasn't home I could at least look her place over, ask around a bit about her and maybe wait a while. I eased the Falcon out of the courtyard by backing and filling. I find this relaxing, though Soames thinks it adds to the air pollution.

Sydney was sweltering. The roads were bubbling asphalt cauldrons and white-hot concrete paths to hell. Most people had managed to stay inside or find some shade, but there were several thousand of us who had to cook slowly inside mobile glass and steel ovens. The crawl through the city seemed endless and the traffic only began to move when it got onto the harbour bridge. Off the freeway into the precipitous harbourside streets, the drive became less of a military manoeuvre and more of a social occasion, with the big cars deferring to each other according to a fine, dollar-determined etiquette of their own.

Mosman looks nice from across the harbour and just as good up close. Mrs Gutteridge's house wasn't quite on top of the highest hill around but there was nothing blocking her view. The house was a gracious old brick job, very broad and deep with plenty of fresh paint on the woodwork and iron. A three-car garage at the side held a white Porsche sports car, a black Alfa Romeo sedan and a boat that looked eager to be off to Monte Carlo and quite capable of getting there.

I parked at a forty-five degree angle outside the house and was walking towards the front steps when I heard a scream. I ran in its direction between the Porsche and the Alfa. Glare from the swimming pool hit me and turned the world momentarily white, but I kept moving towards the two shapes at the far end of the pool. They were struggling and looked like frames from an undeveloped film. As my eyes and brain got back into cooperation I could see a tall, heavy built man trying to hold a woman by the strap of her halter top. He was taking swinging roundhouse slaps at her at the same time. The woman was past her first youth but she wasn't doing so bad; she was ducking some of the swings and getting in a few of her own. But he had the weight and reach on her and he must have landed a hard one to cause her to scream. I moved in behind him and shouted something. He let go and turned. He was hopelessly off balance and I hit him hard and low in the mid-section. All the breath went out of him and he collapsed on his knees by the side of the pool. The woman recovered fast. She stepped in neatly and tumbled him into the water with a half kick, half push to the shoulder. The water was shallow but he went under once and sprawled, spluttering for a minute before pulling himself half over the tiled edge.

The woman was trying to light a cigarette with hands that were shaking like a tall mast in a high wind. She got there, drew smoke deep and blew it out. Her breasts rose firm and full under the halter top and her kicking-men-into-the-pool leg and its partner were pretty nice too.

"You'd better go Ross," she said evenly. "Take the Alfa and leave it and the keys at the office." Ross was big but my punch and the ducking had knocked the fight out of him. His silk and gabardine slacks were going to need some expert laundry work and his suede shoes were probably beyond repair. Water dripped from his thick black hair down over a face that was still handsome despite a badly set broken nose and a criss-cross of scars around the eyes and mouth. His look suggested that he might try to laugh it off, but the woman's face was stony, so he turned away muttering under his breath and squelched off towards the garage. An engine roared a few seconds later. There was a crunch of metal on metal, then a screech of tyres on concrete. The engine noise rose then receded.

"Jesus Christ!" The woman shut her eyes and flicked viciously at her cigarette.

"Who was that?" I said.

"Nobody. Who the hell are you?"

I explained who I was as she poured us both tall glasses of lemon juice and tonic from the fixings on a slat table beside the pool. So far the Gutteridges I'd met seemed to be good at not drinking and kicking things into oblivion. I'd have preferred a bit more drinking and a bit more concern for the lower forms of life.

We sat down in garden chairs and I took a good look while I was talking. She was cool but exciting; there was a lot of work left in her but she looked as if she'd be very choosy about who got the job.

"Have you got any identification?" Her voice was breathy and there wasn't a lot of power in it. She sounded tired and she didn't look very interested in me as she handed back the documents.

"What can I do for you, Mr Hardy?" There was an ironic, unencouraging edge to the standard words. I put the papers away and took a sip of the drink. It quenched the thirst.

"This concerns your stepson and stepdaughter, Mrs Gutteridge."

"Sleeman!" she rapped out.

"Mrs Sleeman," I said quickly.

32

"Miss!"

"All right, Miss, but I'm still here to talk about the Gutteridges."

"That'd be right, private detectives are just about their style."

"What do you mean, Miss Sleeman? Have they used private inquiry agents before?"

She put out her cigarette, lit another immediately and looked at me through the fresh, blue smoke.

"I wouldn't know. Tell me what you want."

I rolled a cigarette and got it going before I answered. She was hard to fathom, she seemed uninterested but it might just have been that she was gathering the energy to be really antagonistic.

"Your stepdaughter's life has been threatened, your stepson wants to find out by whom."

"Let's call them Susan and Bryn, that step this and that routine makes me feel sick. Bryn wants to find out who and why, I presume?"

"The 'why' is my problem at the moment. 'Why' will tell me 'who', I hope."

"Perhaps not," she snapped. "I can think of lots of reasons to do down that little silvertail but they wouldn't necessarily have names attached."

"That's interesting," I said. "Give me some reasons."

She flexed her back, emphasising her best features, and stretched out her long brown legs. It was hard to

33

guess her age; the heavily tinted outsized sunglasses hid some of the signs, her cheekbones were high with the skin smooth and taut across them and her mouth was full of even, white teeth—but the rich can do a lot in those departments. Her figure was full, but firm looking, and if Ross had been taking liberties with her I could easily see why.

"I'm not very interested in this, Mr Hardy," she underlined the statement with a sigh and took in some cigarette smoke. "I don't like the Gutteridge children—that is Mark's children—I appreciate that they're grown-ups in the obvious way at least—for a lot of reasons that I don't care to go into with you. You'd better tell me something to capture my interest or you'll have to go. To be frank, you're boring me."

She pulled over a bottle of suntan lotion which had a $5.50 sticker on it and began rubbing it into her thighs. I gave her a brief version of what Bryn Gutteridge had told me which she listened to with enough attention to call me a dirty name for using the word "stepson" again. She snorted and choked on her third cigarette when I asked her if her late husband had had enemies.

"Hundreds," she said. "He swindled dozens of people, defrauded scores."

"What about you, Miss Sleeman, were you his enemy?"

She flicked the cigarette butt into the swimming pool and waved a hand back at the house.

34

"What do you think?"

I said I didn't know. She yawned and turned her head away to look at the twenty-foot high greenery which separated her swimming pool from her neighbour's. I had a feeling that she was working hard at her tough act but if so she was succeeding well enough.

"Go away, Mr Hardy. I have nothing to say to you. I'm just not interested."

"What are you interested in?"

"Not very much. Making more money, up to a point, and I read a lot."

"I bet you do."

She sneered at me very effectively which is an unusual thing for a woman to be able to do. "Don't try your hard-case masculine stuff on me, Mr Hardy." She lifted her head so that I could see her smooth, brown neck. "I'm forty, just about, I don't look it but I am and I haven't time to waste on men who are busy, busy at their little jobs."

I couldn't afford to let it go at that. I had too little to work on and I didn't want to be thrashing about in the dark when I spoke to Susan Gutteridge that evening. I looked her over again; heavy smoking but not drinking, at least not in the mid-afternoon. She wore a brief but not ridiculous swim-suit that looked as if it'd been wet and dry a few times. At the other end of the pool was a medium high diving board, with well-worn fibre matting. It looked like she dived, swam

35

in the pool and watched her weight. A lot of pool owners dangle their feet in the water while knocking back gin and sailing little boats made of their chocolate wrappers across it.

"You're the best forty I've ever seen," I said. "Who's your doctor? Dr Brave?"

She dropped the bored display of the goods pose. Off came the shades and a pair of hard eyes bored into me. She had a strong-boned face that had never been beautiful but which must always have been arresting, as it was now. A few wrinkles around her eyes put her out of her twenties, but I'd meant what I said. She looked like one of those tennis playing women you see on local courts on the weekends, not aping youth but actually retaining it in the planes of her face and body.

"Why did you say that?"

"About Dr Brave? I don't know. You look like someone who takes good care of yourself, possibly under medical advice. Bryn Gutteridge mentioned Brave this morning, his sister is at his clinic. Bryn's not too happy about it. It just came into my head that as you dislike Mark Gutteridge's son so much you might have a different taste in doctors."

Her hard shell was beginning to split a little. She lit another cigarette with trembling hands and dropped the gold lighter onto the paving. She scrambled for a bit with one hand before giving up and working hard on the cigarette. She looked up at me as if I might just possibly be worth a minute's thought. Her voice was raw with something more than tobacco smoke affecting it. "You're right and wrong at the same time. Bryn's been lying to you. He and Brave are as thick as thieves. Brave's his head-shrinker, handholder and I don't know what else. I detest him."

"Why?"

"I've said all I'm going to say. I don't care if I never see Mark's children again and that goes double for Brave. I want to be rid of the whole bloody crew of them." She stood up, tall and struggling for her natural composure which I'd somehow shattered. "Off you go, Mr Hardy. I'm going to try to have a sleep and forget you ever happened."

I took out one of my cards and put it on the arm of my chair. She didn't look at it and turned towards the house. I stood up, stiff and tense from the pressure exerted by her abrasive personality. I started to walk towards the garage, then I turned towards her.

"One last question, Miss Sleeman." The distance between us was widening.

"Yes?"

"Why isn't Dr Brave listed in the medical register?"

She turned her face towards me and howled, "Go away!" She jerked off her sunglasses and threw them blindly away from her. They sailed through the air, spiralling down like a disabled fighter plane and dropped into the pool.

"Why?" I shouted.

She clenched her fists by her sides and the face she lifted up was a mask of pain. She spoke harshly, grittily. "He's not a medical doctor, he's a psychologist from somewhere . . . Canada . . . somewhere. Now will you please go!"

She marched into the house and I went.

CHAPTER 3

I drove across to The Rocks and bought a paper from a barefoot kid in the public bar of the Eight Bells. The pub is tucked away in a crevice of the sandstone and claims to be directly descended from the first inn built by the waterside in Sydney and maybe it is. Its other main claim to fame is that Griffo drank and fought there, and since Griffo drank and fought in every pub in The Rocks this is incontestable. Seekers after authenticity are starting to discover the pub and pose a threat to its integrity, but for the moment it's holding its own against the pressure to become another unisex, unidrink playground. The counter tea, served early, was steak, salad and chips and I ordered it along with a litre carafe of the house plonk. This made me an eccentric in the saloon bar where workers in singlets were putting down beer with their food and a scattering of executives and trendies were drinking wine from bottles with theirs. They gave me a beer glass with the carafe which suited me fine.

The paper was full of the usual drivel—the Pope pronouncing on sex and politicians claiming to speak for the common man. The lead story was about Rory Costello—standover man and armed robbery expert, who'd been sentenced to twenty years in Long Bay. He'd escaped ten days ago and had been sighted simultaneously in Perth and Cairns. The steak was good and the wine fair. I ate and drank slowly and tried to make some sense of the information I had on the Gutteridge case so far.

I hadn't established any clear connection between the threats to Susan Gutteridge and the suicide of her father, if it was suicide. Bryn Gutteridge hadn't provided any connections out of his picture of his father—an honest, if forceful, businessman. Gutteridge's ex-wife had a different picture of him—unscrupulous and dishonest, with a thousand enemies, any one of whom could be taking it out on the daughter. This view of the late Gutteridge appealed to me most, but that could have been my bank balance and prejudices speaking. Against Bryn's story in general was that he had lied about his attitude to Dr Brave, or a lie was implied in what he'd told me. That is, if Ailsa Sleeman was telling the truth. She was a complex woman who'd seen two tycoon husbands off, but she had no obvious reason to lie on this point. It was easily checked, but that went for Bryn's story too. He seemed to be in dubious control of his cool. Maybe he lied about everything. Maybe he was an eccentric millionaire who liked to send private detectives on wild goose chases. Suddenly, that seemed like a clean, uncomplicated thing to do—to chase wild geese in northern Canada. I ate, drank, smoked and thought until it was time to go and meet the stricken sister.

Leafy Longueville features trees and water glimpses. There's some big money and a lot of middle-sized money around; the middling people are working to keep up with the big people who are looking across the Lane Cove river towards Hunters Hill, where everybody has big money, and wondering if they can afford the move. The people work outside the area, send their kids out of it to school and don't talk to each other. They spend their time cultivating high, privacy-making hedges and looking the other way.

At 7.15 Longueville is quiet. Hoses sprinkle on lawns and the big cars are all sitting in their garages. Nobody and nothing moves in the front grounds of the houses. The terraces and swimming pools out back could be awash with gin and naked women, but you'd never know from the street. The clinic was a block from the suburb's main road. That put it close to the river, and into the heart of the Hunters Hill envy zone. I didn't lock the Falcon because there are no car thieves in Longueville and I didn't take my gun because there are no muggings either. Longuevillians do their thieving in the city five days a week, nine to five, and they get away from it all at home. The Brave clinic was an assemblage of white brick buildings with tinted glass standing in an acre or two of lawn and trees. There were no fountains or benches of the kind that are supposed to soothe troubled minds. Rather the air was of tight security. There was a high cyclone fence with concrete-embedded posts and a glassed-in reception booth which looked a bit too well equipped electrically for the sort of place the clinic was supposed to be. Since my commando days I've always been tempted by cyclone fences—the sadistic instructors must have sent us over hundreds of the bastards at terrific risks to our virility—but not this one. It was wired up to blazes and looked as if sirens would wail if you touched it, while relaying TV pictures of your blackheads to the main block.

I walked up to the booth. Some distance from it a metallic voice bounced off my chest.

"Please state your business."

The guy in the booth leaned forward to look at me through the glass. He wore a white shirt, grey jacket and black tie. Through the thick glass his face was a pale, distorted blob. No microphones were visible. He just spoke in my general direction and I heard him loud and clear. I had to assume he could hear me.

42

"I have an appointment to see one of Dr Brave's patients at 7.30. My name is Hardy."

He pressed a button, a pane of glass slid back. He put his right hand through and snapped fingers tightly gloved in black leather.

"Identification please."

I fished in my pocket and pulled out the licence card. It looks like a student ID card and would get me into Robert Redford movies half-price if I looked twenty years younger and could stand Robert Redford. I handed the card over. More glass slid back and the guard looked me over critically like a Russian customs officer who can be satisfied as to your identification but is pretty unhappy that you exist at all. He nodded, handed back the card and pressed a button; a gate beside the booth swung open.

"Please walk up to the largest building ahead of you, Mr Hardy. Stay on the path all the way please."

I went through. There were a few lights up on poles and some in hatches at ground level. They focused on the wide, intricately laid brick path. There was no excuse for slipping off it onto the velvet grass but I dawdled off to the left and took a couple of steps on the sward just for the hell of it. Closed circuit security TV is even more boring than the public kind, and I might just have made someone's day.

Close up all the buildings had a severe practical look. The main block had heavyweight glass and timber doors at the top of a dozen steps. I went up, pushed them open with a featherlight touch and went into a cool, navy-carpeted lobby with a reception desk set at an artful angle. No blondes. A tall burly guy who looked like an Italian eased himself off the desk and stepped towards me. He was wearing a denim suit with knife edge creases and white shoes. His white silk shirt was open far enough to show a gold medallion nestling in a thatch of thick, black hair. His waist was slim, there was no flab on him and only a slight thickening of his features betrayed how many fights he'd been in. He looked as if he'd won most of them.

"Please come with me, Mr Hardy. Dr Brave is waiting for you."

He inclined his black pompadour towards a teak door at the end of the room. He'd said it before, more or less, but he was still having trouble wrapping his western suburbs Italian accent around the polite words. He was built for action and it was a pity to make him talk. He ushered me through the door and down a long corridor done up in the same style as the lobby. Glass-panelled doors opened off it at frequent intervals and the Italian plucked at my sleeve when I slowed down to take a look through one. The place was getting to me—it looked like a jail for people who were very rich and very sorry for what they'd done. I passed him on the left and pulled open the next door on that side.

"Interesting place this," I said, sticking my head into the room. Empty, sterile, with bars on the windows. A hand fell down on my shoulder and the fingers closed vice-like around the bone. He pulled me back as easy as a kid pulling on a wad of gum.

"Don't do that again, Mr Hardy."

"I'm sorry," I said. "Just curious." I had a feeling that he was trying to hurry me through this part of the building. I wondered why.

"Don't be."

We were side by side when we reached the next door on the right. I hunched myself and cannoned into him blasting him against the wall. I opened the door and stepped in. He recovered fast and moved towards me. When he was half-way through the opening, I swung the door back full into him. He took some of it in the face, some at the knee and the handle in the solar plexus. He collapsed like a skyscraper in an earth-quake. I turned around to look at the room. I caught a glimpse of a man with a bandaged face sitting on a bed before I felt like I'd been dumped by a gigantic wave: a ton of metal tried to tear my head from my shoulders and sandbags crashed into my belly and knees. I went down into deep, dark water watching a pin-point of light which dimmed, dimmed and died.

Everything hurt when I swam up out of the dark. I tried to slide down into it again but I was slapped hard across the face and pulled up into a sitting position on a short, hard couch. I turned my head painfully and saw the Italian dusting off his hands. He looked bad—one side of his face was a purple smear and he stood awkwardly, favouring one leg. But he was on his feet and in better shape therefore than me. Sitting behind a table in the middle of the room was the man I'd seen pulling into Gutteridge's driveway in the Bentley. His face had the colour and texture of chalk. His hair was jet black and there was black hair on the backs of his hands. His eyebrows were thick, black bars that met in the middle; he looked like a chessboard come to life. His voice was soft with a burr that could have been Scots but might have been the echoes and rings inside my head.

"You have been very foolish, Mr Hardy. You were asked to observe certain civilities. May I ask why you did not?"

"I wasn't asked, I was told." My voice seemed to come from somewhere behind me but it would have hurt too much to turn and look. "This place made me feel rebellious."

"Interesting. It's supposed to have the opposite effect. But never mind. The question is, should you be allowed to see the person you've come to see after this behaviour? I have my doubts."

I swung my legs off the couch and wrestled myself into a less invalid position. I felt in my pocket for my tobacco, then I noticed that Brave had the contents

46

of all my pockets neatly arranged in front of him. He waved a hand at the Italian who reached over to the desk top, picked up my tobacco and matches and tossed them into my lap. I rolled a cigarette, lit it and drew the smoke deep. It caught halfway down where everything felt loose from the moorings and I gasped for breath and spluttered. The Italian clouted me hard enough on the back to clear the smoke and rearrange some organs.

"Gently Bruno," said Brave, "Mr Hardy's had a nasty fall."

My voice was wheezy and thin. "You can't stop me seeing her," I said, "not when her brother's OK'd it."

Brave smiled. "Her brother's not her keeper," he said.

"Who is? You?"

"In a way, but not as you may think. Miss Gutteridge is in poor health physically, and she has been under severe strain. Being questioned by a roughneck detective could do her great damage."

Bruno cracked his knuckles to remind me that I wasn't the only roughneck around. I had been out-muscled and now I was having professional rank pulled on me. It seemed time to fight back.

"You're not a medical doctor. I checked the register. What are you, a PhD? They're drip-dry on the hook I hear, at some places."

It upset him. He lifted a hand to his ear and pulled the lobe gently down. He dropped the hand to push my things contemptuously around on the desk.

"Your qualifications are here," he said. "Sleazy and sordid. And your physical powers seem ordinary. What point are you trying to make by insulting me?"

"At the most," I said, "you're a psychologist. You may not even be that, reputably. You're not a psychiatrist, that needs a medical degree. I question your professional and legal right to prevent me seeing anyone at all, especially someone whose nearest of kin has endorsed me."

He gave it some thought, then spoke rapidly, the accent now twanging angrily in his voice. "Who told you that I was a psychologist?"

"I could have worked it out myself," I said, "but since you ask, Ailsa Sleeman."

"I see. Did she know you were coming here?"

"Yes," I lied.

"Who else?"

I kept lying. "A guy named Ross, Miss Sleeman's boyfriend; my answering service; a petrol station attendant I asked directions from; maybe Giles, Gutteridge's man."

Brave looked like the subtle type. I didn't think he really intended to have me dumped in the harbour and he knew I didn't think it, but if he found the threat worth implying I could find it worth countering. But I

48

was getting impatient and didn't want to lose the initiative, if that's what I had.

"How about it, doctor? Do I see her now or come back with a court order?"

"You're being foolish again. Bryn wouldn't take out a court order against me. He wouldn't go against my advice on this."

"You've convinced yourself, you haven't convinced me."

He ignored me. His eyes were as dark as an arctic night under the heavy brows and they seemed not to be registering my presence in front of him at all. I didn't look much. My hair was matted around a wound on the back of my head that was seeping blood and I had the general look of a man who'd been sick for a week and hadn't changed his clothes, but to be looked through quite so devastatingly was disconcerting. He spoke slowly as if talking to himself. "However, they've all been through a lot and it might be best for you to do your clumsy act and run along."

He got up, tall and spare and snapped his fingers at Bruno. "Take him through to Room 38. I'll be along in a minute. He's not to see her until I'm there. Fifteen minutes Hardy!"

"For now," I said.

Bruno opened the door and I followed him shakily out into the corridor. We walked warily, taking a couple of turns to right and left, not chatting. Bruno stopped

49

outside a bolted door which had 38 painted in gold on its smooth black surface. He put his back against the door.

"We wait," he said.

I didn't argue. Balanced and braced like that he was about as movable as Gibraltar and I wasn't feeling rebellious any more. I needed time to think out an approach to the woman whose problems had brought me here, and my condition for thinking wasn't good. I'd come up with exactly nothing when Brave came round the corner. He'd put a fresh white jacket on over his white shirt and dark trousers. His eyes were dark, shining obsidian spheres and he seemed to be carrying himself very stiffly. He might walk and look lit up like that all the time, but there seemed a better than even chance that he'd given himself a shot of something. Bruno stepped aside, Brave drew the bolt, pushed the door open and I followed him into the room.

Room 38 was an expensively appointed sick room; there was a big low bed with a mountain of pillows and acres of white covers, assorted bottles on a bedside table, fruit in a beaten metal bowl, a streamlined portable TV set and a smell of money cloying the air. A woman, on the right side of forty but not by much, was sitting up in bed reading a paperback—*Family and Kinship in East London*. Her hair was dark brown, cut severely, her face was pale, puffy around the eyes. Bryn Gutteridge was right when he'd said that he and his sister weren't look-alike twins. This woman didn't resemble him at any point. Reading, concentrating, she wasn't bad looking, but she wasn't interesting. When she looked up to see Brave standing at the end of her bed her face transformed. She swept her hand over her hair making it careless, pretty. She smiled a good wide smile and something like beauty flowed into the bones of her face. She held out her hands.

"Doctor, I didn't expect to see you again today."

Brave moved around the bed. He took her hands, pressed them, laid them on the bed, not quite giving them back to her. "I'm sorry to disturb you, Susan," he said. "This is Mr Clifford Hardy, he's a private investigator."

Her eyes flew open in alarm, she went rigid for a second then grabbed for Brave's hand. She got it and calmed down, but she was strung up and stretched out and I doubted my ability to get anything out of her without having it filtered through Brave first. And he was making a lot of very strange moves. But I had to try. I stepped past Bruno and went up to the bed, facing Brave across it. I tried to keep roughneckedness out of my voice.

"Miss Gutteridge, your brother hired me . . ."

"Bryn!" Her hands shot up to her face and lines appeared around her mouth and neck which made her look fifty. She'd sweat and twitch if you said Santa Claus too loudly. Like Freud's, most of my clients are middle-class neurotics, but some of them have real problems in a real, hostile world. Some don't have any problem but themselves and I couldn't be sure which category Susan Gutteridge fell into. Brave did some more hand-squeezing.

"Susan, you don't have to talk to him if you don't want, but he has been persistent and I judge that you should see him now, once and for all. I'll stay right here and I promise I won't let him upset you."

Whatever he judged and promised would be fine with her. She relaxed and turned a scaled-down version of the smile on me.

"I'm sorry, Mr Harvey?"

"Hardy."

"Hardy. I'm overwrought, one thing and another. If my brother and Dr Brave think it wise for me to talk to you then I'm sure it is. I've never met a detective before. It's about the threats I suppose?"

"Yes," I said, "and other things."

"Other things?" She looked nervous. Susan Gutteridge's rails were long and narrow and she had to summon all her strength to stay on them for very long. Maybe it was the surroundings—clinics, psychologists, threats—maybe a slight physical resemblance, but I found myself thinking of Cyn, my ex-wife. Cyn, beds, breakdowns, lovers, lawyers: I pushed myself back from it.

"I mean related things, Miss Gutteridge, family things mostly which might throw some light on the problem. Give me something to go on, you understand."

Brave's snort of derision underlined my own awareness of the cliched cant I was spouting, but cops have to say "it is my duty to warn you", and doctors have to say "put out your tongue".

"I'd like to hear your account of the threats," I went on, "and your ideas and reactions. You're a sensitive woman. The threats came from a woman and you might have picked out something that a man would miss."

She looked blank. Wrong tack. I buttered her on the other side. "You have experience of people in need, social problems. Maybe you can guess at the disturbance in this woman's mind, what she wants, what lies behind it." That was better. Smugness crept into her face. She moved her hands away from Brave's for the first time. She smoothed down the covers. It was hard not to dislike her.

"You are acute in your own way, Mr Hardy," she said. "Of course, one of the worst things about this, for me, is the thought of how disturbed that woman must be to be saying those things. The person speaking to me on the telephone was emotionally disturbed. As you say, I have some experience in this area. The language was frightful."

I suppressed an impulse to laugh. "Do you mean it was obscene?"

"Yes, horribly so. I had to burn the letters."

"Were they obscene too?"

She started to look nervous again. "No, not at all, just awful."

"Why did you have to burn them then?"

She plucked at the bedcover, shredding some of the raised nap and balling it in her fingers. "I meant that, well, the filthy language and the letters came from the same person. So I burned the letters."

"You think the phone calls and letters came from the same source do you?"

"Yes, of course."

"Why, of course?"

"They must have."

"Tell me one, just one, of the objectionable phrases in the phone calls."

"I can't, I couldn't say it."

"What were the letters about? The same thing?"

"No—sickness, decay, death."

"Come on Miss Gutteridge, one phrase from the calls."

She glared at me, bunched her fists and hammered them on the snowy bedcover. "Fucking capitalist!" she screamed in my face.

There was a silence that seemed to let the words hang in the air forever. Then she started sobbing and Brave moved in with all systems go. He took her hands and clasped them inside his while murmuring comforting, animal-like sounds in her ear. He swayed above her like a mesmerised snake putting the music back into the pipe. She regained control very quickly. I knew that this kind of command over another person was extremely difficult to obtain and incredibly costly to bring about in time and effort. There was no short cut to it and I wondered why Brave had made an investment of this order in this pathetic woman. There was no time for on-the-spot investigation. At a nod from Brave, Bruno moved forward and took my arm just above the elbow. His grip hurt like a dentist's drill on a nerve.

"You've had your time, Hardy," Brave said. "I hope you're satisfied with what you've done."

If that was supposed to make me feel sorry for the woman it didn't work. Her problems were mine only in a strictly professional sense, but I had to stay with them. At this point I had to assume that Bryn had hired me for reasons other than those he'd stated. That isn't unusual, but you have to sort the real reasons out fairly quickly if you don't want to be the meat in the sandwich all the way. I had to fire a shot in my own war.

"Goodbye, Miss Gutteridge," I said. "I hope you know what you're doing."

"Out," Brave hissed the word like a jet of venom and Bruno swung me round and we trotted out of the room like big Siamese twins joined at the shoulder.

We made the same turns in reverse and Bruno shooed me into the room I'd surfaced in before. I sat down on a chair near the desk and started scooping my things up and putting them in my pockets. Bruno stepped forward and a puzzled look spread over his face as he tried to work out whether he was supposed to stop me or not. He couldn't tell and he couldn't think and hit at the same time. Not many muscle men can and it gives the weaklings a fractional edge sometimes. I made a cigarette as the Italian hovered in the middle of the room looking like a discus thrower turned to stone in the middle of his wind-up.

"Don't worry, Bruno," I said. "I'll wait here for your master and in a little while you'll be able to go off and do something about your face." That gave him something to think of. He put a hand up to his face and pressed gently. "Harder," I said, "maybe there's something broken." He worked his jaw and grimaced. I might have been able to get him to give himself a karate chop but there was no challenge in it. The door swung open and Brave walked in. He sat down primly behind his desk and the first colour I'd seen in his face appeared—high red spots in his cheeks like daubings on a clown.

"You've been very troublesome, Hardy," he said, "and achieved very little, I should imagine."

"Why should you imagine that?"

"I won't fence with you. You are a nuisance, plain and simple. A blunderer into delicate situations. The question is, how to be rid of you."

I wanted to bring his dislike of me up as high as it would go.

"A blunderbuss," I said.

He registered it like a deep internal pain.

"As I understand it," he said slowly, "a private detective is without any authority and credibility if he is without a client."

"You've read too much Chandler," I said.

He looked puzzled for a second but didn't let it stop him. "I think that's so," he went on, "and therefore you represent no problem at all Mr Hardy, none at all. Show him out Bruno."

Bruno and I did our dancing bears act down corridors and through doors and in five minutes I was walking down the path towards the gate. The night air hit me hard and I gave my attention to finding a chemist for my head and a bottle shop for me.

CHAPTER 4

The Green Man and Joe Barassi's All Day All Nite Pharmacy at Drummoyne put me back together. I washed down two red Codrals with a couple of hefty slugs from a half bottle of Haig. I looked at the wound on my head in the mirror of the Green Man's washroom. It didn't look too bad, the blood had stopped seeping and I managed to clean the area up with damp paper towels. Whoever had hit me had known his business and had chosen to give me a purple heart rather than a posthumous medal of honour. I felt vaguely grateful to him and had another nip out of the Scotch bottle for him.

The traffic flowed easily over the Iron Cove bridge. People were all in the cinemas and pubs and there was little competition for me on the drive home to Glebe. I wasn't up to shuttling the car into the courtyard so I left it outside the house with a steering lock on the gearshift which would hold up a good Glebe car thief for about two minutes. My head throbbed and a little laser of pain stabbed over the right eyebrow but I decided to try and make some sense of the night's play before I let another Codral and some more whisky sing me to sleep. I sat in a bean bag with a tall Scotch and soda on the floor beside me. I rolled three cigarettes and set them in the grooves of the ashtray the way Uncle Ted used to. Uncle Ted had a good war, sent back hundreds from the Tobruk two-up games and survived. I'd survived high school, two erratic years at university and Malaya to become an insurance investigator— long hours, high mileage and pathetic incendiarists. The work had coated my fingers with nicotine, scuttled my marriage and put fat around my waistline and wits. The deals and hush-money made divorce work seem clean as riding a wave and bodyguarding noble and manly. Suicides and Svengalis were a different thing though, and I wasn't sure that I was up to coping with them. I was on the third cigarette without having any inspiration, when the phone rang.

I heaved myself out of the bean bag and put the receiver somewhere near my face.

"Mr Hardy?" A woman's voice, drunk or panicky.

"Yes, who's this?"

"It's Ailsa Sleeman, I found your card. I didn't know what else to do. I'm frightened."

"What's happened?"

"It's horrible. Bryn just called me, I don't know why me, I suppose he just doesn't know anyone else . . ."

"What's happened?"

"It's Giles. He's been shot. He's dead."

"When was this?"

"I don't know. Bryn rang me about an hour ago. I've been trying to reach you since then."

"You sound frightened Miss Sleeman. Why?"

"It's hard to explain. Impossible over the phone. It's to do with Dr Brave who you seemed interested in this afternoon. I'm afraid of him. I need help, perhaps protection. I'm willing to employ you."

That was a switch. A few hours ago she was willing to forget me like a bad dream. This would give me two clients on the same case. I wasn't sure it was ethical, it had never happened to me before. But if Bryn meant me to proceed with the investigation maybe I could work out a package deal. If Brave could carry through with his threat, I'd lose Bryn as a client so it would be convenient to stay with it on La Sleeman's behalf. I was hooked on the Gutteridges now, and I felt that I'd got into some kind of conflict with Brave that had to be seen through. I needed a bit more to go on though.

"I'm interested Miss Sleeman," I said in my deliberate voice, "but I need a little more information. Did Mr Gutteridge mention Dr Brave?"

"Yes, they've had a quarrel."

"OK. Can you come in to my office in the

morning?"

"Tomorrow?" The panicky note was back, "I thought tonight . . ."

"Miss Sleeman, I've driven a hundred miles today, been lied to, had two fights and lost one badly. I'm out of action until 9 a.m. tomorrow."

All true enough, but what I really wanted to know was whether she was serious about her proposition and alarm, or was just feeling lonely for the night. She could be one of those rich people who think they have everything they need behind their high walls but occasionally have to send out for some help. Or she might still be in touch with the world outside. I also felt a need to do some talking on my own territory after the lies I'd been told so far. There's something truth-inducing about a hard chair and a smell of phenol in the hall.

"All right," she said. Her voice was steadier, no drink in it. "I'll be in at 9 o'clock. You will help, Mr Hardy?"

I told her I would, made sure she had the address right, made a few reassuring noises and she rang off. The phone rang again almost as soon as I'd put it down. I let it ring a few times while I visited my drink and finished my cigarette. I took Bryn's cheque out of my wallet and spread it out in front of me. It was one of those big, friendly cheques from a big, friendly chequebook. I'd hoped to collect a few more. I picked up the phone.

"Hardy? This is Bryn Gutteridge."

"Yes?"

"A dreadful thing has happened Hardy."

I had to decide quickly whether to let him tell it or to tell him I knew what was up and judge his reaction. The first way seemed to leave me more cards.

"You sound upset. Take it quietly and tell me."

"Giles has been shot. He was in the car, going on an errand for me . . . and someone shot him in the head. He's gone."

"I'm sorry Mr Gutteridge. You've called the police?"

"Yes of course. They've been and gone. They were very considerate. I was surprised."

I knew what he meant but I wasn't surprised. The Commissioner would have got in on this quickly and he'd have kept the public lavatory prowl squad well out of it. "Do you want me in on this?"

"No!" Sacking people was second nature stuff to him. He did it with no embarrassment.

"The police will be prying into my affairs. That's enough. When this is over I'm going away, perhaps for a few years."

"I see. What about your sister?"

"I'll take her with me. We'll get out of this. Drop the investigation Mr Hardy. Thank you for . . ."

"For what? Just for interest, when did you decide

62

to let the investigation drop, before or after Giles' death?"

"Oh God, I don't know. Before, I think. I'm not sure. Why does it matter?"

"It matters to me. What did Dr Brave say to you when you saw him this evening?"

"I didn't see him, he rang." He broke off confused and annoyed with himself for replying. "This is no longer your affair, Hardy."

I didn't have much of his time left. "Did he threaten you?" I said quickly.

"I'm hanging up Hardy. Send a bill."

"You've overpaid me. Have this for free—Giles' murder and the threats to your sister are connected. You can't run away from it." He hung up.

That left me with Ailsa. I took another pill and finished my drink.

I went to bed. The street was quiet, no dog races so my head was spared the roar of punters' Holdens and the purr of the bookmakers' limousines. It was too hot for the street fighters and gutter drinkers to be out lending the area colour and Soames must have had the music down low. I drifted off to the quiet hum of my fan. I slid into a dream in which Ailsa Sleeman, standing tall, reached down for my hands and lifted them up onto her massive breasts.

CHAPTER 5

I woke with a headache that was partly due to the crack
I'd taken the night before. I looked out of the window
across the rusting roofs of Glebe. The sky had a dull,
leaden look—the day was going to be hot. A Sahara
wind was already whipping the ice-cream wrappers
and other crap along the gutters. I made coffee but it
was bitter and I swilled it down the sink. About the
only good thing I've ever heard of Mick Jagger is that
he likes scrambled eggs and white wine for breakfast.
I made my version of scrambled eggs, piled a glass up
with ice and topped it up with hock and soda. I put
the drink down fast, made another, and took it, the
food and *The News* out to the courtyard, feeling better
every minute.

The paper headlined the hunt for Costello, the
police expected a breakthrough hourly, and there were

pictures of beefy guys in shirt sleeves heavying honest citizens. Giles' departure from this vale of tears didn't get a mention. I ran my eye hopelessly over the cryptic crossword and consoled myself with the meteorological report—hot, high winds ahead of a thunderstorm. I skimmed the paper again and was surprised to find an idea forming in my mind. I let it take shape for a few minutes and then gave it another drink in case it went away hurt.

I shaved, took a shower and put on my other suit which is said to be lightweight but always makes me sweat like a pig if I move at a pace above a royal stroll. I was already hot when I slipped into the car. The radio aerial had been broken off just above the mounting and was lying in three pieces across the bonnet in the shape of the mark of Zorro. I swore and swept the pieces into the gutter. Insurance was supposed to cover things like that, but how do you insure yourself against insurance premiums? The car started cheerfully and I moved off towards the city.

I reached my office, two floors up above St Peters Street, close to 9.00. The Cross, or what's left of it after the developers had their way, is just a block north. The whores were already at work, not doing any business among the winos squatting on the pub steps, but keeping in practice. My office opens straight into the corridor, no ante-rooms for people to wait or die in. I inherited it from a clairvoyant who fell under a train. The desk was covered with astrological signs and cabbalistic symbols in inks of various colours—I never had the nerve to rub them out and confined my own doodling to the blotter.

The knock came at exactly 9 o'clock. I sang out that the door was open and she came in slowly and tentatively like a schoolboy coming into the head's study. She wore a light blue mottled smock over tight flared white trousers. Her fine breasts complemented the tailoring of the smock and that length of lean thigh in white denim was something to see. Her low-heeled sandals vaguely matched her tooled leather shoulder bag and there wouldn't have been much change out of three hundred dollars for the set. Yesterday she'd been wearing a scarf or something over her head. Now I could see that her dark, reddish hair was cut short, almost cropped. It lay on her sleek head like a burnished metal cap. She wore yesterday's sunglasses, or maybe she had a few pairs the same. A cigarette came out of her bag almost before she hit the chair and she was one of the fastest people with a lighter I've seen.

She took a quick look around the office which in colour scheme and layout is more like a railway waiting room than anything else. She didn't react to it one way or the other, which probably meant that she'd been in worse places, maybe much worse. She drew hard on the cigarette.

"It must have seemed strange to you," she said, "telephoning like that last night."

"It did, but when people need help they do strange things."

"Can I take up some of your time, Mr Hardy? I have a long story to tell. I'll pay you of course, starting from now."

"Before you start spending money I'd like to know why you've changed your mind about me. I was a fly on the wall to you yesterday."

"That's a fair question. Yesterday I was having a bad time with the man you saw. I'm sorry, it made me testy. Today I need help and I've been thinking. I don't like Bryn Gutteridge, but he's a good judge of people. If you're good enough for him you're good enough for me."

She acted on the "if you have to ask the price you can't afford it" plan and that was all right with me. I nodded reassurance on the point, rolled a cigarette and settled back to listen.

"Today is close enough to fifteen years to the day since I gave up being a dancer. I wasn't bad, I can still do a bit. I'm pretty fit."

"Yes," I said, "you look fine. Put 90 per cent of people to shame."

"Well, I gave up dancing and that sort of life, theatre and so on to get married. I married a man named Bercer. I was twenty-four, he was fifty-nine,

67

I was poor, he was rich. It's an old story and there was nothing very different about it except that it worked out all right. He was nice to me. I liked him and for about three years I thought I'd done the right thing. I read a lot, went to plays I wouldn't have given a thought to before. I improved myself."

"You did a good job," I said, "but then . . .?"

"But then I met a man more or less my own age. I fell for him and we had an affair, a pretty hot one. He was married and I handled it all very badly. I got upset when I couldn't have it all my own way when things went wrong. James, my husband, didn't suspect that I was being unfaithful but he was worried about me and sent me to see a doctor, a counsellor . . ."

"Brave."

"Yes. He was helpful at first, encouraging. I'd lost track of the friends I'd had when I was dancing and they weren't much anyway, pretty wild. I had no one to confide in. Brave was sympathetic and available day and night. I came to rely on him absolutely and I told him about my lover. That was a terrible mistake."

"He blackmailed you?"

"No, not me. He blackmailed James. He told James that there were things about me that would ruin him financially and socially."

"What was Bercer's business?" I knew but I wanted to know whether or not she did and what she felt about it.

"Property development, building, and he did big stock exchange deals. It all hinged on the people he knew, politicians, lawyers, top public servants, even a few military men. We went to hundreds of parties, had dinner engagements six nights a week, sometimes seven. There were lots of smoke evenings, the gentlemen with their cigars and the ladies talking trivia."

I looked down at the frayed end of my cigarette and teased it with my thumbnail. "It sounds terrible."

"It was, a lot of the time. But there were some good holidays, good trips, and the men weren't all oafs and the women weren't all vacuous. It wasn't so bad. I went to a good school, my accent's all right and I could hold my own. But James had to be absolutely clean for his deals to come through, no dubious connections."

"Your lover was a dubious connection."

"He certainly was, the worst. If it got out that he was my lover those important people would drop James cold."

"Why didn't James drop you?"

"He loved me for one thing, but that wasn't all. Brave's line was that James mustn't drop me or he'd spread word about Carl."

"Carl who?"

"It doesn't matter. The important thing is that Brave was bleeding James dry. I found out later that he got over a hundred thousand from him, maybe two hundred thousand, maybe more."

I whistled. "That's big. What does Brave do with the money?"

She set her teeth in a grimace like that of a firing squad commander who has to administer a coup de grace.

"He has expensive tastes in . . . erotica. He gambles like a madman. But we're talking about me, not him."

"Sorry, he's of interest. So are you of course."

She looked impatient and ran a hand over that fine, glowing pelt.

"Right. I'm jumping ahead in telling it this way because at the time I didn't know what Brave was doing. I just saw James getting more and more tense and felt more and more guilty myself."

"Bercer didn't front up to you with it?"

"Never. He just broke under the strain. He started taking bottles to bed and gorging himself on rich food. He blew up like a balloon and had a heart attack. He had two, actually in a few days and he died."

"How did that leave you?"

She was so used to the idea that she didn't even pause to knock the ash off her cigarette—the second since she'd started talking.

"Comfortable, if I'd been careful. I wasn't."

I raised an eyebrow, a stagey trick I'd learned from my drunken, diabetic mother who'd pounded a vampy piano in London pubs and queened it up on the *Oronsay* on the £10 scheme.

"Brave dropped out of the picture when James died. I gave up my lover, unpleasantly, and went a bit wild. Not here—in the States and Europe. I worked through a lot of money and came home a good bit harder. I'd seen a lot, I was too old for dancing and too smart for whoring, so I thought I'd better have another try at what I'd succeeded at before."

She'd gone through it in her mind a hundred times and had made her own role tougher with each run through, but she had intelligence, directness and an awareness of the reality of other people—something real gold-diggers don't have. And her men hadn't been soft-cocked sugar daddies: Bercer sounded like a shrewd operator in a high-powered world and Gutteridge had been smart and tough. But she was telling the story and this was the part she'd assigned herself. I wanted to hear more.

"You did all right again," I said.

"No," she shook her head, "I was getting nowhere for going on a year until I got help. Guess who?"

"Brave again."

"Yes. I met him at a party. I think I'd tried to find him when I first got back but he'd vanished. Remember that I didn't have anything against him except perhaps a bit of resentment that he'd gone off so soon after James died. He said he'd had to go back to Canada. OK, I was pleased to see him and pretty soon I was confiding in him again. He talked to me about needing

71

an anchor in my life, a strong man. He introduced me to Mark Gutteridge."

She was moving steadily through her packet of cigarettes and the room was smoky and heating up fast. My watch put the time at a little past ten which meant that the pubs would be open.

She agreed that it was hot and that a drink would be a good idea. We went down the stairs and I felt my stocks in the building go up several points in the eyes of a dentist with a quiet practice, a hairdresser with big blanks in her appointment book and a guitar teacher whose rooms were smoky and sweet smelling. They hovered about in their doorways as I followed Ailsa's firm white-denimed buttocks down the corridors of their dreams.

The heat hit us like a jet engine blast when we reached the street. Ailsa had slipped the Porsche I'd seen the day before into an illegal but unobtrusive place behind the building. It was unlocked and she stepped in and reached into the glove compartment, also unlocked, for the keys. I wondered if she ignored security the same way in her house. As she pulled out from the kerb I noticed a red Volkswagen pull away half a block behind. I watched it in the rear vision mirror for a mile or so till it turned off or fell a long way behind. I couldn't see the driver. The light wouldn't fall right for me to get a look at him even when the car was close. I directed Ailsa out to Watson's Bay where the big pub on the beach serves the best fish in Sydney. If Ailsa was only halfway through her story it looked as though we could string it out through lunch, and I was on expenses. She didn't talk much. She drove fast and well using the Porsche's power when it was needed and not for show. We reached the pub just before eleven and she slid the car into a patch of shade where a tree hung over the parking bay. She reached over to drop the keys into the glove box.

"Lock it," I said.

She gave me a sharp, unfriendly look and shook her head.

"For me," I said. "Your security's lousy, it's time to start improving it."

She shrugged and locked the car putting the keys in her shoulder bag. We went through the cool lounge, up some stairs and into the dining room which has a view of the boats and the water that puts twenty-five per cent on the price of the food and drink.

"What will you drink?"

"Tonic and a slice of lemon. I hardly drink at all these days."

I gave the waiter the order. I had the same with gin. Out came the cigarettes and she took up her story again without preamble.

"It was all different with Mark. We had a good sexual relationship at the start and he was a very different proposition to James."

"No playing around?"

She shook her head. "Out of the question. It was all much more complicated. Brave can judge people. He'd picked me and Mark as a good fit and he was right. But the fit wasn't all that comfortable."

"The children?"

"Right. Mark doted on them and they were as suspicious as hell of me. He doted, but kept a tight rein on them. He seemed to have them scared. He scared me too at times."

"Where was Brave in this scene?"

"I'm coming to it."

The drinks arrived and I tried not to show an indecent interest in mine. She gave hers only the attention it deserved.

"Brave seemed to be a friend of Mark's in a low-key way. Mark advised him in business matters and helped him to get the land the clinic's built on. You've seen it?"

"Yeah, must have been quite a deal."

"It was. Some old houses came down. Mark had people in his pocket as I told you. I was interested in Mark's business. I thought I'd been wrong not to pay more attention to what James did, it might have kept me closer to him. Well, I talked business to Mark quite a bit. In bed mostly, and he gave me the gist of what it was all about. He was involved in land and property speculation. He got tips from people in high positions and he profited from them. He paid off the people who gave him information, in cash sometimes, more often in land and shares. Sometimes the payments came years after the deal, sometimes the kick-backs went to the wives, you understand?"

I did. If I'd got any kick-backs when I'd had a wife I'd definitely have seen that they went into her Swiss account. But the only kick-backs I've ever had have been of the in-the-teeth variety. I finished my drink and signalled for another. Ailsa's had scarcely lost a drop.

She went on: "Sometimes he told me names, but not often. Sometimes it was obvious to me who he was talking about even if names weren't mentioned. It became a bit of a game with us, a sort of Mata Hari thing, a bedroom game. I'd probe and he'd be indiscreet."

"It sounds like a bloody dangerous game to me," I said.

"It turned out to be. Mark roasted me a couple of times when I let a name slip in company, when I'd had a bit to drink. I watched myself after that. Mark would say that he had things on everyone, there was no one who had anything on him that he didn't have something on in turn. When he was low he even told me that he had something on his children, he never said what, and something on me. I didn't understand and I didn't want to. I used to try to pass it off as a joke. That was hard because Mark didn't have much of a sense of humour, like Susan. He had a dramatic sense, our bedroom spy games showed that, but that's about it. Jokes for him were visible, practical things. You know what I mean?"

I nodded. "Yes. I'd say Bryn's a bit that way too. Speaking of the practical-minded, did Gutteridge keep records of his deals?"

"I'm not certain but I think so. I'll get to that."

She drank down the tonic and lemon peel in a few gulps and refused another. I accepted the wine list, a little early perhaps, but busy people often eat early lunch I'm told. Ailsa sent the waiter for cigarettes and tore them open untidily as soon as they arrived. When she had one lit she went on.

"I used to see Ian Brave occasionally, have a drink with him. I didn't need him as I had before, but he was a confidant of sorts and I still didn't have any friends to speak of. I had problems with Mark's children and occasional bouts of depression. I went to the theatre with Brave twice. The second time he doped me." She sucked in her cigarette and blew the smoke out in a thin, vicious jet. "He took me back to his place—not the clinic, a house he has on the beach. He put needles into me, he questioned me for hours and hours. You can guess what about."

"Yeah. Where was your husband then?"

"Away on business, interstate. He often was. When I came out of it, some time early the next morning, Brave told me what I'd told him. That is, he gave me some snippets, about big names. He thanked me and told me to forget what happened. He said he'd leave me alone."

"I don't follow."

She stubbed the cigarette like it was her last and she was giving it up for life. Except that she lit another straight away.

"Oh shit. He had some pictures. Are you with me?"

"Photographs?"

"Right. He used them to keep me quiet and he used the information I'd given him to blackmail Mark to glory."

"Did your husband suspect that you were the source of Brave's information?"

She fiddled with the cigarette and lined up a napkin, an ashtray and her lighter on the table. "I'm not sure," she said, "I suppose so. He became morose and withdrawn. I couldn't reach him, no one could. My feeling is that Brave had him so cold he didn't care anymore."

"His whole approach to things had been turned round on him?"

"Something like that."

"Did he still see Brave? Socially I mean?"

"No, not to my knowledge. But they hadn't met regularly anyway."

I was interested but there were lots of loose ends.

I played with the menu while I considered them. The story had a ring of truth but it was a bit too close to the first episode of husband and betrayal for comfort. Her innocence looked to be stretched a bit thin. I tried to keep the scepticism out of my voice as I asked the question. "How do you know all this happened? You said you weren't aware of what Brave had done in the case of your first husband. Why are you so sure about all this now?"

The question was important. If she slid about on it the whole thing could be a pack of lies. Dancers can be actresses. Only another good serve of her directness would incline me to believe her. She was direct.

"Brave told me himself," she said. "I went to him one day when Mark was black-minded and told him that I thought he was driving Mark crazy. I threatened to go to the police and accuse him of drugging and molesting me. I said I'd finish him professionally and in every other way."

"What did he say?" It wasn't hard to guess.

"He laughed at me. He said there were good reasons why I wouldn't do what I'd said. He threatened to name me as an accomplice in the blackmailing of James. He said he had so much on Mark that he could play with him just as he pleased and that he could ruin him and put me on the streets. He didn't want to. Mark was making him rich and he was happy with things as they were. If I left him alone, he'd leave me alone. He said he'd ease up on Mark, but I guess he couldn't. He's a greedy bastard."

"How's that?"

"He pushed Mark past the limit, he must have done. Mark was dead about ten days after I had this talk with Brave."

"Are you sure he killed himself?"

"No, I'm not. But he was in a tortured state in the last few days and a gun was found near his body. The coroner's verdict was suicide but I'm sure such things can be arranged."

She stopped when the waiter arrived to take the order. I called for half a dozen oysters naturelle and some grilled whiting. She said she'd have the same and took about half a glass of hock when that arrived. Waiters were hovering about and she smoked and made some small talk until we had privacy again. The golden brown fish fillets and potato chips hid among the salad like Dyaks in the jungle. We pushed them about and sipped the wine. I tried to fill her glass but she glared at me. I munched a few decent mouthfuls of fish and got on with it.

"You think the police didn't pursue the matter satisfactorily?"

She mashed up some fish and salad and pushed the mess aside. She hadn't eaten a single potato chip and I had to keep myself from reaching over and spearing them. I drained my glass instead and filled it from the bottle which was still healthy. She lit a cigarette and more smoke drifted into my face than seemed necessary.

"What are you so cautious about, Hardy?" she asked. "Your licence?"

I shrugged and took in a bit more wine. "You were talking about your husband's death," I said. She nodded and did her cigarette flicking act again. The ash sprayed into the plates and I pushed mine aside.

"Look, this gets back to your question about Mark's records, if you're still interested. Mark died at his desk, in his study. The police found a secret safe in the study, one I didn't know about. It had been opened. It was empty. Maybe Mark kept the records there."

I nodded. "That sounds like a lead for the police, didn't they take it up?"

"No, they didn't take anything up. They rushed on to the inquest and let it go at that. I don't have to spell out what I think?"

"No, you think Brave has the records, maybe killed your husband to get them. Maybe not. In any case he was on the scene pretty quick I assume?"

She nodded, "Very quickly."

"You think he used the records to bring the shutters down on the case?"

She spread her hands quizzically and drew a deep breath. The coffee arrived and she dropped as many grains of sugar into it as you could balance on the head of a nail. I took a gulp of wine and popped the question.

"Your husband's been dead for four years and you've suspected Brave's hand in it all along. Why are you frightened enough to want to do something? To hire me? Brave hasn't threatened you directly has he?"

"Not yet," she said, "but it's only a matter of time. I've done something with the money Mark left me—invested it, got a couple of companies going. I told you this?"

I couldn't remember, I looked non-committal. She went on: "I'm a worthy target for Brave now. He's a leech. But it's more than that." She leaned forward. She had fine broad shoulders and her movements were athletic without being masculine. Her lips were a sculptured counterpoint to the vertical lines of her face. "I think Brave killed Giles. I think he's insane and obsessed with the Gutteridges. I think he's behind the threats to Susan and after Bryn now."

"Bryn's certainly afraid of something, or somebody. I think it connects back to his father's death but I don't know how."

"He's afraid of Brave I tell you. And if Bryn's afraid of him I'm bloody terrified." She slapped down the coffee spoon she'd been playing with and jerked off her sunglasses. There seemed to me to be as much resolution as fear in her face. Her voice was unemotional, businesslike. "You drink too much, but you're intelligent and capable in your own field. I want you to

81

do two things—investigate Brave's affairs and put him out of business, for good. And protect me!"

"It's tough doing two things at once."

"They're two sides of the same thing. I'm sure of it."

She smiled for the first or second time since I'd met her. It was a nice smile but under careful control. "I don't know why you wanted to come out here. The food isn't that good and the view is rather corny. I've been here before."

"Why did you agree to come then?"

"To show anyone who might be interested that I've got protection."

"I guess you hired me a couple of hours ago then."

"Well, yes, I did in a sense. But are you interested in the complete job now you know what's involved?"

I gave it about half a second's thought. Handled right it would keep me clean of guard duty and the cheap rooms and caravan parks for weeks. I had too much good wine inside me to think of much else. I believed at least half of Ailsa's story and that was enough. I told her my rates and conditions of work. She pulled a chequebook from her bag and wrote words and digits on it with a gold pen. I put it in my wallet, not too far from Bryn's cheque so that the two of them could debate the ethics of it.

I had just enough cash to cover the bill and I was feeling clever and successful when we walked out into the parking lot. The sun was beating down hard and the shade had retreated from the Porsche leaving its rear bumper shimmering and reflecting like a white hot steel mirror. Ailsa stepped up to the driver's door, pressed the button in and pulled the door free. She had it three inches open before my half-stewed brain got the message. I took two rabbity leaps across the melting asphalt and swept her off in a diving football tackle. Her bag came adrift from her shoulder and flicked the car door full open as we hit the ground. The Porsche burst into flame like a Molotov cocktail on impact, the bonnet lifted and the windows cracked in quick succession like rifle shots. Hellish heat surged towards us as I rolled Ailsa over three more times in the gravel and tar.

"You should always lock your car," I ground into her ear as we came to rest twenty feet away from the inferno.

CHAPTER 6

We were both shaking as we brushed the grit of the parking bay off our clothes. Ailsa's white pants were a ruin and her smock was smeared and torn. My trousers had a great three-cornered tear in the knee and blood from a bad graze was seeping into the ragged edges of the tear. The car was burning fiercely, the tyres were bubbling like lava and the vehicle was sinking slowly, lopsidedly onto the rims. There was a stench of burning rubber and vinyl and a cloud of dark smoke had settled in the still hot air over the parking area. I put my arm around Ailsa's shoulders and helped her across to the steps in front of the hotel. Staff from the place were thronging about and Ailsa accepted a woman's offer of help to a toilet where she could clean up.

The manager came out and mumbled about calling the police. I told him I'd do it myself if he could show me to the phone and produce some brandy. He seemed relieved to escape the job and took me into an office which contained a desk, chair, a telephone, a pot plant and a bar. I'd always wondered what hotel managers did in their offices. This one must have twiddled his thumbs and drank. He left me in the room telling me to help myself. I mixed a strong Hennessy and soda, sat down with it behind the desk and dialled a number. The voice at the other end was tired and unsympathetic. It had answered ten thousand telephone rings and never once heard good news.

"Police, Evans speaking."

"Grant, this is Cliff Hardy."

"Oh good, you're going to pay me the money you owe me and take me on a holiday to Coolangatta."

"This is serious, I need your help. And I might be able to help you with something you've got on your plate."

"Yeah? What would that be?"

"I can't tell you just now."

"That's terrific. Well I'll just drop everything here. It's nothing much, a couple of murders and a multi-million dollar extradition job and hurry on over to your place. What shall I wear?"

"Stop joking, I've been bombed."

"You're always bombed, tell me something new."

"I mean really bombed, detonator, gelignite, explosion, flames. I'm OK and my client's OK but a Porsche is dead."

85

"You've got a client and he's got a Porsche? Maybe you will pay me what you owe me."

"She has one. It's dead now, but she'll have another tomorrow."

"You sound more or less sober. Are you dinkum, Cliff?"

"Yes, blood oath I am. Here's what I'm asking. If you've got some cars that aren't busy picking up the take, send them over to the pub at Watson's Bay. The sightseers will need dispersing, the car will need towing to your forensic parlour, Miss Sleeman will be requiring a lift to Mosman and I'd like to come down and see you."

"Charmed. Consider it done, anything else?"

"No. See you soon Grant."

"Yeah. I don't like that crack about the take, Cliff."

"That's because none of it ever reaches you, mate. You've got to put yourself forward, make friends."

I hung up on his stream of obscenities. Grant Evans was ex-army, ex-Malaya, like me. His sense of humour wasn't his strongest point, but he was fairly honest like me. That made us mavericks in our respective professions and useful to each other. We were also old friends who'd been under fire and under the weather together too many times to count.

The manager was hovering outside the door. I told him the police were on their way and that I'd probably be able to see that the matter was kept pretty quiet. He looked pleased and showed me through to where Ailsa was sitting in a private room. She doused her cigarette and came up out of her chair to meet me. We put our arms around each other and stood together, not moving. It felt like the most natural thing in the world to do—coming that near to death seemed to draw us close.

"The police are coming," I said after a minute or so, "they'll take you home."

"You saved my life," she said.

"And mine don't forget."

She didn't move away. "The tough guy's tough guy."

"Not really. I nearly spilt the brandy they forced me to drink."

"You're a drunk, but you seem to be lucky for me. Will you stay with it? This doesn't change anything?"

I told her I would and it didn't and we were still patting each other like timid middleweights in a clinch when the manager came in to let us know that the Rose Bay cops had arrived. Ailsa continued not to do silly things. We walked out to the parking lot and she barely gave the burnt out wreck a glance. She answered a few basic questions from the senior uniformed man and then turned things over to me. Grant had clued the men up and they were willing for her to go home and for me to go down town and give a detailed account of the bombing. A cop picked up Ailsa's bag from where it had landed after being blown clear by the explosion of the petrol tank. He handed it to her and ushered her into the back of one of the patrol cars. She mouthed "Tonight" at me and I nodded. The cop slammed the door and the car took off. I was surprised to find that I wished I was going with her, but it was time to start earning her money by playing the "bumping pitch and blinding light" stuff with the law.

On the ride I tried to work out how to play the cards I had, or thought I had, but I found myself spending more time admiring the driving of the young detective at the wheel. He whipped the big Holden Kingswood through impossible gaps and caught every light from Watson's Bay to East Sydney. He didn't say a word on the journey.

"Great driving," I said as I got out in front of the central police building. He looked at me and jerked his head at the steps. A specialist.

I went into the building and gave my name to the desk sergeant. He lifted a phone and spoke briefly to someone in Grant's inner sanctum. The sergeant lifted old, tired cocker spaniel eyes to me.

"You know the way?"

"Yeah. OK to go up now?"

He nodded wearily and turned his attention back to the stolen car sheet. He read it like a form guide maybe hoping that if he spotted a few on the way home he could get out from behind the desk. Then again, maybe it was just a stunt the police PR boys put him up to as something that would impress the public. I went up three flights in the creaking lift. The view from the corridor windows was dull, out across the commercial buildings of East Sydney. The park on the other side was a better eyeful. Grant was still on the dull side but I knew he hoped to go up a floor and cross over. I might be able to help him if I could persuade him at this point with nothing. I pushed open the door and went into the office he shared with two other senior men.

Grant was alone. He was sitting at a desk which was untidy with papers, coffee cups and full ashtrays. He pushed himself back from the desk and waved me into a chair. He took hold of his spare tyre and pinched it.

"I'm getting fat, Cliff, not enough action. Are you going to give me some?"

I sat down. "Could be Grant, could be. I'd better fill you in."

I told him the tale, an edited version which left some things out and under-played others—especially the events at Brave's clinic. Grant listened closely, making occasional notes. He ran his hand ruefully across the thinning dark hair on his skull. He was one of those men who took the disintegration of his body hard. His wife still appeared to think of him as the twenty-five-year-old paratrooper she'd married and his three daughters thought the sun shone out of him, but he bemoaned each lost hair and extra ounce. He'd been a superb fighting machine in Malaya and he'd killed three men on active duty as a cop, three hard men. He'd saved my life once in the jungle and kept me out of jail a few times since then. I usually played court jester to his gloomy king.

"Well, you seem to have yourself a nice case," he said when I'd finished talking. "Well-heeled client, real Lew Archer stuff. What do you want from me?"

"Can you sit on the bombing for a while, keep it quiet?"

"Yeah, I think so. No one really wants to know about car bombings. Everyone assumes they're about crims and punters welshing on debts. Mostly they're right. No reporters there?"

"No, not that I saw. The management won't talk, that's for sure."

"Naturally. All right, quiet it is. What's in it for me?"

I rolled a cigarette and offered him the makings. He hesitated then took them and expertly made a cigarette. We both blew smoke at the stained, cracked ceiling.

"I want to know something about the Gutteridge case. Four years ago, remember it?"

"Yep, I was on it for a while."

"Did it get sat on? I hear there were some loose ends—an open safe for one."

"That's right. He killed himself though. I was the first to see him and it looked real to me. I've seen a lot of dead men who got dead in different ways. I'd say this was an auto."

"Or set up by an expert."

"Maybe. Unlikely."

"What about the safe?"

"Puzzling."

"Look, was it a bloody cover-up?"

He stubbed the cigarette out and dusted his hands. It looked as if he was trying to stop smoking again. He'd tried it a dozen times to my knowledge and it always made him mean. His face set in one of its tough, bloody-minded official masks.

"You're asking everything and giving nothing. If you want to offer me something juicy out of the Gutteridge case forget it. I don't want to know."

"No, it's not that. I'm working on something connected with the Gutteridge case and I want to know all there is to know about it. It might give me some leverage. I'm pretty confident I can put your name in lights over something which has nothing to do with Mark Gutteridge's death."

"Give me a clue."

"I can't. You wouldn't buy it at this stage."

Grant sighed. He reached into his pockets, pulled the hands out empty and did an isometric exercise against the edge of the desk.

"You weren't in Sydney when this thing came up?"

"No, I was on a country job, Broken Hill and Melbourne after that. I had a holiday in Fiji on the proceeds, I must have missed it all."

Grant looked sour, I shouldn't have mentioned the holiday, but he went on: "OK, well it made a fair splash in the papers. The open safe was hinted at in one of the papers, but that was as far as it went."

"Who called you?"

"Servant, an old one, she'd been with the Gutteridge guy for years, nothing there. Nothing much for her in the will."

"Who else was around?"

"The lot, from memory, a driver, two gardeners as well as the old housekeeper—that's the underlings. Then there was the wife and a son and daughter. Probably ran out of places to spend their money in and had to stay home."

"Now Grant, don't be bitter. They have their troubles just like you and I. The fix came in, did it?"

"Yeah, the photographer arrived fast and fired off a few but the support squad had some heavies in it and they took over—OK Cliff, you've got the inside dope. Make me feel good about it within twenty-four hours," he said, "or I'll call it all square, all round."

The pressure of his job was getting to him, or maybe it was some other trouble. Whatever the case, now wasn't the time to sketch out my suspicions. Just now he'd rather fight than think.

"I think I can promise you that," I said.

"Lovely," he gave me a tired smile. "Now, I got something off my chest and I've got your promise, my day is made. Shoot through Cliff. I'll be expecting to hear from you." I got up and patted him on the shoulder. He faked a collapse into his chair and picked up the top file in his IN tray.

I walked down the corridor and took the lift again. From the noise it made I might just have caught it on its last journey. The desk sergeant called me over and handed me the phone. It was Grant.

"I forgot to tell you to take care of yourself," he said.

"Why do you say it now?"

"I keep up with what's going on. Bryn Gutteridge's chum was shot once, close in but very neat. Whoever did it had done it before."

"I'll sniff every hand I shake and watch for bulges under jackets."

"If you meet him you probably won't have time for one wisecrack." The phone went dead. I hung on to it for a second listening to nothing.

CHAPTER 7

I realised how beat up I looked when I hit the street and how ill-equipped I was for the weather. The storm that had been brewing broke when I was in the police building. Rain sheeted down bringing clouds of steam up from the pavements. The water soaked into my torn pants and dirty shirt which was pinkish from diluted blood. I had a change of clothes back in my office and I decided to complete the picture of ruin by taking the short walk there despite the rain.

I started out and caught sight in an oddly angled shop window of a red Volkswagen. It was well back and crawling along in the thick traffic. I took a turn and walked slowly down the street. A look in a parked car's side mirror showed that the VW had stopped at the top of the street after making the turn. I still couldn't get a glimpse of the driver.

I walked back to St Peters Street the most direct way, cleaned up, changed my clothes and came down after checking that there hadn't been any calls. The rain had stopped, the air was moist and clean-tasting and all the city's photochemical sludge was running down the gutters to the sea. I got the Falcon out of the tattooist's backyard and took off going south-east. The VW picked me up and stayed with me through Taylor Square, Moore Park and Kensington. He was doing it quite nicely, like a pacer, one out and one back, and then letting me get away a little. I cruised past the University and took the turn to Maroubra.

The used car yards cuddled up against each other on both sides of the road over a short stretch of ugly Australia. I made a late turn left, a quick one right and pulled up under a heavily over-growing row of plane trees the council pruners must have missed. I pulled the Smith & Wesson out of its clip under the dashboard and jumped out of the car onto the road. The Volkswagen came round the corner and I faced it fifty yards ahead with the gun up. I counted on the element of surprise to bring the car to a stop but I was wrong. The driver slowed a fraction, then accelerated and came straight on like the Light Brigade. I swore, jumped aside, hit the Falcon hip and thigh and dropped the gun. The little red car roared to the end of the street, brakes screaming, then it slewed around in a full turn taking some of the sidewalk to do it, and came belting back towards me. Dead end street. That gave me a chance to reverse the roles. I picked up the gun as the VW passed me and had my car turning before its tail whipped around out of what had been a quiet little street twenty seconds ago.

The Volkswagen was new and the Falcon was old, but the horsepower was all on my side. I had the car in sight as it turned onto the highway and kept with it through thick and thin. The traffic thinned as we got into Maroubra and I moved up closer. The driver appeared to be small with frizzy dark hair and I saw the flash of light on wrap-around sunglasses on one of the turns. From his driving I assumed that he was worried, it was jerky and he wasn't timing things well.

We moved on down towards the beach and then turned right up a steep hill flanked by tall apartment blocks with names like "Nevada" and "San Bernadino".

I crowded the VW near the crown of the hill opposite "Reno", but the driver found a little more speed and went into a cheeky slalom down the other side. I took evasive action, conscious of my lack of insurance, but I was hard on its twin exhausts when we turned into a long, flat run parallel to the beach. A mistake, I'd surfed along this beach for ten years and knew its geography like the back of my hand. It was deserted now, dark clouds were boiling up out over the sea and the road was slick with oily rainbow patches showing between the puddles.

I closed up behind the VW, timed the move and brought my black paintwork up alongside the red. I pulled my door handle down and held the door ajar. I blared my horn and gave the little car a quick flick with the door. It slewed away and shot through the only gap available—into a fenced parking lot which reached down to a toilet block and changing sheds on the beachfront. The VW driver struggled for control and then had to pull up within twenty yards. He made it, just. I ran in after it and brought the Falcon skidding in on an angle that closed off all exits.

I killed the engine, grabbed the .38 and moved around my car. The other driver was sitting quietly, hands on the wheel, crying softly and shaking. The frizzy hair was short and black as pitch, the thin shoulders in the dark T-shirt were heaving and her face when she turned it up to me was dark as chocolate and beautiful as a rose. I put my hand on her shoulder and gave it a gentle shake. The flesh under my hand was soft and the bone felt like a fine steel rod.

"Take it easy," I said, "I'm not going to hurt you. Calm down and tell me why you were following me."

She kept on shaking and sobbing and she dropped her head, the crisp hair curled on the nape of her neck like black metal filings. I wanted to touch them and moved my hand up.

"Don't! Don't touch me!" Her voice was lilting with an accent, not American. I stepped back and rubbed my tired face with the hand holding the gun. She jack-knifed from the car and sprinted for the beach bent low and balanced, legs pumping. I yelled and brought the gun up but she was too fast. She rounded the changing shed and was into the scrub before I'd taken a step. I lumbered after her but the day had taken its toll; there was no one in sight on the sodden beach and the flickers in the scrub a hundred yards away could easily have been branches in the wind.

I gave the car a quick once-over. It was a recent model which had been well kept. The clean vinyl and interior paintwork probably carried hundreds of fingerprints but I couldn't see any point in collecting them. There was a service book in the glove box and a street directory in the driver's side pocket. A folded copy of *The News* lay on the back seat open at the international news page. There was a pair of pliers and a roll of insulating tape in the passenger side door pocket; no cigarette butts, no night club matches, no soil obviously from the lower eastern slopes of the Great Dividing Range. For no special reason I wiped off places I'd touched in the car and wrote down the licence number. There were no keys in the ignition. That could mean one of two things—the car was stolen or the crying had been an act put on after she'd had the presence of mind to take the keys out of the lock. I pulled the bonnet release, yanked back the cardboard housing and looked in at the panel—nothing across the ignition terminals. Fooled again, Hardy.

It was after six and a warm drizzle had settled in when I got back into my car and started the motor. The Falcon protested the change in the weather by coughing and it flooded before I got it running reasonably. I swung her around, pulled out of the parking lot and took the road back to town. I stopped at a hamburger place and picked up one with all the trimmings. I got a six-pack of beer from a pub full of used car salesmen working on late afternoon marks and tired-looking men putting off going home to their wives.

CHAPTER 8

I ate the hamburger and swigged the beer as I drove. The traffic was light and I made good time to Longueville. Lights were on in the front rooms and the colour TV sets were semaphoring comforting messages to each other across the deep gardens and quiet, damp streets. I parked about a hundred yards from the entrance to the clinic on the opposite side of the road, and focused my night glasses on the relevant point. I could see cars approaching and turning into the reception booth from the other direction and I had a good view of the ones that passed me to get there. I figured I had about an hour at most before someone inside might tally up comments about the tone of the street and come out to investigate.

So I gave myself an hour with the thought that I might sneak an extra fifteen minutes if nothing happened. I was pretty sure something would happen —enough shit had been hitting the fan over the last twenty-four hours or so to produce some reaction in this area. I risked a cigarette or two, drank the beer, now heating up a bit but not too bad, and waited. The first car came about ten minutes after I arrived. It was a Rover, nice car.

The street light caught its number plate nicely as it made a purring turn to the reception booth. I had the glasses on it and wrote the number down. I was too far away to be sure, but I thought there was a driver in front and one passenger behind. Fifteen minutes later a car came up from behind, moving fast. I hunched down in the seat but it roared past. I sat up and then went down again as another car came from the same direction. A light coloured Fairlane swished past me and took the turn, too fast and not quite steady, into the clinic. The light didn't hit this one as well as before, but he had to back out and take another run at the drive so I got the number with no trouble.

Ten minutes went by to the whisper of the falling rain. The Rover slid out onto the road and went back to where it came from. I checked my reading of the number plate and found I had it right. The second car left and the third arrived almost simultaneously. The Fairlane lurched out onto the road, collected the kerb and almost collided with an Italianate sports model which was gliding up towards the clinic and me. The

101

driver flicked out of the path of the Ford and neatly whipped around to stop perfectly aligned with the gates. The number plate was a blur through all this. I swore and settled down to wait for the car's reappearance. I felt edgy and exposed, I was pushing my luck.

After eight minutes lights went on in the compound and I heard a dog bark. Warning bells rang in my head and the name of every prison I'd ever heard of flashed through my mind. I didn't have all the information I wanted but I had enough.

The Falcon threatened to flood but relented. I revved it firmly, did a tight U turn and got the hell out of Longueville.

Mosman seemed a hundred miles away and all of it uphill. I washed down a few caffeine tablets with a swill of beer and concentrated on navigating the greasy roads. I was tired or I would have noticed it at least ten minutes sooner—an unchanging pair of headlights centred in my rear vision mirror like bright, sparkling diamonds. The driver knew nothing about tailing, which was comforting, but I felt I'd had enough of that scene for one day. He would have followed me down a sewer and it was child's play to fake a right turn and then run him into the kerb. When he stopped his left front wheel was up on the concrete and the genteel, muted neon lights of the Waterson & Sons funeral parlour were flashing in his eyes.

I got out cautiously and kept the gun down in my jacket pocket. The car was an old FB Holden and the driver was not all that much older than it was. He had damp blond hair, pretty long, but there wasn't enough of it to be worth spending much time on. There wasn't much of him all round—he looked almost childlike sitting in the car with his sports jacket collar turned up. I could see a tight grin on his face and he was fumbling inside his breast pocket as I approached the car—he was so amateurish it was almost funny.

I leaned on the car and rapped on the driver's window. A wallet and some papers spilled out on his lap as he pulled his hand out to wind down the window. He leaned forward to recover the papers presenting me with a thin, clean neck that I could have broken between my thumb and forefinger.

"I have identification." His voice squeaked a bit and was young and educated.

"Let's not worry about who you are first off," I said. "Everybody has identification, everyone is someone if you get what I mean. Why were you following me?"

"That's connected with who I am."

He seemed determined to tell me and I thought I'd better sit down to receive the impact. I walked round the back of the car and climbed in on the passenger's side at the front.

"Right. This is cosy. Now, who are you and why were you following me?"

He pushed the wallet over. Tucked in one of its compartments was a press identification card with photograph. The name on the card was Harry Tickener and it was him all right on the photograph; he had to be the only one of his kind in captivity.

"OK, you're an artist. Let's have the answers."

"I work on *The News*. I just got up to the political reporting team last week, from sports, you might have seen the byline?"

"I don't follow the volleyball all that closely. Come on, get to the point."

"I haven't done much yet in the political line. I've mostly run errands for Joe Barrett."

Now that *was* a name with clout. Barrett was by way of being a crime-busting political reporter and he'd made some fat faces very red in his time. *The News* occasionally gave him his head on a story and he was very good for circulation when they did. He went a bit wild sometimes so they used him sparingly. Tickener pulled out some thick plain American cigarettes and got one lit after a struggle. He puffed, didn't draw back and the Holden turned into a fair imitation of a second class smoking compartment on the New South Wales railways. I reached across, pulled the cigarette out of his mouth and threw it out the window.

"If you want me to say 'Quit stalling' I will. I'll pull a rod and do a Cagney impression if you insist, but how about just telling me in plain and simple English what you're up to."

He nodded and the words tumbled fast. "I took a call for Joe. She must have thought she had got on to him direct, anyway I didn't get time to say who I was. She said she had a tip on a big story and if I . . . if Joe wanted to get in on it he should start taking an interest in Dr Ian Brave. She said she'd call again if she saw any signs of interest at our end."

"So you took the job on?"

"Yes, there didn't seem to be any harm in it. Joe's in Canberra for a few days. I thought I could do the initial poking around and let Joe take it from there. Or maybe he'd let me follow it through, I don't know. Anyway, it sounded interesting so I went out tonight to have a look at Brave's place. I saw you parked and watching the clinic, so when you left I followed you. I thought you might lead me to someone, maybe the woman who rang."

"Where were you?"

"My car was two blocks away. I watched you from the garden of the house on the corner of the street you were in."

He looked wet enough for it to be true and the story sounded straight.

"Tell me about the woman's voice."

"It was nice, educated, with an accent."

"What sort of accent?"

"European, not Italian, maybe French."

It checked. The net was getting thrown wider all the time and it seemed like the moment to bring in some keen, unpaid help. I was thinking how to put it to him when I caught sight of my face in his rear vision mirror. It looked like it had been made out of a kerosene drum; my skin was pale and creased and my nose and jaw were sharp and cruel. I tried to produce a smile out of this unsuitable material and to get a halfway human tone into my voice.

"Look Tickener, we could get together on this. I think there is a story in it and you could have it. If I call you in it's your story, not Barrett's. That tip was incidental, get it?"

He nodded slowly. "It isn't quite ethical, but . . ."

I broke in. "Ethical is what doesn't keep you awake. It's different from one person to another, that's what's interesting about it. Do you want to hear more?"

"Yes."

I gave him some of the details, stressed the political implications and the likelihood of high level police involvement, hence the need for security at the investigative end. He came in like a well hooked trout. He was eager to do anything, he'd go anywhere, meet me anytime. I almost regretted the impulse to use him, faithful dogs can get in the way, but I felt that events to come would justify co-opting him. I gave him the licence numbers—of the Volkswagen and the cars that

106

had visited the clinic that night—and told him his first assignment was to get the names and addresses of the people to whom they were registered. He said he had a contact in the right place for this dating from the days when he used to follow football players to get a line on what clubs they might defect to. I felt better about him. We agreed to be at our respective phone numbers at a certain time the next day. We shook hands. I got out of the car and he drove off, probably with dreams of Watergate in his head. I eased myself back into the traffic and headed for Mosman where the drizzle would look romantic falling on the lapping waves and the mansions.

CHAPTER 9

The Alfa was looking racey and the boat toey when I arrived at Ailsa's place. I parked the Falcon next to the boat and took the steps two at a time to test my wind. It seemed to take ten minutes to reach the top and I wondered how Ailsa made out on fifty smokes a day. The door was made of oregon pine with glass panels. The curtains inside drew across what looked like a hundred yards of glass on each side. I gave the handle an experimental turn. It was locked, as befitted the front door of a lady whose car has been booby trapped with gelignite. I pressed the bell and waited. Ailsa's voice came from inside, back a bit and to one side. Good.

"Who is it?"

"Cliff Hardy."

To judge from the sound she was drawing a bolt and undoing a chain. She said "Come in", and I opened the door and pushed aside a section of the heavy curtains. Ailsa was standing well inside the room, with one hand up to the electric light switch and the other full of a big, black gun pointing at my navel. We looked at each other for a full quarter minute.

"That's good security," I said. "Congratulations."

"Thank you." She lowered the gun to her side and took a step towards me. I took three or four and put my arms around her. She pressed in close and we kissed expertly and carefully. She pushed me away gently and handed me the gun.

"Put it down please, I hate it."

I thumbed forward the safety catch and put the big automatic down on a chair.

"You looked like business."

"I've never fired it, I don't think I could."

We circled around each other for a while in the kitchen and living room while she made me a drink and tea for herself. She'd spent the afternoon in bed and had taken it quietly in the evening, fixing herself a meal and watching TV. She was wearing a silk chinese-looking robe, all red and black with wide sleeves. It suited her, she looked rested and good. We sat side by side on the floor of her den which was book-lined and comfortable. The wind whipped some branches against the window. The soft, warm rain pattered down and I sipped my drink while telling her about my comings and goings in her service. Some kissing spun the story

109

out and after two drinks, with her head on my shoulder and my hand on her breast inside her robe, I was feeling miles away from coffee coloured girls in red Volkswagens and rainy vigils outside hospitals. She brought me back to it with the big question, or one of them.

"Who do you think the woman with the French accent could be?" I stroked her breast drowsily, it seemed the right thing to do when considering French-accented women and was very nice for its own sake too.

"Brave has Canadian connections you tell me. Maybe that's the answer, some French Canadian woman. But since talking to Tickener I'm not so sure. She put him on to Brave. They could have fallen out I suppose, but I'm not wild about the whole theory."

"Why not?"

"Brave and bombing don't go together, he's more subtle. Still, there's Giles' death to consider. Can't rule Brave out on that and therefore he could be involved in the bombing."

"It's getting very complicated, isn't it?"

"It is, that's why you need a specialist in complicated criminal cases."

"Like you?"

"Like me."

Her breast was warm under my hand and her fingers on my thigh reminded me that it had been a long, long time. I pulled her to her feet and we did some more kissing and eye gazing. She broke away and led me off by the hand—it felt like the fifth or sixth time, when you know enough to take it slowly and be touched by it. We undressed each other in her timber-beamed, white-bricked bedroom and closed like tired but healthy and experienced animals. She finished before me and opened up warmly beneath me. I went down and around and moaned out my gratitude.

She seemed to feel the same thing—a gratitude and release and we each smoked a cigarette and made mildly dirty remarks in each other's ears. It was an exchange of needs, strengths and weaknesses and both of us knew that was all it was for now. She rolled away from me and slipped her hand between my legs.

"Go to sleep." Her hand soothed me beyond the power of food, drink or money. "I might catch you again before morning."

We woke soon after first light and moved in on each other urgently and hard. It was a different event, less tender, more athletic and she got out of bed almost as soon as we'd finished.

"Tea or coffee?"

She wrapped a cheesecloth cloak around her and ran her hand over her hair. I wanted to pull her back into the bed but the look on her face told me she wouldn't be playing. She looked preoccupied, withdrawn and anxious to get on with some task to divert her from the reality of a man in her bed.

111

"Coffee, black please."

"Do you want anything to eat?"

I pulled the sheet up over my head. She snorted and went out. I unsheeted and looked around the room. It was austere with built-in wardrobes, a low camphor-wood chest with a lamp on it and some paperbacks, and a full length mirror. The outlines were muzzy in the early half-light, softening down the lines of the neat, not self-indulgent decor. It was a fine room to wake up in. I got up and pulled back a little of the curtain. The pool was immediately outside—you could dive into it from the decking if you were good enough or drunk enough. I wandered around the room and into the compact ensuite bathroom. There was a man's shirt, several sizes too big for Ailsa, hanging on the back of the door. It was slightly soiled and monogrammed RH on the breast pocket. It was silk, very expensive. I took my empty bladder and the little puzzle back into the bedroom.

Ailsa came in with the coffee on a tray as I was riffling through one of her books—*The Day of the Jackal*, good stuff by a guy who wrote passably and had something good to write about. She kept the cloak on and sat down on the bed away from me. She handed me the coffee which was strong and hot.

"I suppose you want brandy in it?"

"It has been known. What is the H in RH for?"

She put down her cup and looked away from me, at the mirror.

"That's it," she said. "I was waiting for the thing you'd say that would be all wrong, and you come out with that."

She reached for her cigarettes but I checked the movement and pulled her down beside me. She didn't resist, didn't comply. I stroked her hair.

"I'm sorry," I said. "That was a question to ask a suspect at midnight. I'm sorry love, I'm off on this case again. I didn't think."

"It's all right, you don't have to soothe me. I'm not going to cry or anything like that. But you're not being completely truthful. You saw Ross' shirt, right?"

"Right."

"Well, what does it mean to you?"

"Jesus! Not a 'what does it mean session' this early."

She pushed herself up and away from me angrily.

"You're a ripe bastard this morning, aren't you? Is this your usual style? Do you fuck your clients and piss them off in the morning and keep the retainer? Nice work."

She got the cigarettes this time and lit one shakily. I recovered my coffee and drank some trying to work out how to calm the storm. Maybe she was right, I'd woken up with clients before and worked my way out by the shortest route. But I wasn't feeling like that this time.

"Ailsa, it isn't like that. There's loose threads hanging everywhere in this case. I saw your fight with

113

this guy Ross. I just want to fit him into the picture a bit more clearly. If he's in the picture."

She tapped ash off her cigarette and drank some coffee, not looking at me.

"Very well," she said tightly. "Yes I suppose Ross is in the picture, or was. He's been my occasional lover for a year or so. Mostly we fight, sometimes it's nice . . . was nice. I don't expect it to be any good again. That fight was beyond the limit."

"What was it about?"

She drew on the cigarette and looked at me, her head nodding slightly.

"You know men aren't all that attractive in the morning," she said. "Bristly, stinking a bit of tobacco and bad teeth. You're no major exception Cliff Hardy. You'll have to warm up a bit to get anything more out of me. Would you admit to being jealous?"

"Under pentothal."

She finished her cigarette and coffee, dropped the butt in the dregs and slung herself down on the bed beside me. She put her hands behind her head and drew her knees up until she was sitting in a sort of yoga posture.

"OK, the full story, for your files. Ross came to me a few months after Mark's death. He had some references, pretty impressive ones. I was just getting around to thinking I'd have to do something with the money Mark left me. Ross had ideas."

114

"Like what?"

"He knew about setting up companies and minimising taxes and quite a bit about the share market. He made some nice killings for me there, early on. I've got a fashion business, manufacturing and retail, I've even gone international with it in a small way. I've got a vineyard—that'd interest you—and some outlets for the wine. I've got a company to co-ordinate things and Ross is second in charge."

"Who's in charge, you?"

"No, only nominally. The real boss is a man called Chalmers. He's a chartered accountant and the dullest man in the world. He's ultra-cautious and he's never lost me a penny. That's why he's in charge."

"Ross has lost you pennies?"

"A few. A couple of times, that's why he hasn't got the job. I work on old Sophie Tucker's dictum, 'I been rich and I been poor . . .,' you know it?"

"Yes."

"Most people just take it on faith. I know it's true. But I'm not a maniac about it. I just like being rich and I don't intend to get poor by going into wildcat schemes."

"That's Ross' style?"

"Yes, it is now. He wants to be in charge of everything or failing that to play a few hands without Chalmers' interference. I don't feel like staking him."

"And that's what the fight was about?"

115

"Yes. He's been getting very pushy lately. He was pressing me to go into a mining deal and I'm not interested. He got nasty and started putting me down. I'm a lot older than him and he pointed it out. You saw how it went."

"You were doing pretty well, you might have won it on your own. How's it going to be, business-wise, if you break with him?"

"He'll just have to accept it or move out. He hasn't got a contract and I know he's not short of women. He gets a good salary and the usual perks. He's useful, he knows people. I think he'll stay."

"The silver spoon?"

"I don't think so. I'm not sure. He's never told me anything much about his background."

We'd got over the hump and she relaxed letting her long legs slide down the bed. We kissed for the sheer pleasure of it. She rubbed her hand over my face.

"Bristly, black-bearded bastard."

"Virility," I said. "Tell me about Chalmers."

"Christ, you like your work don't you. What do you want to know?"

"Just one thing, was he connected in any way with Mark Gutteridge?"

"Yes," she spoke slowly, beating her hand in time to the words on the bed. "He was Mark's chief accountant for many years."

I did the same. "And how did he come to work for you?"

116

"He approached me. I don't know exactly why he picked on me. I do know that he couldn't get on with Bryn."

"In what way?"

"I don't know. Ross once said something about Walter being a repressed homosexual, that could have something to do with it. But Ross isn't reliable on the subject of Chalmers."

I thought about it. There were more connections back to the Gutteridge trouble for Ailsa than I'd realised. I still felt that the car bombing related back to the harassment of Susan Gutteridge, but I didn't know how. Ailsa had given me some more people with possible motives, but Brave was still out in front and my main concern as well as hers. He was Harry Tickener's concern too.

"I'm going to be very busy on your behalf today love," I said, planting a firm kiss on her shoulder.

"And your own. Your rates are moderate verging on extortionate. Do you make a lot of money?"

"No. Overheads are high and I have long slack periods. Most of what I make goes on booze and books anyway."

"I can imagine. And on women?"

I disengaged myself and rolled off the bed. "Very little on women. Use your shower?" She nodded. "Are you married Hardy?" she said. "Was. Tell you about it sometime." I started for the shower and turned back. She was sitting up again and lighting a cigarette. With the cream coloured fabric draped around her she looked like a young, scared Christian about to go to the lions. I walked back and put my fingers in the hair at the nape of her neck. I massaged her neck gently.

"We'll have lots of time to talk," I said. "Today I've got ten men to see and six houses to break into. Can you write me down the addresses of Chalmers and Ross . . . what's his other name?"

She rotated her head cat-like under my fingers. "That's nice. All right. Ross' other name is Haines." She got up, crossed to the wardrobe and got out a thick towel. She tossed it to me and I caught it and went into the bathroom. When I came back into the room she handed me a page torn from a notebook. The names and addresses were written in neat capitals. She made a grab at the towel around my waist and I backed off. She looked amused and got out another cigarette. I pulled on my clothes, bent down over the bed and kissed her on the head.

"You could have typed it out," I said.

"Can't type, never learned."

I nodded. "What are you going to do today?" She blew smoke at the mirror. "Since I evidently can't stay here with you," she said, "I'll go into the office and check a few things. I might go to the library. Where's my protection by the way?"

"You should be safe enough if you stick to doing

118

what you say. Take taxis and stay with other people. You can do it all the time if you try."

"Taxis, OK. That reminds me, what about the police and my car? Will I have to talk to them again do you think?"

"I don't think so, I've squared it for the time being."

"Fully insured, I'll get someone in the office onto it today. Good car, I think I'll get another one the same."

"You do that," I said.

She flared. "Don't be supercilious with me. I employ a lot of people, I spend my money. I do the best I can and I'm not hypocritical about it."

"Like Susan Gutteridge?"

"Yes."

"You've got a point. I'll call you about six, maybe we could have dinner, then have some things to do."

"Tonight?"

"Yeah, it could be all over tonight if things go right."

"You're being mysterious."

"Not really, if I told you all about it you'd think it was so simple you wouldn't feel like paying me."

She laughed and came up to me. I pulled her in and we kissed and rubbed together for a minute or two. I promised to call her at six, come what may, and left the house.

CHAPTER 10

I took the first drink of the day in an early opening pub at the Quay. My companions in sin ranged from a tattooed youth, who was playing at looking tough and doing pretty well at it, to a grizzled wreck who was mumbling about the Burns-Johnson fight at Rush-cutters Bay in 1908. He claimed to have been the timekeeper and maybe he was. I bought him a schooner and he switched to Sullivan-Corbett which was a bit unlikely. A scotch would probably have got me Sayers and Heenan. I had a middy of old and tried to anticipate the results of Tickener's inquiries. The smell of toasted sandwiches interrupted this train of thought and I put the matter aside in their favour. I ate two cheese sandwiches and had a second beer. The rain had cleared and the day was going to be warm. Students and the unemployed would be on the beaches, accountants would be at their desks, private detectives would be peeling secrets off people like layers of sunburnt skin.

I got a shave in the Cross at a barber shop where I'd once seen Gough Whitlam, before he became Prime Minister—I figured he'd know where to get a good shave. The Italian razor man was neat and economical and let me read the paper while he worked. He was coming on strong with garlic and aftershave but I fought back with beer and I guess the honours were about even. *The News* had put Costello on the second page and had splashed a government statement about unions across the front. There was a front page picture of a cricket player kissing a paraplegic girl to remind everyone that God lives and life is still all fun and games.

I got to the office, checked the mail and the incoming calls with the answering service. There was nothing of interest in either. I rang the number which Harry Tickener, newshound and wordsmith, had given me the night before. He must have been sitting on top of the phone because it was snatched up the second it rang.

We established identities, confirmed that we were both in sound health and got down to business. The records branch of the motor registry never shuts down to accredited people and Tickener's contact had got what we wanted during the night. In a voice as thin and reedy as himself, Tickener recited the facts: "The Rover is registered to Dr William Clyde, 232 Sackville Drive, Hunters Hill, the Fairlane to Charles Jackson,

114 Langdon Street, Edgecliff, the VW to Naumeta Pali, Flat 6, 29 Rose Street, Drummoyne."

"Good. Do you know anything about these people?"

"Not a thing. The only Charles Jackson I know of is a cop, Detective Inspector, CID. I don't know where he lives or what he drives. Never heard of the others, could find out though."

"Right, you take Clyde, call me in an hour."

I tidied my desk, throwing away bills and advertisements, and paid a couple of modest accounts with cheques I could cover by lodging Gutteridge money. I phoned Grant Evans at home. It was delicate but I was getting more confident.

"Grant? Cliff, I'm getting closer but I need a piece of information."

"How big a piece? I'm feeling weak."

"Not big, but close to home. You have a colleague by the name of Charles Jackson?"

"Yeah, what about him?"

"Your assessment."

"No comment."

"What does he drive and where does he live?"

"A Fairlane, he lives in Edgecliff somewhere."

That spoke volumes. Evans trusted me but not enough to give out information on anyone for whom he had any regard. I had a character sketch of Jackson from those seven words.

"Anything else Cliff?"

"Not until tonight. You on duty?"

"Yeah, seven to three."

"Good men with you?"

"Good enough."

"I'll call you at eight."

"You'd better come through on this, Cliff. There's a bit of flak about the car bombing and some bright boy has got on to the Gutteridge connection. I'm not sure how long I can sit on it."

"Just hold the lid on until tonight. What I've got will be big enough to make you smell like a rose."

He rang off without saying any more. Grant's position in the force was secure, but it would add to his troubles if the promotions didn't keep coming. If he got stuck on a rung too long he'd dry up with frustration and snap like a dead branch. He needed to get up to the top and get there soon. I hoped I could help him make it. Tickener's call came through at 10.00 precisely. It tied things up.

"Dr Clyde's a plastic surgeon," he said without too much interest. "What about Jackson?"

"He's the cop you've heard of."

"Yeah?" He sounded keener. "What's it all about?"

Suddenly I had doubts about telling him, not about his honesty but about his control of his tongue. If he went around talking to the wrong people for a day, word could get about and the whole thing could be blown. If Gutteridge's files existed and were being put to use there could be prominent people in all sorts of places treading the high wire and alert to anything in the breeze about Brave and the Gutteridges. I decided not to risk it.

"It hasn't quite come together yet," I said, "but I expect it to tonight. I'll call you at eight and you can be in on it from the start. Meanwhile I'd dig up all I could on Brave's background if I were you. You're going to need that sort of stuff for your story. And keep quiet about Jackson, he's a small fish. How are you fixed in there? Is Barrett around?"

"No, still in the ACT."

"Good, do you know Colin Jones, the photographer?"

"Yeah, a bit."

"Line him up and be there at eight."

He said okay and for his ego I told him to be sober and to have a full tank of petrol in the FB. That wrapped things up in that direction as far as I could see. I was sure that Costello was at Brave's clinic. Jackson was covering the police inquiry end and Dr Clyde was doing the face job. They'd been alarmed when I'd blundered into the clinic and seemed to have held some sort of conference the following night. But they hadn't moved Costello yet and perhaps they couldn't. It mightn't be medically advisable. If they were going to move him it would almost certainly happen at night and I had plans to head that off. I wished I had a man to watch the clinic in the daytime but I didn't and there was no use lamenting it.

All this planning was thirsty work and I left the office to repair the damage. Before I took off I put a handful of shells for the Smith & Wesson in my pocket and added a plastic wallet of easily assembled burglar's tools. I had a licence for the gun but no one has a licence for skeleton keys and lock slides.

CHAPTER 11

I drove to a pub near the University where you can sit in the shade, drink old beer and eat passable rissole sandwiches. I took my street directory into the pub and looked up the addresses of Haines, Pali and Chalmers while I worked on the food and drink. Students around the place were talking in their derivative argot and preparing themselves to fall asleep in the afternoon lectures. One hairy intellectual studied me for a while and then announced that I was obviously in real estate—so much for higher education.

The addresses were more or less on the same side of the city. Geography determined the order of my visits—Pali, Haines, Chalmers. I finished my drink and got up. The pub was emptying but the vocation spotter seemed to be putting off the evil hour. He was rolling a cigarette from makings he'd bludged from one of his fellow seekers after truth. I caught his eye as I stood up and pressed a finger to my lips. As I passed his table I dropped one of my cards, face up, into the beer puddles.

Naumeta Pali's flat was in a six storey red brick building which was a wound in a wide street flanked by neat terrace houses. The flats were built over car parking space and there was a wide expanse of those smooth white stones that are supposed to replace grass around them. The whole set-up was modern, tasteless and medium expensive. The parking area was divided into bays of white lines; each bay had a flat number painted on it and there were a couple of signs around warning the public that this was private space. The space allotted for flat 6 was empty. I went into one of the lobbies in the building and located the flat. It was three floors up. In Glebe there'd have been milk bottles and cats on every landing and you'd have to fight a gang of kids for every inch of territory. Here there was nothing.

I knocked on the door of flat 6 and heard the sound echo about emptily inside. After a second try a woman put her head outside the door opposite.

"She ain't in," she said.

The voice jarred with everything around and I turned around to take a good look at its owner. She was fortyish, fat and a good advertisement for cosmetics—black circled eyes, rouged cheeks and fire engine red lips. She'd had a few drinks but not enough for her to forget that she had to hold herself together. She had some help from corsets and a bra that pushed her breasts up out of the tight floral dress towards her loose chin. She wore gold, high heeled sandals. I looked closely for a cigarette holder but she didn't seem to have one just then.

"If you're looking for the darkie she ain't there." Her voice was city slummy with a touch of country slowness.

"Do you happen to know when she'll be back Mrs . . .?"

"Williams, Gladys Williams. Who're you? Is she in trouble?"

"Why do you ask that?"

"Well, you know them. She comes an' goes, all hours like. Must be doin' something shady."

"I see. Do you mind if I ask what you do Mrs Williams?"

"Nothin', not any more."

I raised an eyebrow and she gave a lopsided grin. "Nah, not that either, not for years. Married now."

I nodded. "Husband's a bookie," she went on, "in Lithgow. That's where we live. He comes to the bloody city meetings once a week, bloody dumps me here."

"Why don't you go with him?"

She shook her head, the frizzy red tendrils danced about like the Gorgon's snakes. "Sick of 'em, rather stay here. Might go out tonight. Hey, why're you askin' all these questions, wanna drink?"

I'd only asked three that I was aware of, but she was ready to open up like a sardine can and her qualifications as an observer of her neighbours were impeccable. I produced a card from the insurance days.

"A drink would be very nice," I said, moving towards her so she couldn't renege on the offer. "I'm an insurance investigator. Miss Pali isn't in trouble exactly, but any information you could give me might help to clear things up a little."

She wanted it to be trouble. "Fiddlin' a claim is she?" We moved through the door straight into the living room. It was over-furnished and over-cleaned, the blinds were drawn to enhance the television viewing—the real day closed off to allow the fantasy one fuller rein.

"I'd rather not say Mrs Williams. It's rather unsavoury in some ways."

That was better. She nodded conspiratorially and went off into the kitchen. She made noises out there and came back with two hefty gin-and-tonics. She handed me one, sat down in a quilted armchair and waved me into another. She tucked her legs up under her and took a long pull at her drink.

"I understand," she said throatily. "How can I help youse?"

I sipped the drink. It was something to take in slowly over half an hour with a novel.

"What can you tell me about Miss Pali? I understand she drives a red Volkswagen, is that right?"

"Yeah, like I said she comes in at all hours of the day and night. Makes a bloody awful noise that thing."

"What does she do for a living?" She wasn't stupid, she gave me a suspicious look. "Don't you know?" I cleared my throat and took another sip trying to look guarded. "Well, we're not sure, that is . . ."

"Umm, well I dunno. Seems to have plenty of money to judge by her clothes, not my taste of course but they aren't cheap—slack suits and that. Could be some sorta secretary, 'cept not in an office. She's home a lot an' types for hours. A couple of blokes come and bring . . ." she made a vague gesture with her hand. "Files," I suggested, "papers?"

"Yeah, somethin' like that. Folders and that."

"I see. How many men?"

"Couple."

"Can you describe them?"

"One's a big bloke, bigger 'n you and younger. Other one's dark, not a boong, more dagoey looking, sharp dresser."

"All business is it?"

She looked sly, "No way, young man stays the night sometimes."

130

I took out a notebook and pretended to write in it. "You keep your eyes open, Mrs Williams."

"Bugger all else to do here. I stay down sometimes see, go to a show and go up to Lithgow at the weekend. Got a coupla relations in Sydney."

I wrote some more gibberish. "Can you describe them more closely, her visitors?"

"Nah, never looked that close. Both wear good clothes, better 'n Bert's."

"Bert?"

"Me husband. Bert wears old fashioned clothes, he reckons bettors don't like trendy bookies. I reckon they don't like bookies full stop, but you can't tell Bert a thing."

The gin was getting to her and she was wandering into the dreary deserts of her own life. I only wanted the spin-off from that—the fruits of her boozy, envious snooping.

"I see. What else can you tell me? Does she have other visitors?"

"Yeah, course she does, other darkies mostly, but they piss off when the white blokes arrive."

It was time to wind it up. "When did you last see her, Mrs Williams?"

"Yestiddy mornin', didn't come home last night don't think. No sign of her this mornin'."

"Is that usual?"

"No, always comes home sometime, *he* comes there, see. I dunno, suppose it's all right, black and white and that. She's a funny sort of blackie anyway, not an Abo', comes from some funny place, New . . . somethin', saw the stamp."

The gin had hit her, she was coming apart and I pressed in for just this last scrap.

"New Guinea?" I prompted.

"No, I heard of New Guinea, Bert was there in the war. Never heard of this place, New . . ."

"Hebrides?"

"No, don't think so."

"Caledonia?"

"Yeah, that's it, New Caledonia. Where's that?"

I told her, thanked her for the drink and eased my way out. She slumped down in her chair muttering about a cruise.

Strictly speaking, it was a little too late for me to be making another call. I'd meant to give the Pali flat a quick once-over and be on my way, not get stuck drinking gin with a lady whose best days were behind her. Still, I'd learned a bit and this encouraged me to stick to my schedule and tackle Haines next. The traffic would hold him away from home for at least an hour after office hours, if he observed them. If he didn't, then one time was about as good as another for what I had to do. It was a short drive but my shirt was sticking to my back and my throat was oily with the humidity and the almost neat gin when I turned into Haines' street. It was a migrant and black neighbourhood which surprised me a little from what I'd heard of Haines, but perhaps he liked slumming. His flat was in a big Victorian town house, free standing with massive bay windows on both levels. Someone enterprising had made the building over into flats about thirty years ago and it was now in a fair way to return a thousand dollars a month. There was a small overgrown garden in front of the house and a narrow strip of bricked walkway down each side. At the back the yard had been whittled away to nothing to allow four cars to cuddle up against each other under a flat roofed carport. There were no cars at home.

I took this in from a slow cruise around the block formed by the street onto which the house fronted, two side streets and a lane at the back. I parked across the street and a hundred yards down, took the Smith & Wesson from its clip, dropped the keys under the driver's seat and walked up towards the house. My car blended in nicely with the other bombs parked around it. Two black kids were thumping a tennis ball against a brick wall. I gave them a grin and they waited sceptically for me to pass. The iron gate was off its hinges and leaning against the fence just inside the garden. I went in and took the left hand path to the back of the house. It turned out to be the correct side; a set of concrete steps ran up to a landing and an art nouveau door with

133

slanted wooden strips across it and a swan etched into the ripple glass. I coaxed the door open with a pick lock and slid inside leaving the door slightly ajar.

It was what the advertisements call a studio apart-ment—one big room with a kitchenette and a small bathroom off to one side. A three-quarter bed was tucked into the bay-window recess, and a couch and a couple of heavy armchairs were lined up against one wall with a big oak wardrobe facing them across the room. A low coffee table and a few cushions filled in some of the space and an old wooden filing cabinet stood in a corner away from the light. The rug left a border of polished wood around the room; it had been good and expensive fifty years ago and still had much of its charm.

In the kitchenette were the usual bachelor things and there was no one dead in the bathroom. There were no papers in the filing cabinet, just socks, underwear and folded shirts, all high quality. The drawers of the wardrobe held tie pins, cuff links, a couple of cigarette lighters and some dusty stationery. I flicked through the suits hanging in the long cupboards, four of them with custom labels, nothing in the pockets. Nothing either in the bathrobe, trench coat, duffel jacket or two sports coats. The shoes were in the bottom of one of the cupboards, formally aligned like waiters at a wedding breakfast. There were no bathing suits, no tennis sneakers, no camera, no records or cassettes. There was a small transistor radio, but no television and there wasn't a book in the place.

I found the personal papers in a drawer in the base of the bed—on the side turned to the wall. They occupied one large manila envelope and it took me about two seconds to spread them out on the coffee table. They didn't amount to much: five photographs and five pieces of paper. Unless he carried them around strapped to his thigh, this guy had made a point of not accumulating the usual pieces of plastic and paper that signpost our lives from the cradle to the grave. That in itself was interesting.

If they haven't been kept with any special care, a collection of photographs is fairly easy to arrange from the earliest to the latest and so it was with this batch. The earliest picture, yellowed and a bit creased, was of a building I'd never seen before to my knowledge—a nasty red brick Victorian affair with a wall around it and the look of a women's prison. Next oldest was a muzzy snapshot of a woman in the fashions of twenty years before. A young woman with flared skirts and plenty of lipstick—she looked vaguely familiar but it might just have been the clothes; my sister had looked much the same at the time. Number three, according to my layout, was a careful shot, taken with a good camera, of a landscaped garden—a beautiful job with rockeries and tiled paths and garden beds spreading out over what could have been an acre or more. The fourth picture was a booth print, passport size, of

Ross Haines taken about five years ago. He had a dark bushy beard and was slimmer than he now looked; he was wearing a department store shirt and tie and a suit which, to judge from the cut of the shoulders and the lapels, had come off a fairly cheap hook. Haines wasn't smiling or scowling or pulling any kind of face, just presenting his puss neutrally to the camera. The most recent of the photos could have been taken yesterday—it showed Ailsa Bercer Gutteridge, nee Sleeman. She wore light coloured slacks and a denim smock and her eyes were slightly crinkled up against smoke from a cigarette which she was holding rather stiffly in front of her. She looked a bit surprised, a bit off guard, but she wasn't doing anything she shouldn't unless you disapprove of smoking.

The documents, all but one, dated themselves. There was an extract of birth to the effect that Ross Haines had been born on 8 May 1953 in Adelaide, South Australia. It was only an extract so no parents' names appeared. There were two references from employers dated October 1970 and November 1971, both letterheads were of plant nurseries and garden suppliers and landscapers in Adelaide. They established the solid credentials and serviceable talents of Ross Haines in this line of work. The other dated document was a diploma from a Sydney business college. It detailed the creditable performances of Haines at typing, shorthand and commercial principles and practice. A map of the Pacific Ocean completed the personal papers of Ross Haines. It folded four times, down to the size of a ladies' handkerchief. I opened it out. There were no marks, no circles, no pin-pricks; at that scale most of the islands were dots or straggly shapes like ink-blots in a vast and trackless sea.

I couldn't make much of this very selective preservation of the past. I studied the photographs of the building and the women closely so as to recognise the originals if I ever saw them and then put the whole lot back in the envelope and the drawer just as I'd found them.

This piece of illegality had taken longer than I'd expected, over half an hour, and I felt an itch at the back of my neck that told me it was high time to go. I went out onto the landing and pulled the door shut behind me. I froze as I heard a car engine being cut under the car port twenty feet away. A door slammed and leather-soled shoes started hitting the bricks. I risked a look down and saw a short, heavy-set man with a head as bald as an egg move briskly down the path and turn into the doorway of the front flat on the ground floor. I let out a stale, sour breath and went down the steps and out through the spaces in the car port. Flat 1's space was taken up by a red MG sports model with wire wheels and kerb feelers. I sneered at it and walked through the lane and up the street to where the Falcon stood with its rust patches and bald tyres gleaming in the late afternoon light.

I had just enough time to try a long shot which would round off the day's work. I drove against the flow of traffic, which was thick and moving as slow as a senile snail, across to the University. I arrived when the day students were pulling out and just before the evening sloggers took up all the space. I got a parking place near the east gates and strolled across the lawn to the main library. I had once done a little research into architecture when I was investigating an insurance fraud on a fire in a Victorian hotel and I remembered where the architecture section was in the library. I looked along the rows until I found Chiswick's two volumes on *The Public Buildings of South Australia*. The book had been very expensive when it was published thirty years before and the quality of its photographs was excellent. It was meticulously indexed and it only took a few minutes to find out that the building of which Haines had kept a picture wasn't a prison. Another few minutes showed that it wasn't a school. Perhaps it was a combination of the two though: I found it on page 215 of the second volume, the picture was taken from a slightly different angle but it was undoubtedly the same forbidding edifice—St Christopher's Boys Orphanage. The short history of the building wasn't interesting but I read it through just the same. I put the books back and left the library.

CHAPTER 12

The part-timers, looking tired already, were getting out of their cars as I got into mine. I decided to make for a pub and have a few drinks before calling Ailsa. I'd been hired to help a woman I found I cordially disliked and had ended up working for one about whom I had quite different feelings. It was a big changeabout in a short space of time and I wondered what effect it was having on my judgment. I wonder better over a glass of something, so I put off the effort until I had the conditions right. After a scotch in a place near the dog track, I picked the right money out of my change and put it into the red phone at the corner of the bar. The wall was scarred with a hundred telephone numbers and the names and numbers of innumerable horses and dogs. The directory was a tattered ruin. I read the record of losing favourites and one-leg doubles as I waited for

Ailsa to answer her phone. It rang and rang hopelessly and I hung up, checked the number and rang again. The result was the same and the repeated buzz on the line chilled and sobered me like a bucket of ice water in the face.

I ran to the Falcon and unparked it regardless of duco and chrome. I ripped my way through the late afternoon traffic towards Mosman.

There were no cops about and I set records through the winding roads towards the Bridge. I hit the Harbour Bridge approach and pushed the Falcon to the limit cursing it for its sluggishness and refusal to steer straight.

I ran into Ailsa's drive too fast and nearly spun the car around full circle in bringing it to a stop in front of the house. I unshipped my gun and went up the steps at a gallop. I hammered on the door and wrenched at the handle but it was locked so I kicked in the glass pane next to it. The thick glass shattered and splintered where my foot hit it and the rest of the pane came crashing down like a guillotine. I went in through the jagged hole and raced through the house, poking the gun into each room and calling Ailsa's name. I found her in the bedroom. She was naked and her clothes had been torn in strips to truss her up and tie her to the frame of the bed. She was breathing harshly through puffed, split lips and her body was criss-crossed with long, heavily bleeding scratches. There were round, white-flaked burn marks on her forearms and the room smelled of singed hair and skin. I grabbed the bedroom phone and called for an ambulance, then I untied the strips of fabric and lifted her up onto the bed. I tucked a pillow under her head, her pulse was strong but she was rigid and sweating and there were now lines in her face that looked like they would stay there forever.

I got some water from the kitchen, went back to the bedroom and lifted her head a little to the rim of the glass. She opened her eyes and lapped at the water. Her eyes showed that her body was a package of pain. She looked at me reproachfully.

"Some protector," she croaked through her battered lips.

"Ailsa, I'm sorry," my voice sounded like grit in ball bearings. "Who did it love, why?"

"Bryn . . . and another man. I let them in. Other man slapped me and stripped me. Bryn just watched."

The effort of speaking was doing her no good, she was in deep shock and her face was pale and waxy, but I had to know a little more.

"Listen love, just answer in one word or shake your head, understand?"

She nodded.

"What did Bryn want?"

"Files."

"Gutteridge's files?"

A nod.

"Did Bryn touch you?"

A shake, no.

"Just the other guy. Was Bryn there all the time?"

A shake.

"Why did he leave? What did you tell him?"

"Brave."

"You told him Brave had the files. Is that true?"

She closed her eyes and I eased her back down onto the pillow. "You don't know," I said almost under my breath. "Good girl, that was smart." There was one last thing I needed to know. I smoothed down the cap of hair which was sweaty and sticking up in spikes. "Ailsa, I have to know this. When did Bryn leave, can you tell me?"'

"You rang," she whispered, "he left."

That made it half an hour or so, a little more. If he went to Brave's place directly he'd be there within an hour. Maybe he wasn't there yet and perhaps I could still spring the trap. Ailsa seemed to have lost consciousness, I checked her pulse again, still strong, I pulled a sheet up over her body and was just watching the blood ooze through it when I heard the sirens.

"Where?" the shout came from the front of the house.

"Back bedroom," I bellowed.

Two ambulance men charged into the room carrying a stretcher.

The young fresh faced one stopped short, he

hadn't done much in this line of work before. The older man took a glance then busied himself preparing the stretcher. His face was an expressionless mask.

"Anything broke?"

"I don't think so."

He pulled the sheet aside carefully and gently lifted her arms and legs an inch or so; he put his ear to her chest.

"Think you're right. Has to be moved anyway, needs treatment fast. OK Snowy, stop gawking. On the stretcher."

The boy did his share smartly enough.

"Who did this?" he said as they were fastening the straps.

"A friend."

"God, I'm sorry."

"Thanks, he's going to be sorrier."

While this was going on I found Ailsa's address book and the name and number of her doctor. I wrote them on the back of my card and tucked it into the older guy's overall pocket.

"I'm admitting her. Her doctor's name and number are on the card, it's my card. Her name's Ailsa Sleeman, double e. Where will she be?"

He raised an eyebrow and seemed to be going to protest until he got a good look at my face. "St Bede's," he said nervously. "You should admit her personally, but I guess you're going to be busy."

"That's right."

I told him I'd contact the police and he offered no argument to that. They carried her gingerly out of the house, down the steps and put her in the ambulance. The siren screamed and the vehicle wailed off towards the city.

It was early for my calls to Evans and Tickener, but perhaps too late. A packet of Ailsa's cigarettes was lying on the floor near the bed and I took one out mechanically and put it in my mouth. Then I looked at the floor again. Three long butts had been squashed out into the deep pile of the carpet making charred holes as big as five cent pieces. I spat the cigarette out, grabbed the phone and dialled. Tickener's voice was flat, bored, he wasn't expecting me yet.

"This is Hardy," I said, "things are breaking. Here's what I want you to do . . ." He interrupted me. "Listen Hardy, I've been looking into this Brave. He's weird, he . . ."

I cut in. "Yeah, I know. Tell me later. I want you to get out to the clinic as fast as you can. Colin Jones around, is he?"

"Yes, matter of fact he's right here now. I had a word with him, mate of yours I understand . . ."

I cut him off again. "Bring him! The cops won't be far behind you and I won't be far behind them. Give the place a bit of air the way you did before, OK?"

"OK Hardy. We're busting Brave?"

"Wide open," I said, "and you're an A grade from tomorrow if you handle it right."

I rang off and dialled Evans' number. He answered testily.

"You're early, you're never early, it can't be you."

"It's me, I was pushed. My client's been cut and burned and our men aren't standing about. Can you move now?"

"Yeah, but give me something for the sheet."

"Put what you like on it, but don't put this— Costello."

"Shit!"

"Right. I think Brave has him at his clinic in Longueville. Your mate Jackson is running interference and a Dr Clyde is doing the remodelling of Costello's dial. I want Brave. Costello's just a by-product to me but I haven't got any time for him anyway. Suit you?"

"And how!" I could hear the scratch of his writing across the line. I gave him the address and a few other details. I was praying that Bryn's trip to Longueville would delay things out there enough so that all the principals wouldn't be on planes to Rio by the time the law, the press and I got there.

I got up off the floor with creaking knee joints and needles of pain in my skull. I looked around the room, at the bloody sheets, the cigarette ends and the ripped clothes. Some light was coming in from an opening in the curtains and I could see the swimming pool still

145

reflecting light challengingly close, but I doubted that Ailsa would ever feel like reading her novels, smoking her cigarettes and being warm and loving in that room again. It was a room I'd liked more than most, and it made me sad to know how it'd been used by the worst sort of human being to create the worst sort of pain.

There was a small clutch of neighbours across the road standing on a second level balcony exhibiting well bred interest in the proceedings. They had glasses in their hands as if they were toasting the most excitement seen in that part of the world in years. I gave them a rude gesture and drove off leaving them twittering and fluttering like birds who've been thrown a handful of seed.

I was getting to know the route out to Longueville well enough to drive it in my sleep. I pushed the Falcon flat-out. A few solid citizens shook their heads disapprovingly as I passed them and two bikies gave me an outrider escort for a mile for the hell of it. The day was dying and a soft, limp night settling down on the suburbs and hills when I reached Longueville but I was thinking of Ailsa and wailing sirens and it seemed to be raining blood to me.

CHAPTER 13

Tickener's Holden was standing around the corner from the clinic and half a block back along the street. Across from it were two unmarked cars carrying four men who could only have been cops. I pulled up behind Tickener. Grant Evans got out of his car and walked across to the Holden. He got on the front seat and I got in the back. I sat down next to a small, relaxed looking guy who wore a Zapata moustache and an intelligent expression. Evans spoke first.

"You didn't tell me that the press were in on it, Cliff, I could get my arse kicked for this."

"You won't," I assured him. "The fish are too big and too many people are going to be scared shitless to worry about you. You'll do yourself a lot of good. Oh, by the way, Harry Tickener, Inspector Grant Evans." They shook hands warily. Tickener half-turned and nodded at the photographer sitting next to me who was fiddling with what looked like twenty different camera attachments. "Colin Jones," he said. Evans stuck out his hand and Colin gave it a quick shake and went back to his cameras. He'd been a man of few words when I'd met him as a reconnaissance cameraman in Malaya, and he hadn't changed a bit.

"This should be right up your street, Colin," I said. "Here's how it stands. I think Rory Costello's in there getting a face job. There are legitimate patients in there too which poses a bit of a problem and there's plenty of muscle. A boy named Bruno who can handle himself and at least two others who can dish it out. And Costello of course, but I imagine he's out of action. He was bandaged up like a mummy when I saw him, if it was him."

"It better be," Evans growled. "Weapons?"

"Didn't see any but sure to be some. The guy on the gate is almost certainly armed and he's our first problem."

"That booth looks like a fortress," said Tickener.

"It's pretty formidable," I agreed, "but the problem is that it relays pictures and alarms to the main building. The fence is electrified and there are TV cameras about."

"So it's no go to divert the guard and go over the fence?" Evans leered at me. "What are we going to do, parachute in?"

Jones spoke up. "Have you been inside the fence and the building, Cliff?"

I said I had. "Did you hear any constant background noise of any kind?" All I'd heard was a lot of talk and a lot of ringing inside my head after I'd been hit. I tried to remember the feeling of being inside the place, lobby, corridors and rooms. "No," I said, "No background noise." "Any flickering in the lights?" Jones asked. I thought about it. "No."

"Then it's no problem." He slung a camera around his neck. "No generator, they're working off the mains supply—amateurs. You knock out the supply lines temporarily or permanently and in you go."

"Is it hard to do?" I asked.

"No, a cinch, I can do it."

"Can you now?" said Evans thoughtfully.

The cameraman smiled at him. "I was trained in Her Majesty's armed service, Inspector. It's easy if you know how, I'd need a hammer and a couple of big nails and a screwdriver."

"I'd have them over the back," said Tickener. "I'm building a shack up the Hawkesbury."

"All right for some," Evans muttered as the reporter got out of the car, went round the back, dropped the hatch and started a few seconds of noisy rummaging. My nerves screamed at the clanking of metal on metal and I was anxious to be moving. Evans sat there shaking his head gently and looking resignedly out into

149

the night. Tickener came up with the nails and tools and put them on the bonnet of the car.

"Assuming we get in OK," Evans said, "how do you read it from there, Cliff? No warrant, no nothing."

"They'll react. They'll shoot, I think. That lets you in."

"True, true. Shooting's illegal." Evans began to enjoy himself. "Right, I'll leave two men in a car outside to mop up or follow us in if need be. The rest of us will go in—you, me, Varson, Tickener and Jones. The objective is Costello, right?"

"Right," I said, "and Brave if he's there. I think he will be."

I had my own thoughts about others who might be there and it probably wasn't fair not to tell Grant about them, but I had plans about what to do if Bryn and his mate got within pistol distance and I didn't want any interference.

Jones spoke again. "Do you want the blackout permanent or temporary?"

"Temporary," said Evans, "I want to see who I'm arresting."

"OK." The photographer deposited his equipment carefully on the seat and got out of the car. "Let's find the power line. Oh, I forgot to tell you, if it's right outside the front gate we're stuffed."

Evans, Tickener and I got out of the car and followed Colin. Evans beckoned to the car behind,

150

a man got out and jogged to catch up with us. He had a quick confab with Evans, ran back to the car to fill his colleagues in, and was out of breath when he caught up with us again. We set off to pick up the perimeter of the clinic at the north end. Evans' offsider was a big, bald-headed man with a bald man's look of hostility at the world. From the bulge under his coat I guessed he was carrying a fair sized gun and I was glad that he was on my side. I assumed that Grant was adequately armed, I had my .38, fully loaded, in my jacket pocket.

We walked around the fence with Jones looking up and down every few yards. After walking the full length of one side of the block and half of the next, Jones stopped and clicked his tongue softly.

"This is it, a cinch."

He pulled his belt from his pants, took off his jacket, put the nails and screwdriver in his pants pocket and shoved the hammer inside his waistband. He buckled the belt on the first hole and looped it over his shoulder. The lamp post stood about twelve feet back from the fence and it was a good twenty feet up to the cross beam. Jones whistled to himself as he shimmied up the post using hands, knees and feet like a south sea islander after coconuts. He reached the cross beam and slung the belt over it. He steadied himself by hanging onto the strap and began to hammer and probe the electrical equipment. Two minutes later he slid down

151

the pole. He was carefully holding a piece of wire in his hand when he hit the ground.

"Always plenty of spare wire up there," he said cheerfully. "This is all set up. One pull and the lights go out all over Europe, another tug and they go on again. You trip a switch and untrip it, see?"

"I believe him," I said to Evans who grunted. The other cop spoke for the first time since he'd joined us. "How do we handle it? Do we go through the fence or the gate?" It was a pretty good question. Evans looked at Jones. "You're the one with all the ideas at the moment, what d'you think?" Jones paused, he was probably thinking of his compound-storming in Malaya and he'd been in on some tough ones.

"The gate's the easiest. The guard's going to be as blind as a bat when the lights blow. Should be easy to grab him and keep him quiet. We can get the gates open and drive in. Of course, someone'll have to stay here and do the pulling."

"That'll be you, Ron," Evans said to the cop, then he waved a hand at us. "Sorry, Hardy, Jones, Tickener—Ron Varson, rough as guts."

We nodded at him. Varson didn't look happy with his second fiddle job but he took Evans' description of him as a compliment and looked grimly determined. Evans was in control of it now. He issued his instructions briskly and authoritatively. We checked our watches and agreed on lights-out time and three of us headed back towards the gate. Varson stood holding the wire and looking up to where it connected with the switches. He still looked a bit unhappy with the job, as though he was about to flush himself down a giant lavatory.

We proceeded in a huddle as close as we could to the main gate without being noticed. We decided to take Tickener's car because that meant the reporter and photographer could go in with a maximum of cover. Maybe Evans was hedging his bet a little, but no one argued. Jones huddled down in the back of the FB, Tickener hunched over the wheel. We waited. The clinic grounds and the reception booth were almost floodlit, very bright. Evans eased a black automatic out of his holster and checked it. I patted my gun. There was no traffic within earshot and the quiet of Longueville at that moment was just the sort of quiet the residents had paid all that money for.

The clinic blacked out suddenly as if it had been covered by an old-time photographer's cloth. Evans and I sprinted for the reception booth. By the little moonlight and the street light we could see the guard flailing around pushing buttons. Evans fronted the glass cage and pointed his automatic at the guard's nose. He reached for a sawn-off shotgun which rested against the wall of the booth but he was too slow. I had the side door open and my gun in his earhole before he could grab the weapon.

"Easy does it friend, you don't want to die for five hundred a month."

He saw the wisdom of it and let go the shotgun. Evans came into the booth and prodded the guard out. The guard walked towards the car, moonlight glinted on the barrel of a pistol which one of the detectives held out of the car window trained on his chest.

The light came on again and Grant pushed a couple of buttons on the instrument panel in the box. The wide gates swung open. I grabbed the shotgun and went out and through the gates at a run. Evans took a swipe at the control panel and followed me. Tickener came burning up to the gate and we ran along beside him as the FB roared up to the clinic. He wavered on and off the brick path and the wheels churned furrows up in the smooth green grass on either side. There were three cars parked near the main entrance and I was shouting at Tickener to block them when a red and blue flash came from a window in the main block. Glass shattered in the car and I heard a yelp from Jones. Tickener stalled the motor and we crouched down behind the car. Another flash and a bullet whined off the Holden's bonnet. I peeked around and snapped two shots at the window. Evans crouched double and ran for the porch. He went up the steps, fired twice into the glass doors and jumped aside. A bullet from inside splintered a panel on the door and I made it to the other side of the porch in six heart-in-the-mouth strides. Footsteps pounded up the path and the gun behind the window opened up and Varson dropped like a stone. I couldn't tell if he'd been hit or not. Evans kicked the shattered door in and we both went into the lobby, almost on our bellies. It was empty. Then the door at the end of the room opened and Bruno fired a quick shot at Evans before ducking back. He missed and Grant took a chance. He rushed through the door and flattened himself against the wall. I went through and pasted myself against the other side. Bruno was halfway down the corridor and his next shot whistled between us. Evans dropped to one knee, sighted quickly and fired. Bruno screeched and went down like the last pin in the lane and his gun skittered crazily along the polished floor.

Two men came out of a door on the right. One of them snapped a shot at me and they jumped over Bruno and rounded the bend at the end of the passage. I was vaguely conscious of movement and sound behind me and took a quick look. Tickener was crouched down near Evans and slightly hampering his attempt to take a shot, his face white and his eyes wide and scared. Jones was standing up behind Evans, snapping and flashing. A man lumbered out of the door the other two had come from. He was big, dark hair spilled through the unbuttoned top of his pyjamas coat and he was groping at the tie of the pants. His face was heavily bandaged and the pistol he carried was pointed nowhere in particular.

Evans shook Tickener away and bellowed. "Costello, police, let go the gun."

The blind-looking bandaged face turned slowly towards the sound of the voice. Jones stepped forward and snapped. The bulb went off and Grant threw up his hand to ward off the glare. Costello lined him up like an Olympic shooter with 20/20 vision. I swung the shotgun on him and fired. The charge hit him in the chest, lifted him up and slammed him against the white wall. He slid slowly down it, leaving a bloody trail behind him like a wolf shot high up in the snow country coming down the slope to die. Jones walked up and took a careful picture. His hands were as still and steady as Costello's corpse.

I put the shotgun down. Evans was leaning against the wall. His gun was pointing at the floor and his lips were moving silently. He knew how close he'd come.

"There's more of them, Grant," I said quietly.

As I spoke the door behind us opened and Varson came through it sideways, propping it open with his back. He waved a man through with a quick gesture of his enormous, gun-filled right hand. Dr Ian Brave strolled into the passage.

"I got him outside," said Varson, "he was leaving."

"He stays," Evans said.

Brave looked at the crumpled, bloody ruin on the floor. His face had a vacant, other-worldly look—for my money he was floating high and free somewhere a long way off. Along the corridor Bruno groaned and tried to pull himself up against the wall; everyone had forgotten him.

BOOK TWO

BOOK TWO

CHAPTER 14

The quiet tableau broke up after a minute or two. Jones backed off down the passage and took a quick picture of Brave with Varson looming over his shoulder. Brave was Varson's prize, all he had to show for the night, and he kept close to him like a nervous spouse at a party. Evans, Tickener and I went into the room which Costello had come out of to die. The window leading out into the shrubbery at the side of the building gaped open.

"He had two goons with him the other day," I said, "one of them socked me but I guess they weren't shooters."

Tickener scribbled on a pad and Evans grunted. "Looks that way."

"Two hopped it just after I shot the Italian. That makes four on the loose. I hope the boys at the gate got them, but it's a lot to handle." He brooded on this for a moment and then shrugged. "You didn't quite level with me about the strength of the troops, did you Cliff?" I opened my hands apologetically. "Never mind," he said, "we done OK." Varson called his name and he went out into the corridor. Tickener looked at me inquiringly but I turned away from him and looked out through the window thinking my own murderous thoughts. Tickener walked out. I rolled a cigarette, lit it and followed him.

Susan Gutteridge was standing in the corridor along with a woman with wild hair and eyes. They both wore severe calico nightdresses. Brave was trying to do his hand-holding act with Susan but Varson was shouldering him aside. Jones had left the scene and Bruno had passed out. The other patient was staring at the body on the floor. Suddenly she collapsed to her knees and pitched forward over it. Blood soaked into her nightdress and she daubed it over her face and body.

"Sally," she moaned, "oh Sally, Sally."

Evans started pushing the buttons. He told Varson to take Brave in and book him for harbouring an escapee. He pointed at Tickener who was still scribbling and poking his long thin nose into rooms off the passage. "OK, Tickener," he roared, "you've had your ringside seat, now do something useful. Get on the first phone you see and call an ambulance. Call police headquarters and tell them I want a police doctor out here right away."

Tickener turned away obediently and Evans rapped out a few more words. "And a nurse or two, tell them about the women." I was next. "So you know these ladies?" he snapped.

"Take it easy, Grant. Yes, I know the younger one, she's Susan Gutteridge." He rubbed his hand over his eyes, then looked down surprised to see that the hand was still holding a gun.

"OK, OK," he said tightly. "Get her away somewhere. Jesus what a mess!" The older woman was still embracing the corpse and sobbing. I took the Gutteridge woman's arm and led her down the passage.

I didn't remember where her room was, so I let her lead me. She plodded on not saying anything until we came to room 38. I pushed the door open and she walked in ahead of me. She still hadn't spoken a word. I had nothing I wanted to say to her, but I felt an impulse to stir her from her trance if I could. Perhaps I didn't want her to have the luxury of a cotton wool wrapping while people were dying around her.

"Do you remember me, Miss Gutteridge?"

"Of course I do," she snapped, "do you think I'm crazy like Grace?"

"Grace?"

"Grace Heron, back there." She jerked her head at the door.

"No, no I don't. But you've had a shock, I thought . . ."

163

"I'm all right I tell you," she cut in. "What's been happening here? I heard shots."

I was surprised at her composure. When I'd last seen her she was as fragile as a spider web, ready to be torn apart and dismembered by the slightest harshness, now she seemed to have put together a tough, no-nonsense personality. But it was hard to tell how real it was or how enduring it would be. She sat quietly on the bed while I gave her an outline of events as they related to what she'd seen in the hall. She nodded occasionally and once smoothed down the rough material over her thighs—they weren't bad thighs—otherwise she kept still and attentive. I didn't mention Ailsa in this explanation, but when she asked me directly who I was working for now, I told her, including what had happened to Ailsa that night. I didn't bring Bryn into it. She said something reassuring and patted my arm so there must have been some indication of how I felt in what I said. It might have been the automatic, professional touch of the social worker, but it felt sincere.

"Well, Mr Hardy," she said, "you've really got yourself tangled up with the Gutteridges, haven't you? Have you any idea yet who was threatening me and did these other things, I mean to Giles and Ailsa?"

"I don't even know if the same people are involved," I said. "Ailsa thought Brave was behind it all." I waited for her reaction to that. She bit her lip and pondered it so I decided to go on. I wanted a drink badly, but it seemed possible that this new woman with the mind of her own might help me do some reappraising of the case at this point. "That could be," I continued, "if he's fallen out with an accomplice. You saw a ferrety-looking guy out there?"

She nodded. "Yes."

"He's a reporter. A woman phoned him at his paper and tipped him off about Brave. She had an accent that sounded French. It could be the woman who phoned you."

Her face screwed up in distaste. "Yes, I suppose so, her voice could have had a French sound to it. I'm not much good at that sort of thing. I was rotten at languages at school."

I was liking her more. "Me too," I said. "Then again, your brother might fit. He could have killed Giles himself and put the frighteners on you and arranged for the bomb in Ailsa's car. But there's one thing wrong with that line of theory."

"What's that?"

"Why would he call me in in the first place?"

She gave it some thought. "It seems to me that in books, you know, detective stories, the guilty person sometimes hires the detective. Doesn't it ever happen in real life?"

"Yeah, sometimes it does, it can be a good blind. But Bryn seemed to be genuinely distressed about Giles, it didn't look like an act to me. It's still a possibility

165

though, if he was tied in to some deal with someone else and they fell out."

"What someone else?" she asked.

"God knows. I'm just trying the idea out. Brave maybe? But I get conflicting reports on Bryn and Brave's relationship. I just don't have any firm candidates."

"Well, I can fill you in a little there, on Brave and Bryn. God, it sounds like a stage act, doesn't it? What do you want to know?"

"For a start whether Bryn and the doctor were on good terms and whether Bryn trusted him. And secondly, who really advised you to come to this place and put yourself under Brave's care?"

The cigarette I'd lit fifteen minutes before was dead between my fingers. I fumbled for a match and lit it, it tasted bitter and stale and I crushed it out into an ashtray on the night table beside the bed. I rolled a new one and fiddled with it. She watched me with a look of concentration on her face. I lit the cigarette.

"Bryn and Dr Brave became very close after my father died," she said. "Bryn saw a lot of him socially and professionally. You know what Bryn's like, his . . . orientation?" I nodded. "Well, he's got it sorted out most of the time and Giles is . . . was good for him. He functions in business life very effectively and in private life pretty well. He's been doing better at it in the last two years, but he does know some terrible people, vicious, depraved people. Dr Brave helped him a lot, trying to get Bryn to control and channel his impulses. Bryn can be very cruel. I'd be very surprised if there was any rift between them."

"Bryn told me there was," I said, "and he also said that he was against you going into the clinic."

"That's just not true." She frowned and spoke quickly. "Ever since my diabetes started playing up and I began having these bad spells Bryn has urged me to rely on Dr Brave."

"When did this trouble start?"

"Oh, fairly soon after my father died. Diabetes can be affected by emotional upset. I just couldn't seem to stabilise myself again, and I'd been stabilised for years."

"When did the diabetes set in?"

A shadow seemed to pass over her face which surprised me, but I was adjusting to the new personality and forgetting about the old, fragmented one.

"I was sixteen when it started," she said shortly. "After Mark died I started working harder and harder for charity and other causes. Dr Brave encouraged that too, but I got very tired and I came here more frequently."

She seemed now to have a completely different attitude to Brave from the one I'd seen before and it puzzled me. At the risk of breaking up her present helpful mood I decided to ask her about it.

"You seem able to talk pretty objectively about Brave now," I said. "Do you feel differently about him?"

She nodded. "Yes, yes I do. I seem to recall thinking you were a perceptive man when I met you before." I tried to look modest. "You are," she went on. "I felt differently about him the minute I saw him in the passage with all that blood and that man standing next to him. Is he a policeman?"

"Yes."

"I thought so. Dr Brave doesn't control him. He controls everyone here you see and he was controlling everyone at home—me, certainly, and Bryn to a large extent. I suppose not having the treatments for a few days might have something to do with it."

"What are the treatments?"

"I've been on a course of injections, hormones. And I have hypnotherapy sessions with Dr Brave."

"What goes on in them?"

"I don't remember very clearly. They seem to be mainly about the day Mark died. I was the first one in the family to see him. Dr Brave seems to think my trouble is psychosomatic, stemming from finding my father like that. I had a sort of memory lapse, a breakdown, you know."

I knew. "And Brave questions you about this under hypnosis?"

"Yes, at least I think so, it's hard to remember when I come out of it."

"Does it do you any good do you think?"

She wrinkled her forehead and drew a deep, slow

breath; she was treating the question as if it contained a mint fresh idea she'd never heard before.

"I thought it did at the time," she said, "now I'm not so sure. No, that's not true, now I don't think it did. On and on about safes and things . . ."

"Safes? Brave asked you about safes?"

"I think so, yes. But I don't know anything about safes. He said they were symbolic, the womb and all that. I couldn't ever seem to satisfy him about it."

She was getting tired and all this forced recall was making her edgy. She still looked a lot better than she had when Brave was doing his Svengali bit all over her though. I told her to get into bed and she did it.

"There'll be a nurse here soon. You might as well spend the night. Then in the morning, if you feel up to it, I think you should check yourself out and go see a good doctor. Get the diabetes straightened out. Will you?"

She sniffed and wrinkled her nose before answering me.

"What's that smell?" she said.

I lifted my hands. "Cordite, I've just fired a shotgun."

"Did you kill him, the man with the bandaged face?"

"Yeah."

"He looked blind."

"He was meant to, he wasn't though."

169

She nodded, then glanced across at the dressing table, on it was a white plastic case, about four inches tall, with a screw top, and a roll of cotton wool. She gave the kit a look I'd seen before—it was her lifeline and her cross.

"Do you inject yourself?" I asked.

"Mostly, not in here though. Do you know anything about diabetes?"

"Not much. My mother was one, but she was a drinker. When she was on a binge it used to go all wrong and she'd get in a bad way."

"I'm not a drinker," she snapped.

"No, but you've got a problem with your condition just the same. Will you see another doctor?"

She lifted the sides of her hair up and let her fingers slip through the soft waves. She still looked tired, older than she should, but there was some shine in her eyes that could just possibly be hope.

"I don't know why I should let you tell me what to do," she said. "But yes, I will. I'm still interested in your investigations. Will you let me know how they proceed?" I said I would. "And I'd like to see Ailsa in hospital," she went on, "if I can be of any help I will."

I had some red Codrals from the night before in my pocket and I offered them to her as a sedative. I thought she might need them to get to sleep in a building where a man had died the hard way. She took them.

"Thank you, Mr Hardy. Dr Brave would never allow any kind of sedative. I'd lie here for hours some nights. Thank you."

"Good night Miss Gutteridge." She swallowed the tablets with some water and let herself slide down the bank of pillows. "Susan," she said. "Goodnight, Mr Hardy."

I'd been dimly conscious of some car noise and other flak from outside while I'd been talking to Susan, so I wasn't surprised when I found only Tickener's FB and one other car outside the building. There were lights flashing at the end of the drive and a certain amount of shouting and hurrying about. I started towards the gate and had covered about half the distance when a figure loomed up in front of me and pointed a pistol at my hairline which is low and just in front of some pretty vital parts of my brain.

"Put your hands on your head slowly," the shadow said. He took a flashlight from his pocket and shone it in my face.

I raised my hands. "I killed Cock Robin," I said, "take me to your leader." The flashlight beam wavered and the gun muzzle looked a fraction less eager.

"You Hardy?" he growled.

"Yeah. Is Grant Evans still around and can I put my hands down?"

"You can. Have to be very careful, Mr Hardy. One of the heavies who was with Costello is still loose, we got the other one."

"Dead?"

"No, my partner winged him and he's talking a blue streak already."

"Good," I said. "What about the other two?"

"They got away. There's another way out around the back. We reckon they lay low while the shooting was going on, then hopped in one of the cars at the front and scooted out. They went over garden beds and all. We had other men coming and they reported a car moving fast on the road but they didn't know the score and let it go. Bad luck. Anyway, Inspector Evans is down there."

He jerked his chin at the gate and went off to shut the stable door a bit tighter. I was thinking that it was partly my fault, I hadn't noticed another exit. I reached the gate where Evans was in a huddle with some cops in uniform and some men in plain clothes. Tickener was looking serious and about ten years older. Jones was photographing two white-overalled men sliding a long, white-wrapped bundle into the back of an ambulance. Bruno was lying on a stretcher which had little fold-out legs to keep it up off the ground. I jolted it a bit as I came up.

"Careful," he groaned and turned his head to look at me. I grinned down at him. His elegant flared trousers had been slit to the crotch and there was a large dressing around his knee. He didn't look happy.

"How's it going Rocky?" I said. "I bet the police surgeon'll do a great job on that knee. You'll be back kicking old ladies to death in no time."

"Get fucked," he snarled.

I tut-tutted him and walked over to Evans.

"Back exit, Cliff," he said, "it'd never have done for Malaya."

"True," I said. "What car did they take?"

"Fiat, sports model."

"That'd be right," I said wearily.

"How's that?"

"Never mind, Grant. What's the drill now? Head-quarters, statements and such?" He nodded. "OK," I said, "see you there."

I trudged over to the Falcon, climbed in and turned the key. The engine leapt into life as if it had thrived on the action.

CHAPTER 15

I was at police HQ for over four hours. It would have been longer and tougher if Grant Evans hadn't been on side. I made statements about my earlier call on Brave. Evans allowed me to leave the Gutteridges with a very low profile in the whole thing. The Costello affair was what he was interested in and what Tickener's readers were interested in as well. They were both happy for me and my involvements to take a back seat. I told Grant that I might have something soon on the Giles killing and he said that would be nice in an uninterested way. I read on a message sheet on his desk that "attempts to contact Senior Detective Charles Jackson and Dr William Clyde had been unsuccessful". Bulletins were out on them. In a break from the recording and questioning, I got on a phone and called Bryn Gutteridge's number. There was no answer. The same ten cents bought me a call to St Bede's hospital and the information that Miss Sleeman had responded well to transfusions and a saline drip and was sleeping peacefully. When I gave my name the desk attendant said that the police were anxious to contact me in connection with Miss Gutteridge's injuries. I told her where I was calling from and she seemed satisfied. I hadn't heard anything about it at headquarters and I didn't want to if I wasn't going to be there until mid-day.

Brave, Bruno and the thug who'd been picked up in the grounds were securely booked. The third man had sung like a bird and there was a bulletin out on his mate, a long-time hood with an impressive record and a history of association with Rory Costello. Nobody put pressure on me to identify the two men who'd escaped in the Fiat and I kept quiet about it. Evans prepared a statement for the press and went into a huddle with Tickener and Jones about their respective rights to the glamour and gore of the evening. They sorted it out and the pressmen, looking pretty pleased with themselves, came over to shake my hand before leaving.

"Lucky I followed you, Hardy," said Tickener. "Instinct, eh?"

We shook. "I guess so," I said. He hadn't handled himself too badly and he'd be well clear of the sports page and Joe Barrett's errands now. Also, he now owed

175

me something and it's handy in my game to have a pressman in your debt. Colin Jones looked like he needed some sleep, but if he was going to get his pictures into the morning editions he probably wouldn't get it. He let go my hand and slapped one of his cameras.

"Miles to go before I sleep," he said.

"You're the only educated cameraman in the west, Colin."

"Yeah, it gets in the way. Thanks for letting me in, Cliff, it made a change." They wandered off to put the final touches on the thrills in store for their readers over the yoghurt and crispies.

I'd exhausted my packet of Drum and drunk all the autovend coffee I could stand. It was 2 a.m. and I felt like I needed a new skin, a new throat and quite a few other accessories. I had an Irish thirst and the image of the wine in my refrigerator beckoned me like the damasked arm of the lady in the lake. Evans started slipping papers into folders and his telephone had finally stopped ringing hot. I was sitting across from his self-satisfied look. He reached into a drawer of the scarred and battered pine desk and fished out two cigars in cellophane wrappers. He offered me one.

"Keeping 'em since Jenny was born. Thought it might be a son. This is the next best thing, have one?"

I shook my head. "Wouldn't have a cold beer would you?"

He smiled, lit his cigar and leaned back blowing a thin stream of the rich, creamy smoke at the ceiling. "Piss artist," he said indulgently. "Case closed, Cliff?"

"Yours or mine?"

"Mine is like a fish's arsehole. I mean yours."

"I don't know yet." I was lying, I suspected it was just beginning and that there were many little corners of it still unexplored and a great highway of truth still to put through the lives of the people concerned.

"Well, anything I can do, just let me know." He looked at his watch and I took the point. We shook hands and I trudged down the corridor and took yet another chance on the lift. We made a nice couple as we wheezed down to ground level and I closed its wire grille gently; with care and kind treatment we might both just last out the decade.

I picked up my car which was looking sheepish and barely roadworthy among the powder blues in the police parking lot, and drove home through the back streets and quietest roads. I tried to think of Ailsa battling with her pain in hospital, and Susan Gutteridge coming out of a long slide, and Bryn cruising and cruel like a harbour shark, but all the pictures blurred and the people receded far off into the distance. A truck backfired when I was within fifty yards of home, and as I sidled the Falcon into the yard my ears were ringing with the noise and I could smell the smoke and feel the shotgun heavy and deadly in my hands. I went

177

into the house, drank a long glass of wine and made coffee, but I went to sleep in a chair while waiting for the cup I'd poured to cool. I swilled it down cold and went to bed.

Tickener made a good job of it. His headline was lurid but his story was sharp and clear. Evans got a splash verbally and photographically and there were lots of adjectives scattered through the writing like "fearless" and "masterly". I got a few mentions and anyone reading between the lines would come away with the knowledge that I had killed Costello, but who reads between the lines any more? The name Gutteridge didn't figure in the story and it seemed that a combination of brilliant investigatory journalism and enterprising police work had delivered the goods. That suited me. The last thing I wanted was pictures of myself in the papers and my name a household word—it might feel good, but it would play hell with business if kids came up to ask you for your autograph while you were staking out a love nest.

I read most of this sitting on the lavatory while a warm, soft Sydney rain darkened the courtyard bricks. Back in the kitchen I made coffee and welsh rarebit. Ordinarily, I'd have been at least semi-relaxed. I was on a case, on expenses and earning them and hadn't had any bones broken in the past twenty-four hours. But this one was different, my client was special and she was in hospital and I was partly to blame. The villain was in custody as they say, but villains were coming out of the woodwork and the past was sending out tentacles which were winding around the necks of people living and dying in the present. It's a dying trade I'm in.

I called the hospital and was told that I could visit Miss Sleeman at 10 a.m., seeing that I was the one who'd admitted her. I took a long, hot then cold shower, which made me feel virtuous. I capitalised on this by taking the flagon and a glass out onto the bricks along with my electric razor and my razor sharp mind. I sipped the wine and ran the tiny, whirring blades over my face. The sun climbed up over the top of the biscuit factory and beamed heat down into the courtyard. The bricks started to steam and sweat began to roll off my chest down into the thin layers of fat around my waist. I resolved again to walk more and to cut out beer and that was as far as my thinking took me. I towelled off the sweat, dressed in cotton slacks, shirt and sandals and played inch by inch with the Falcon out onto the street. There was a sweet, malty biscuit smell in the air as I drove past the front of my house. Soames had just put on his first record of the day. Pretty soon he'd take a peek over the fence, shake his head at the empty flagon and roll his apres-muesli joint.

I don't like hospitals. My mother and father and Uncle Ted died in them. They all smell and look the same, all polished glass and lino and reek of disinfectant. Ailsa was on the fourth floor in a ward past the maternity unit. It was crammed full of rosy cheeked mothers smothering babies, black, white and brindle, against their chests. It made me feel my childlessness like a burden and I wondered if Ailsa felt the same way. Perhaps she didn't need to. She hadn't mentioned any children, but then I had only got a pretty episodic biography of her, perhaps she had twins being finished in Switzerland. Dangerous thoughts for someone for whom marriage was a busted flush and kids were something not to shoot when out on business. I had wanted kids but Cyn hadn't unless I was going to be home at six o'clock every night and I couldn't give her that guarantee. I was in an intensely self-critical mood when I arrived at Ailsa's ward. A roly-poly matron who hadn't heard how dragon-like she should be showed me to the door and told me I could have an hour. I went in.

Ailsa was sitting up in bed wearing a white cheese-cloth nightgown. She had no make-up on and had lost a lot of colour in her face, her eyes were shadowed and huge so that she looked pale and fragile like a French mime. The bronze hair was newly washed and a bit curly and she had a scrubbed clean look as if she was about to be delivered somewhere. Her face and lips were still puffy and bruised, but when she looked up from her book she managed to work her features into a smile.

"Hardy," she said, "the great protector."

I moved up, took the book away and grabbed her hands. She winced with pain and I swore and let her go. She reached out slowly and stiffly and put her hand on my forearm, it rested there light and feathery like a silk stocking across a chair.

"You're hopeless," she said, "no fruit, no magazines. How'll we fill in the time?"

I gave her a leer and she smiled before shaking her head. "Not for weeks," she said. "But when I can you'll be the first man I call."

I was relieved. We'd seemed to be plunging into something very heavy and I wasn't sure I could handle it yet, or ever. Her version of the way we stood, even though it was determined by her injuries, accorded with my feelings and relaxed me. I patted her hand and we sat there quietly for a minute or two feeling something like trust and understanding flow between us. I eased back the loose sleeves of her nightdress and saw that her forearms were bandaged. I told her again that I was sorry I hadn't been there.

"Don't be silly, Cliff," she said, "how could you have known what was going to happen. The whole thing has got out of control. I don't understand it properly, do you?"

"No, I can't make the connections. It's all hooked up. Brave, Bryn, the files and the threats, but I don't know how they're linked exactly. That makes it hard to take the next step with any confidence."

"What are you going to do then?"

I looked at her and ran my finger lightly across her high, sharp cheekbone. The skin was stretched thin and tight across it like a rubber membrane over a specimen bottle. "I haven't finished checking all the possibilities I was working on yesterday. Brave is out of circulation of course." I nodded at the newspapers lying on a bedside chair.

"Yes," she said, "thank God for that." She was looking tired already and spoke slowly. "But I want it seen through, you'll stay with it won't you? Bryn's dangerous, he's got to be put away, and the bomb . . . !"

"I'll stay with it," I said. "I was hoping you'd want me to."

"You should have known."

I nodded and we did some more quiet sitting. After a while her eyelids flickered and she said she was tired. It was partly that and partly the dope they were giving her. I got up from the bed but she motioned me closer, she patted her chest with one hand.

"Touch me here, Cliff."

I did, she felt warm and firm. She reached up with both hands, grabbed my hands and pressed them hard against her breasts, her face contorted.

"Cliff, the pale one, he was going to . . . to do something there next."

I felt a rush of atavistic rage. I gently freed my hands, smoothed her hair and kissed her forehead.

"Don't worry love," I said harshly, "it'll be all right, it'll be over soon."

I promised to call the hospital twice a day and to visit whenever I could. She smiled and nodded and slid down into a deep sleep that the dope was calling her to.

CHAPTER 16

When I left the hospital I intended to finish yesterday's job by checking on the residence of Mr Walter Chalmers, but sitting in the car with the engine running and the street directory beside me, I changed my mind. It suddenly seemed a hundred times more important to track down Bryn and his inquisitorial mate. Bryn was my starting point for this twisting, turning affair and it seemed like the right moment to check back to the beginning. And I was looking forward to a meeting with the man with the cigarette butts and the razor blades. I turned off the engine and reflected. Men like Bryn, with money like his, have houses scattered about the countryside—mood houses, hobby houses. I'd known one millionaire who kept a $50 000 hunting lodge on land which cost him $5000 a year to lease because he liked to go deer shooting about once every three years. He got shot to death up there on one of his rare visits but that's another story. It was a sure bet that Bryn had hideouts on the sea and in the mountains, but they wouldn't be public knowledge. How to find out about them? Easy. Susan Gutteridge, the lady on the mend. I tried to remember whether I'd mentioned a particular diabetes doctor or not and decided I hadn't. But there was no doubt as to who was the best diabetes man in Australia, Dr Alfred Pincus. He charged like the six hundred, but there was more information about diabetes in that polished, clever dome of his than in a shelf of textbooks. I'd seen him on the subject on television and he was so interesting about it he almost made you wish you were a sufferer. Susan Gutteridge would contact him as sure as her bank balance was in the black.

I walked back to the hospital lobby and looked Pincus up in the directory. His rooms were in Macquarie Street naturally, a half mile away. I went back and locked the car. This was as close as I could expect to park to the address anyway. I tramped down the street which was lined with coffee bars and chemist shops the way streets around hospitals and medical offices are. I found the three storey sandstone building which Pincus shared with a dozen or so other top-flight men on top of the hill which gave it a commanding view of the water. The brass nameplates told me that several of Pincus' co-occupants were knights. The lift was ancient like the one in the police building, but it had been better serviced and it slid up its cable like a python up a tree. I got out at the second floor and fronted up to a door which had Pincus' name and degrees and memberships of this and that engraved on it in a prince's ransom of gold leaf. I pushed the door open and looked straight into the eyes of the secretary. She was worth a look, a Semite with raven dark hair and a pale golden face like the image on a Mesopotamian coin. Her nose jutted and her brow sloped back to where the sleek mane of her hair began. Her voice was deep and sweet coming up from well below a pair of heavy, firm breasts.

"Are you Mr Lawrence?"

"No," I said, "I'm Hardy, who's Lawrence?"

She smiled to show she understood but withheld approval. "He telephoned, he's been referred to Dr Pincus. Have you been referred?"

"No, I don't want to see the doctor, at least, not yet. I want some information." She picked up a pencil and tapped it against her big, strong white teeth. "About what?" she said.

"I want to know whether a Miss Susan Gutteridge has contacted Dr Pincus and whether she gave her address." There'd been no number listed for her in the directory.

"I can't possibly tell you that."

"Then she *has* contacted him?"

"I didn't say that."

186

"You, as good as did. Look, I referred her to Dr Pincus. She was having trouble with her diabetes, I knew he was good, the best."

She unbent a little. "I still can't help you, Mr Hardy," she said, "I can't give out information about patients."

I took out my wallet and showed her my card. I found Bryn's cheque with his name stencilled on it to establish my connection with the family. She was inclined to help but a tough professionalism held her back. I noticed a copy of *The News* tucked into a basket beside her chair.

"Look, Miss . . .?"

"Steiner, Mrs."

"Mrs Steiner, this is a serious business, it's connected with things that happened last night. The story's in your paper. I'm mentioned. Take a look."

She pulled out the paper and ran her eyes over the story. She looked up at me with huge dark eyes that seemed to invite you in for a swim.

"I haven't time to explain," I said. "Miss Gutteridge was at that place last night, I saw her. I advised her to see the best diabetes man in Sydney and now I need to see her again. I don't know where she lives."

She gave a convinced nod. "I believe you Mr Hardy." She flicked over the pages of an appointment book. Pincus looked to be booked solid until the end of the century. "Miss Gutteridge has an appointment for tomorrow," she said, "she gave her address as 276 Cypress Drive, Vaucluse. She called from a private phone so I assume she was at home."

I thanked her and took back my licence folder. I gave her a smile and a half-bow as I left, but she was too busy re-reading the story in the paper to notice.

I went back to the car and drove out to Vaucluse again. Life went on out there as it always would, the traffic flowed smoothly as traffic does in places where no one has to get anywhere at a particular time. Cypress Drive was a notch down from Bryn's lofty eminence, but it was still nothing to be ashamed of. The house was on a rise and the grass, shrubs and trees had never lacked fertiliser. A concrete driveway led up to the house like a stairway to paradise. There was no way the Falcon could have coped with the grade, so I parked it outside the wrought iron gates and took my exercise for the day—keeping my promise to myself to do more walking.

I was short of breath and sweating when I reached the top of the drive. The house had too many arches and white-painted, sculptured pillars and railings. It looked like a wedding cake by a baker who'd let his passion for decoration run away with him. I sat on a set of marble steps to catch my breath and then went up two more flights of marble to the door. The bell was the eye of a tightly curled, plaster moulded snake. I shuddered and pushed it waiting to hear the William

188

Tell Overture inside. In fact a few clear, plain notes sounded inside. It was loud and audible even through a house of twenty squares, but it got no response. I tried again with the same result. I pushed at the door but it didn't give an inch. I went down the steps and around the house on the right side; pebble-strewn garden beds bordered the house from front to back and the windows were at least fifteen feet from the ground all around. There was a slight look of neglect about the lawn edges and shrubs as if they were feeling embarrassed to be caught in such a state.

The back door of the house was reached by a railed set of concrete steps that led to a tiled patio, but the garage took my attention first. It would hold four cars but there were signs of frequent occupation—tyre marks and oil stains—in only two of the bays. A third bay had a very slight tyre mark and a small grease spot. Above the garage was a long, low structure which looked like quarters for the staff.

I went up the steps to the flat and pushed the door open. I stepped straight into a neat kitchen and announced my presence by rapping on the wall. There was no answer. I went through to the next room which was pleasantly furnished with a good timber table, a serviceable divan and some built-in cupboards. A man was lying on his back on the divan, snoring quietly. There was a two-thirds empty brandy bottle and a sticky glass on the floor beside the couch. The sleeping man was short and spare, beak-nosed like a jockey, with thin, sandy hair and bad teeth. His mouth was open and he smelled like the Rose and Crown on a Saturday night. There was a rinsed glass on the kitchen sink indicating that someone had helped him on his way to oblivion.

I went out fast and took the steps to the back of the house three at a time. The back door was locked, it looked solid but wasn't, it sprung open at my third kick. The house was an exercise in total comfort, total push button luxury, total soullessness. It was intended to be clean and tidy at all times but it wasn't now; the bed in one of the large bedrooms was a tangled mess, the mattress was slewed off the base and there were clothes, books and make-up strewn about. A sleeve ripped out of a satin nightgown lay on the floor in a passageway and objects had been knocked and spilled from tables through the house. Susan Gutteridge had given whoever had carried her off quite a fight, but it appeared to have been a fight with rules because I didn't see any blood.

I went back into the bedroom and began a search of Susan's belongings. One thing was clear—whoever had taken her wasn't interested in her papers or possible hiding places. Nothing was disturbed in the dressing table drawers, there were no edges lifted, no seams ripped, no books disembowelled. It wasn't money either. Susan's purse was on a sideboard in the living room; it had all her personal tickets in it as well as four hundred dollars in cash. It also had what I was looking for—an address book. There were four addresses for Bryn listed along with telephone numbers—one in the city, Vaucluse, one near Cooma in the snow country and one at Cooper Beach on the Central Coast. I slipped the book into my pocket and wandered across to a window. There was a harbour view of course. The early rain had cleared and the day had turned into the sort of Sydney special that persuades Melburnians to give up their football and settle. I saw in a series of mind-made movie stills images of Bryn Gutteridge sitting on his sun deck potting at sea birds with his air pistol. His skin was saddlebag brown and he was a heliophile if ever I've seen one. He'd be at Cooper Beach. The scene around me screamed for a telephone call to the police, but I'd had enough of desks and blotters and forms in triplicate for a while. The guy in the flat should wake up in a few hours and would probably call the cops. That left me with a fairly clear conscience and about as much of a start as I needed.

I was congratulating myself on having thought this out when a slight sound made me turn. I couldn't tell at first whether it was a man or a woman. There were flared purple slacks and a flowered shirt, shoes with metal buckles and a stiff brimmed black hat on top of a head as pale and fair as a lily in a snow field. I decided that it all belonged to a man, and that the man was holding a gun. He was almost albino, slightly pink around the eyes and he spoke with a high voice, lisping a bit.

"Hold your hands out like this." He fluttered a hand at full arm stretch. "If I do, can we be friends?" I said. He didn't move a muscle in his face and the gun was steady on my navel.

"Just do it!"

I did it.

"Now turn around."

"Oh, don't take advantage of me."

He'd heard it all before and it didn't touch him. I felt as if I was digging my grave with my teeth. I knew I should stop riding him, but the words seemed to come out wrong.

"I might have what you want," I said.

Still no reaction.

"Just turn, I'll let you know when to stop."

I had nothing to lose. He looked as if he'd enjoy killing me and his only problem would be where to put the bullet for maximum enjoyment. I reached into my pocket. He did none of the things an amateur would do. He didn't clutch at the trigger or move back; he knew he had me cold and maybe he just wanted to see what sort of gun he was up against. I flicked the address book out of my pocket and threw it at him with a jerky movement as I dived for his legs. The book missed him by a mile. He sidestepped a fraction and swept the side of his gun down onto my perfect target of a skull. The blow hit the same spot as before and the blood must have flowed like Texas oil. I blacked out for a second and when I came to I couldn't breathe and my heart seemed to be missing three beats for every one it caught. I heard the paleface say, "Shit, he's dead." I thought for a minute that I was but that was quickly replaced by fear. If he thought I was dead that was fine with me, even an animal like him wouldn't want to kill me twice. Through half-shut eyes I saw him pick up the address book and go off towards the back of the house. I tried to pull myself up but my arms and shoulders couldn't take the strain. I went down hard and blacked out again.

CHAPTER 17

I was out for about ten minutes. I was rubbery legged like an unfit businessman pushed through a three mile run when I came to. I had flickering vision and the hemispheres of my brain seemed to be competing for the space. I propped myself up against the nearest wall, wiped blood out of my eyes and debated whether to look for whisky or die. I opted for the whisky and found some in a small room got up like a cocktail lounge. I had a choice of nearly full bottles of four different brands and decided on Teachers. I took a long, breath-cutting swig of it. The liquor fused my double-sided headache into one which was slightly less painful overall. My hair was matted with blood and an external clean-up seemed to be the next thing indicated after the internal treatment. I staggered off to find a bathroom, dimly aware of what sort of figure

I'd cut before a policeman, a judge and twelve citizens good and true.

I lapped water up into my face and eyes and waited for the snowstorm vision and morse code heartbeats to stop. I lowered myself gently down onto the edge of the bath, soaked a face towel in water and mopped carefully at my scalp. After a few painful minutes of this and a close look in the mirror I decided that the experience hadn't aged me much more than ten years and that I was up to doing some thinking. It didn't take much—the albino was Bryn's offsider, the torturer; Bryn had sent him back for something, probably the address book. He was going to catch Bryn up somewhere or maybe Bryn was waiting for him. It didn't matter because he thought I was dead. I closed my eyes and brought the writing on the page of Susan's notebook back and up into focus. I got it—24 Seaspray Drive. I dried my face and ten minutes later I was in my car heading for Cooper Beach.

I stopped in North Sydney for petrol and water for the car and tobacco for me. I pelted through the north shore suburbs up to where the Pacific Highway joins the Newcastle tollway. The old road holds close to the hills. Driving it you call in at a couple of pleasant little towns. It's nice but slow and Bryn wouldn't have taken it. The tollway rips through the country defiantly, it sits on huge concrete pylons over valleys and it passes through thirty-metre-high rock cuttings that look as if they've been carved by the hand of God. You get a different picture of the country from this route. The Hawkesbury looks a mile wide, and little beach towns look like pretty fishing villages instead of the take-away horrors they are.

The car coughed a little on the hills and I felt a bit unsteady on the bends, but I used some more of Susan's whisky which I'd brought with me and that helped. It took three hours from the Harbour Bridge to the rickety wooden affair that crossed Cooper Creek. Seaspray Drive was on the beachfront at the northern end of the town. Bryn's house was a modest two-storey timber and brick hideaway that probably had solar heating and an indoor pool. The Fiat I'd seen before and a Land Rover were parked in the driveway, the gates were shut and there was no air of imminent departure. I drove past quickly. It was after three o'clock and I felt light-headed from the beating, the whisky and the lack of food. I went into one of the town's two pubs and persuaded the stringy, faded barman to get me a toasted sandwich although the food went off at 3.00. I got a beer from him first, breaking my promise of the morning, and he went grumbling off to the kitchen.

He came back with two great steaming chunks of toasted bread, meat and tomato that had been prepared by an artist. He accepted my offer of a beer.

"Wife made 'em," he said, pointing to the food.

"They're great." I couldn't see why he was so woe-begone. The beer seemed to lift his spirits a bit though, and I thought he might be good for a few questions.

"Do you know a Mr Gutteridge, Seaspray Drive?"

He took a deep pull on the middy. "Yeah, rich bloke."

"That's him, see much of him?"

"Not much. Now 'n' then. Doesn't come in here but, sends for some grog occasionally. Why d'y wanna know?"

"I've got some business with him, just want to get him sized up a bit. What do you make of him?"

"Well, I don't know him properly like, just talked to him on the phone a coupla times and seen him up the house when I've been delivering the grog. He's a homo."

I nodded. He finished the beer and I fished out the money for two more. He pulled them, looking closely at what he was doing. He put mine in front of me and lifted his own.

"Thanks, cheers. Well, we get plenty of them up here, their business I suppose. Gutteridge himself seems all right to me, but there's some funny jokers up there with him sometimes."

I finished the second sandwich, terrible for the waistline and for getting shot on, but good for morale.

"Have you ever seen a very pale man up there, white hair, just about albino?"

"Yeah, he's the one I had in mind. Something off about him."

"Like what?"

"I dunno. Partly just the weird bloody look of him, but I seen him shoot a seagull once, pointblank with a .22. Bloody cruel. I reckon he's not the full quid."

I left the pub with the brisk step of a man on business although I was very unsure of my next move. The beer had fuzzed me up a bit so I decided to take a walk along the beach to clear my head. I took off my sandals, rolled up my pants and walked along in the shallows for a mile or so until the rocks running down in sharp spines to the beach turned me back. The beach was clean and white with a light scattering of driftwood on the squeaky, powdery sand above the tideline. Like everyone who lives in the city and draws their bread and butter and stimulation from it, I indulged in some dreams of a seaside hideaway where I could cut down on my drinking and be free of pollution, mortgages and everything else. But mortgage was the native tongue in the hills above this beach and on the walk back I consoled myself with the thought that many of the residents of Cooper Beach were deeper in debt than I was.

It was five o'clock. I sat on the sea wall while a little of the daytime warmth seeped out of the air, but not much. I put on my sandals, glanced over towards the pub and saw a man in white denims and a pale blue shirt going into the bottle shop. His hair was silver white and among the expensive sun tans and liquor complexions on the street he stood out like a bishop in a brothel. The Land Rover I'd seen in Bryn's driveway was parked across the street from the hotel. Getting the grog in was a good sign, it meant they didn't intend going anywhere in a great hurry. You don't send your minions down to the inn for Campari if your next move is a dash to the airport and a plane to Paris. My car was parked under trees around the corner from the Land Rover and it was unlikely that Pinkey would see it. I was congratulating myself on this when he came out of the pub. The barman I'd been talking to was with him, carrying a carton and nattering away. Pinkey was nodding his head and looking up and down the street like a circling hawk watching for chickens. He pointed across to the Land Rover and went back into the pub, maybe for a drink, maybe to phone, no way to tell. In any case it seemed like London to a brick that my presence in Cooper Beach was soon going to be known about in all the wrong quarters. I'd been careless and slow and the thought came to me, not for the first time, that I might be getting too old for this line of work.

I ran across the street and came up on the Land Rover from the other side. I got in the driver's door and climbed over into the back. There was the usual mess of tools, rope and groundsheets that every four wheel drive freak collects, and I huddled down in a corner behind the passenger seat and pulled a light tarpaulin over me. The door opened, glass clinked and cardboard scraped on vinyl. The door closed. I wished like hell that I had a gun and that made me think of Bryn and his guns and the possibility that he might keep one right here. I risked a quick peep out of the window. No sign of the albino. I rummaged about quickly and found lengths of pipe, two fishing rods, a pump and a .22 rifle. The rifle was in a waxed paper sheath and there was a box of bullets taped to the side of the sheath. I pulled out the magazine, put six shells into it and worked one up into the breech; I put the safety catch on and laid the gun down on the floor parallel with the seat. I pulled the tarp up again and waited. Sweat rolled off me and I wanted to scratch in ten places, the tarp was damp with sea water and I felt as if I was slowly pickling like a joint of meat.

He moved like a cat, as I'd seen before. He was in the driver's seat and starting the motor in one smooth motion and hadn't made any noise outside that I could detect. His driving was also smooth and efficient and we'd made a few turns and were heading for home before I'd had time to plan the next move fully. The car wouldn't be visible at the gates I decided, and it wouldn't be audible, what with the Pacific crashing in a hundred yards away and the breeze roaring through the Norfolk Island pines. I had to hope that the gates were closed. They were. He pulled up a car's length from them and as he set the handbrake I came up and poked the end of the rifle barrel into the nape of his neck.

"Put your hands on the wheel," I said.

He did it.

"This is a rifle, feel the sight." I slid the end of the gun round and rubbed the front sight into the back of his ear, not gently.

"Convinced?"

He didn't answer, he was thinking and I didn't want him to. I jabbed the sight into the ear hard, it made a ragged tear in the flesh and blood seeped out.

"OK," he said, "it's a rifle."

The voice was still thin and lilting, there was no fear in it and I realised that I sounded shakier than he did and that I was afraid of him. I started gabbling even though I knew I shouldn't.

"You hurt a lady I like and you hurt me. I wouldn't mind killing you, so be careful."

He let out a light, reedy laugh. "You're talking too much, you're scared shitless."

His voice had a hypnotic quality and I felt a little mesmerised. He was right. I hadn't done anything positive apart from putting the gun on him. His calmness was getting to me. If it went on like this he'd have me presenting him with the rifle and opening my mouth for him to shoot into. It was no time for subtlety and I was losing at badinage. I reached out my left hand and grabbed one of the lengths of pipe. He made his move—a grab into the door pocket on the right side. But before he got there I hit him left and right with the pipe and the barrel of the rifle. The rifle smacked into his ear and the pipe landed lower down and further back on his skull and he slumped forward and slammed his forehead into the stem of the steering wheel.

I climbed into the front seat and pushed him aside. He slumped against the cardboard box. The motor was still running and I crunched the vehicle into a gear of some sort and kangaroo hopped the thing around to the right of the gates. It stalled close enough up to the fence to be hidden from the house and not at such an unnatural angle to attract attention from the road. That just left me and him. I got some wire out of the back and trussed him up as tight as I could without paying too much attention to his circulation. The gun in the door pocket was a beautiful old Colt automatic. I pushed it into the waistband of my trousers and got out of the Land Rover. I took another look at the albino. He was tied up tight but he could still make a noise so I stuffed a piece of stinking oily rag into his mouth. I grabbed the rifle and set off along the fence to pick an entry point that would give me cover and easy access to the house.

I went over the fence at a point where a gum tree conveniently dripped some branches over it and approached the house from the rear through a few thickets of shrubs and one great maze of a privet hedge. By hopping between the outbuildings I was able to get up close to the back door without breaking cover for more than a few seconds. I sidled round the corner of the house and listened at the kitchen window. I could hear voices but it was hard to tell where they were coming from. There didn't seem to be anyone in the two rear rooms on the ground floor so I decided to go in. I parked the rifle by the back door, checked the pistol and inched open the fly wire door. It came easily, the door handle turned smoothly and I moved into a glassed-in porch. The kitchen was well-gadgeted, but plain. It was about six o'clock and I thought nervously about the possibility of someone coming into the kitchen to get the drinks, then I remembered that you didn't go to the kitchen to get the drinks in a house like this, the booze had a room of its own.

I went through a door into a dining room and through that into a hallway dominated by a carved staircase, painted white. From near the front of the place I could hear Bryn Gutteridge's voice. I moved forward and flattened myself against the wall outside the room. This was the den or something such, ice was tinkling in glasses and I heard the soft hiss of the springs giving in an armchair when Bryn got up. I could hear

203

every word spoken. Bryn sounded nervy, impatient.

"I just don't believe you," he was saying, "it doesn't make sense, you have to know something."

"If I do, I don't know what it is." It was his sister's voice, fairly calm and even. "I know it sounds like nonsense," she went on, "I almost believe that I do know what you want me to know. But I can't remember . . ."

"That's bullshit, Susan. Brave says you didn't forget anything important, and this is important."

"Brave! What would he know? He isn't a doctor. He's in jail now and serve him bloody right. God, how you two have put me through it. What the hell do you think you're doing now?" There was strength in her voice. She hadn't gone back to the vegetable kingdom where they'd been keeping her and she seemed to be standing up to Bryn nicely. That took some doing because, along with the edginess, there was a menacing quality in his voice which was pretty telling in combination with the usual authority.

"You know very well what I'm doing, Susan. I'm going to force you to tell me where those files are. It has to be you, no one else could have got them. You always were a sly bitch, Susan. You found out the combination to that safe somehow, you took the files when you found Mark dead."

"I didn't! You can talk till you're blue in the face. I didn't know there was a safe, let alone the combination."

"You're lying, Susan. Brave knew you were lying but he was too gentle with you. You'll tell me here and now!"

"You're mad, Bryn. How do you know there were any files? I just don't know what you're talking about. You've got everything screwed up, you need help."

"Know what I'll do sister dear, just to prove to you that I mean what I say? I'll tell you something. Someone's been using those files. Someone knows a hell of a lot they shouldn't know about some very big people. They wouldn't be able to put the pressure on they have unless they had Mark's own brain inside their heads. So it *has* to be his files. There are some very scared people about, some politicians, a judge, a couple of lawyers and developers. They're very scared and they're getting at me. They think I'm the one and I'm not. It has to be you or someone with you."

"It isn't, I swear it isn't. I've been ill for so long . . ."

"Well, you would be," said Bryn with a sneer in his voice.

"What do you mean?"

The springs creaked again. I guessed that Bryn was leaning forward trying to impose physical as well as emotional pressure on her. There was heavy silence in the room like when old lovers go over the ground and discover how hopeless it all was from the beginning. My scalp was crawling and I sneaked a look behind me, but it wasn't a threat from outside that had produced the sensation, it was some kind of inbuilt resistance to hearing people expressing their deepest hostilities and antagonisms with no holds barred.

"I've been doctoring your insulin for ages, Susan, or having it done. You've been eating yourself up, literally."

"You bastard!" They were twins alright. Susan had exactly the same kind of venom in her voice now. "I wouldn't tell you anything even if I could. Christ, I've felt so rotten, so weak, and Brave nagging away at me, all that stuff about clearing my mind and starting afresh. Well your man Hardy put a rocket under him!"

"Hardy," Bryn said slowly, "yes, that was a mistake."

"Why did you hire him?"

"I thought he might stir Brave up, I didn't think he'd bust him. But let's get back to you."

"Yes, let's. At least I understand it now, that's a relief. I was doing everything right, the shots, the diet, the exercise and it wouldn't come good. You're a sadistic bastard Bryn."

"I had to do it, Susan, I . . ."

She cut him off. "Like hell you did. I thought I was mad in that place sometimes. Now I know I'm not. Thanks Bryn, thanks for telling me. I despised myself for being such a dishrag, I'd rather be normally dead than what I was. I don't know a damn thing about Mark's files and I don't give a damn what you think or do."

Gutteridge was coming apart, I could hear him sloshing his drink about and fidgeting in his chair. When he spoke his voice was a low moan. "Susan, I'm about at the end. They killed Giles, God knows how many of them are after me. You must help me."

"I can't, and I wouldn't anyway."

"Don't say that, you'd have done anything for me at one time . . ."

Susan let out her breath in a long hiss and a glass crashed to the floor. Her voice was so different in tone and quality that it sounded as if a third person had materialised in the room.

"You rotten little queer," she said, "I hope they kill you slowly."

Chair springs, a slap and a scream and I was in the room with the Colt gripped tightly in my hand. Bryn had his sister by the hair and was reaching back for another slap. Susan's knees had buckled and she was falling, trying to cover her face and keep him back. I chopped him in the ribs with my left hand but he seemed bent on scalping her, so I slashed the sight of the pistol across his wrist. He yelled, freed the hair and collapsed on the floor. Susan twisted away and fell back into a chair sobbing and scrabbling her fingers in her tortured hair.

When she'd recovered a little she held out a hand to me. I fended her off. "He's still dangerous," I said, "and he might have some help around."

She pulled back and composed herself in the chair.

"I don't think so," she said. "There was just Bryn and the albino man from the beginning." A look of panic appeared in her face. "Where's he?" she said quickly. "I'm afraid of him, he's terrible."

"I don't care for him much either," I said, "but he's out of action for a while. I surprised him, he's tied up down at the gates."

She breathed out noisily. "That's good. I hope you tied him tightly. I hope it hurts."

"It does."

Bryn was crouched on the floor listening and not moving. I couldn't tell how badly I'd hurt him but I guessed it wasn't much. He was strangely resilient.

"Into the chair, Mr Gutteridge," I said, "you've got some talking to do."

"Mr Gutteridge." His voice was heavily ironic and he'd recovered his breath fast. "Are you always so polite to people you pistol whip, Mr Hardy?"

"Only to ex-employers and you never can tell when it'll stop in your case. Why did you bomb Ailsa's car?"

Confidence and control were flooding back into him. He looked bored and just slightly puzzled.

"I didn't."

It was my turn to look puzzled, I believed him and my attention must have wavered for a split second because he came up out of the chair and launched a flying kick at my head. It isn't supposed to work against a well prepared man with a gun but it did. I took it on the shoulder and went down clumsily against a chair. I dropped the gun, scrambled for it and by the time I got it Bryn had rolled over neatly and was out the door moving fast. I got up and started after him. Susan moved in all the wrong directions and I cannoned into her. We both went down and I lost time extricating myself and apologising.

CHAPTER 18

Susan held me by the arm longer than seemed necessary—some instinct to protect such close flesh and blood I suppose—and by the time I'd shaken her free Bryn was out of the house. I craned my neck up over the foliage from the back step and thought I saw him moving through the shrubs, already halfway to the road, but I wasn't sure. I ran across to the Fiat, the keys were in it but I lost some time figuring out how to drive it. When I got the right buttons pressed it roared down the drive in great style. I lost more time opening the gate and when I got out I saw the tail end of the Land Rover disappearing behind a corner a hundred yards ahead. I followed fast, thinking that if he stuck to the roads he didn't have a chance and if he took to the bush I didn't have a chance—a nice even money bet. I also tried to remember whether the rifle had been still leaning against the house where I'd left it. I couldn't remember and it was important to the odds in a showdown between Bryn and me.

The road from Cooper Beach north is all ups and downs with a long drop to the sea on one side and high, densely timbered slopes on the other. It's a place for closely concentrated driving at the best of times. Bryn handled the four-wheel-drive job like an expert; it looked new and must have been in top condition because it touched seventy when the grade permitted and it whipped around the bends like it was on rails. The Fiat was almost too fast for me; it was so long since I'd driven a good car that I had trouble controlling it. Bryn couldn't get off the road and as I got the hang of driving the sports car I drew closer to him and I could see a shape swaying about in the front seat—the albino. Bryn wouldn't have had time to untie him, which was a point or two for me.

We screamed along in tandem, thirty feet apart for about five miles. The narrow, winding road was empty both ways and we burned down the middle towards the long, twisting descent to the salt-flat and lake country. If he reached the bottom first, Bryn could pull off into the salt pans and ti-tree and take all the points. I hadn't driven the road for fifteen years, but it hadn't changed much and I remembered the tight, cruel turns and bad cambering we were entering. Bryn was using all his power and all the road he needed to stay ahead and get a break on the flat. I lost a fraction of time and an inch of speed correcting a slide but I was in command of the car when a timber truck came lumbering up around a bend. The Land Rover swung desperately into the shoulder and missed the truck by the thickness of a coat of paint. I slid past easily and when I rounded the bend I saw Bryn's vehicle sliding and fish-tailing down the road fifty yards ahead. The road coiled into a wicked S bend and he didn't make it—the Land Rover shot over the edge and began scything down saplings. I hit the brakes; the Fiat stopped straight and true. I set the lights flashing and ran to where Bryn had gone over. A hundred feet down the vehicle was wrapped around a tree and before I could move an inch it exploded with a roar and a yellow and blue flash like an incendiary bomb.

I sat on the edge of the drop waiting for the truck driver to come back and compel me to become an honest citizen. There were going to be a few questions about this accident—a brand new Land Rover goes over a cliff with a healthy young man at the wheel, beside him is another man who was unhealthy before he got dead. The fire would do incredible damage to them both, but there was no mistaking baling wire and it wouldn't take long to trace the car to Gutteridge. A bomb, a murder, a raid, a torturing and a fatal crash all with the name Gutteridge included—Grant Evans wasn't going to sit on that too long.

The truckie didn't come back and no one else happened along. I was left to make my own moral decisions.

I scooted back to the Fiat, pressed my luck by making a three-point turn and drove back to Cooper Beach as fast as Italian engineering could take me. I sneaked a few looks in the rear vision mirror and from the high points on the road I could see an orange glow from Bryn's funeral pyre. The penalties for leaving an accident scene in this state were tough and my investigator's licence was forfeit from the second I'd got back into the car. But the truck driver, who must have heard the explosion, was the only one who could tie the Fiat to the Land Rover, and he wasn't playing. The odds on getting back to the house unspotted and gaining a breathing space seemed pretty good. I could use the breathing space to get Susan back to town, report to Ailsa and keep my credentials on the case good and tight. The thought occurred to me that there was a reason to bring Susan and Ailsa together at this point, but I couldn't quite clinch it. I was thinking about how to handle the bright lights and sleeplessness of a police interrogation when I swung the Fiat into the late Mr Gutteridge's immaculate concrete driveway.

I put the Fiat back where I found it, reluctantly. It would have done wonders for my professional and neighbourhood image, but I wouldn't have been able to afford to have its oil changed. I wiped it clean and gave its bonnet a pat reflecting that probate on it alone would be six months' earnings for me. Pity the rich. The rifle wasn't where I'd left it. I went through the porch and kitchen and was heading for the den when I froze like an ice-trapped mammoth—Susan Gutteridge was sitting on the staircase about ten steps up and she had the rifle trained directly on my middle shirt button. Her face was dead white and her mouth was set in a hard, concentrated line. She looked more determined than nervous and I wasn't sure that she recognised me.

"Miss Gutteridge." It came out as half-croak, half-giggle. "It's Hardy, put the rifle down please." Nothing moved in her face or hands. Some people say a .22 is a toy. Don't believe it—at that range and with a bit of luck it can be just as final for you as a .357 magnum. I drew a breath and tried again in a more confidence-inspiring tone.

"Put the rifle down, Susan. I'm here to help you, just put it down slowly."

"I thought you were Bryn." Her voice was calm and detached, as if it belonged to no one in particular.

"No."

"Bryn or the other one. I was going to kill you."

"There's no need. I'm a friend."

She looked at me for the first time. I must have looked a pretty unlikely object for a friend in her circle, but she got the message. She stood the gun up, not inexpertly, and handed it to me with the muzzle pointing safely away. She'd had it cocked and the safety catch was off. I wouldn't have fancied Bryn's chances if he'd come into view. I worked the action and shook a shell out of the breech.

"Come and sit down." I held out my hand to her. She took it and we moved towards the den.

"You said something strange just then," she said.

I thought I'd been making good, solid sense, but she pressed it.

"It was odd I said I was going to kill Bryn and you said there was no need."

"That's right. It was just an expression though."

"But he's dead already?"

I nodded. "His car went over a cliff, it burned."

We sat down in one of the den's deep chairs, then she jumped out of it and moved across to another chair. I went to the bar and hunted for whisky. I found an empty decanter and held it up to Susan inquiringly. She pointed to a long cupboard, like a broom cupboard, in the corner of the room. I opened it. A supersize bottle of Johnnie Walker swung inside a teak frame; it looked like it held ten litres or more of the stuff and it was still half full. I filled the decanter and poured two stiff ones over ice. I sat down in the chair Susan had deserted and took a few restorative gulps. She did the same and in a strange way we seemed to be toasting her dead brother.

"Have you reported this to the police?" she asked.

"No." She asked me why and I tried to explain stressing that I didn't know how she wanted her kidnapping handled, but I also pointed out how deeply I was involved and how being held by the police would hamstring me. She saw it.

"Well it's not going to matter to Bryn," she said, "in a way it might please him, the end of it all. He had a sort of Byronic . . . no, satanic streak, he cultivated it. You might have noticed?"

Byronic was closer I thought. "Yes, I did."

She was quiet for a minute, thinking God knows what. I let the good liquor work on me and sat being soothed by the sound of the waves on the beach and the feel of the deep piled carpet under my feet. There was a hell of a lot Bryn hadn't been able to take with him. I wondered if Susan was his heir and what she'd do with all the loot if she was. I wondered about everything except the essential point—what to do next. Susan broke up the reverie by asking me exactly that. I had a few smaller questions of my own, like was Bryn telling the truth when he denied all knowledge of the bombing of Ailsa's car, and did Susan really know nothing about the files? But I was too tired to pursue them or to come up with any plans for interstate flights, midnight meetings on lonely airstrips or hard drinking, incognito, in low-life taverns.

"Let's get back to town," I said, "we can talk a bit on the way."

It was a mundane suggestion, but she sloshed down her drink and took a quick look around the place. A trifle proprietorial and previous, but who could blame her? I'd have been making an inventory and marking the levels in the bottles. We turned out the lights as we went through the house and I pulled the back door locked. I gave it a test tug but Susan waved me on.

"Don't worry about the house, or the car. Someone from the town comes up to look after it."

I hadn't liked her when she had no personality at all and I wasn't too keen on this one emerging. I snapped my fingers.

"Of course, silly of me," I said.

Her head jerked sharply round to look at me. She grinned, then tossed her head back and laughed. "Fair enough Hardy," she said when she finished laughing. "Don't like rich bitches, eh?"

We were tramping down the drive now and it didn't seem to occur to her to ask why. Maybe she trusted me, in any case her stocks with me were climbing a bit.

"Not much," I said. "I feel awkward around large amounts of money, I don't get enough myself to practise on."

"That's a pity, we must see to that."

We went through the gate, she stopped and looked around.

"Where's the car?" she said.

"What car?"

"Your car!"

"It's parked back in town, I caught a ride with the albino. We're walking."

She shook her head. "No way, it's too far."

I was getting a bit tired of her and my voice wasn't gentle.

"Look Susan, you have three choices, walk, wait here for me to drive back from town or go up to the house again and call a cab. It's late but you might just get one to take you to Sydney, if you do he'll ask why you're not using the Fiat. You'll have to lie, later you'll have to explain to the cops why you lied. You can wait here if you want to, but who knows when things are going to break. I think you'd better walk."

She nodded and we started out. It was dark, the road was rough and Susan's thin-soled slippers weren't ideal for the job but she didn't complain for the whole forty-five minutes. She didn't talk except to confirm the direction a couple of times. I tried to draw her out about the house and the family connection with Cooper Beach, since she obviously knew the area pretty well, but she wasn't responsive.

Bryn had gone over the high side closer to the next town, Sussman's Wharf, than to Cooper Beach, and I was hoping that the police and ambulance action would come from there when the wreck was discovered. That's the way it happened; when we trudged into the little township the streets were as quiet as a Trappist prayer meeting. One milk bar cum eatery was open at the far end of the main street and the pubs were still serving a thin scattering of hard cases. My car was where I'd left it and the keys were where I'd left them. There was no obvious sign that anyone had taken any interest in it, but I prowled around it a bit just to be sure. Susan obviously thought I'd lost my mind, she sat on the grass looking beat but not downhearted until I was satisfied. She got in looking dismayed at the peeling vinyl and the general air of ruin. It was probably the oldest car she'd ever been in apart from vintage models in rallies with some of the chaps from her brother's school.

"Why were you crawling about in the dark just then?" she asked after we'd got moving and she'd found that the passenger side seat belt didn't fasten. I told her about the bombing of Ailsa's car again and asked her if she'd forgotten.

"Stop trying to trip me up Hardy," she snapped. "I'm not crazy."

"You're cool, I'll say that."

"What do you mean?"

"Your twin brother's dead and you're here exchanging insults with me."

We were on the winding road up to the tollway and I couldn't get a look at her until we made the highway. When I got on it and could glance across I could see that she was gripping the sides of her seat and weeping silently.

219

"I'm sorry," I said, "that was cruel, you've got the right to feel whatever you feel."

"That's the trouble," she said, "I don't think I feel anything. I think that's why I'm crying." She brushed her hand across her face and made an effort to steady her voice. "I've got some questions for you, Mr Hardy."

"I have some for you," I said.

"Well, let's try a few as far as we're each prepared to answer."

"OK, you first."

"Do you think Bryn and Dr Brave were behind everything that's been happening, the bombing, Giles and so on?"

"No."

"Who then?"

"Someone else, or others, plural."

"Who?"

"I don't know, I have suspects, just that."

"Are you going to try and find out for sure?"

"Yes."

"Can I hire you to do that?"

That conflict of interest seemed infinite. "No," I said, "afraid not. Thanks just the same for the compliment."

"Why not?"

"I'm already retained on the job."

"By Ailsa?"

"That's right."

"And just how do you feel about her?"

"You just reached the end of your questions, my turn."

She rummaged about in the glove box among the odds and ends and spent Drum packets and slammed it all back in frustration.

"Haven't you got anything to smoke except this vile tobacco?"

"No. Do you know anything about the files?"

"Not a thing, I wish I did."

I let that pass to avoid side-tracking her. "What did Bryn mean when he said you would once have done anything for him? You reacted very strongly." She jerked up in her seat. "Nothing, nothing at all," she said quickly, "we were once very close that's all."

"I see. This may or may not be related. What did your father have on you and Bryn that kept you in line?"

"Who told you that he had something?"

"Never mind, what was it?"

"No." She slumped down and ran her fingers through her hair, lifting and dropping the wings, her voice was old and thin as it had been back in the clinic. "No more questions."

"One more, do you remember exactly who was around the night your father died?"

"I could, I have an excellent memory when conditions are right. I'd have to sit down and think about it."

That brought it back to me, the reason I'd had a flash about bringing Ailsa and Susan together. The key to all this was somewhere back four years ago when Mark Gutteridge had killed himself. I needed to know all I could about that night. It didn't seem like the right time to put this to Susan, so I let her answer stand and we drove on together in silence towards the smoggy lights of Sydney.

Susan gave me the address of a friend she could stay with for the night and I took her there. I stopped the car outside the place, a tizzed-up terrace in Paddington, got out and went around the car to open her door. She stepped out and put her hand on my arm.

"Thank you, I'm going to see Dr Pincus tomorrow," she said.

"I know," I said. Then an idea hit me. "Try for St Bede's."

"What?" She looked at me, puzzled and deeply tired.

"If he wants to put you in hospital, ask to go to St Bede's."

"Why?"

"I hear it's the best anyway, so you'll probably go there as a matter of course. But as well as that it might help me if you're there."

She was too tired to pursue it, she shrugged her shoulders, pushed open the stained wood and iron gate, and climbed the steps to the house. I saw light flood out from the open door and heard a woman's voice say Susan's name in startled but welcoming tones. The light went out.

CHAPTER 19

It was after midnight and I was low on everything—energy, alertness, courage, the lot. I drove mechanically away from Paddington towards Glebe. The car felt as tired as me, unresponsive to the pedals, resistant to the wheel, dull as lead. I needed rest very badly and I couldn't think of anywhere to get it except at home. I vaguely considered crashing at Evans' house but rejected the idea. Motels were out for psychological reasons—I'd lie awake all night thinking of death.

I turned into my street and killed the engine and lights outside my house. I was fumbling about with the key in the front door lock when a beam of light hit me in the eyes and a hundredweight of hand fell on my shoulder. Another hand reached out, took the keys and dropped them into my jacket pocket. I tried to shield my eyes from the light to get a look at them but they weren't co-operative. One twisted my arm up behind my back just short of breaking point and the other jammed his torch into the end of my nose. The torch-carrier's voice was like rocks rumbling about in an empty oil drum.

"We hear you're tough Hardy, care to prove it?"

"Not just now," I said, "I'm short on sleep. I'll be tough again tomorrow."

The other one laughed. "You won't be tough tomorrow mate," he said. "You'll be soft, soft as jelly." He emphasised the prediction by putting another fraction of an inch strain on my arm.

"Whatever you say. How about easing down on the lighting and the strong arm stuff and telling me what this's all about?"

I was getting used to the light and was able to make out the general shape and size of them. Even under these imperfect conditions they were obviously cops, the kind that start off as slim, eager youths on traffic duty and end up as big, beery corrupt bastards shoving the citizenry around for kicks. The bulk of one of them looked vaguely familiar, the one with the torch.

"Is it yourself, O'Brien?" I said, all mock bog and peat.

"Don't be a smart arse, Hardy, just come along quietly and you won't get hurt unnecessarily."

"I haven't said I wouldn't. Who's the half-nelson expert?"

"The name's Collins, Hardy," he said, "and I'd really like to break your arm, know that?"

"I can sense that you love your work, yes."

O'Brien switched off the torch and turned me around by the shoulder. Collins wasn't quite ready for it and it turned me partly out of his grip, I stumbled and my clumsy foot came up sharply into his shin.

"Oh, sorry Collins," I said. He swore and reached for me like a bear in a bad mood. O'Brien pushed him back.

"Leave it, Colly," he said, "this guy's a fancy prick and he'll have us doing something we'll regret later if he gets to us."

"He's fuckin' got to me already," Collins ground out, "why's he got to arrive spick and span?"

"If you can't figure it out for yourself there's no point in telling you," O'Brien said with an air of tolerance for weaker intellects. "Let's just take him in as we found him, he doesn't look in such good shape anyway."

He was right, I wasn't. A little adrenalin had flowed over the past few minutes, but all the guns and king hits and karate kicks of the past twelve hours had worn me down and left me in good condition to be leaned on. I still felt cheeky though.

"Do as he says sport," I said. "Grant Evans will explain it all to you just before they cut you down to Constable Colly."

226

O'Brien gave out with his basso laugh again and Collins chuckled along in chorus.

"That's where you're wrong, Hardy," O'Brien said, "Evans is on leave, sort of a reward for his good work handed down from above. Someone up there isn't too happy so there's a bit of shit coming down all round. Inspector Mills is copping it and he wants to unload some on you. Let's go down town and talk about it."

They eased me down the path and into the car. It's a pity Soames wasn't watching, it would have made his day. I slumped down in the car and tried to think but nothing came. I was in a very bad spot without Evans to protect me even if they hadn't placed me at all the scenes I'd visited that day. If they had, and they didn't want explanations, it was going to be some time before Hardy walked proud and free again.

Collins got behind the wheel and O'Brien sat in the back with me. I'd left my .38 and the albino's Colt in my car which was lucky, but I didn't like the air of confidence hanging around the two of them.

I tried pumping O'Brien for some information so I'd know what to expect at Headquarters but he just told me to shut up and sweat it out. I did. Collins drove like a maniac, jumping lights and bullying everyone on the road. O'Brien shook his head at a couple of the more flagrant breaches of road decency but in general he seemed to regard his partner as beyond redemption. I was almost glad when we arrived at the Police

Building. Collins slammed the tyres into the kerb and cut the ignition just as he gave the motor a last, lead-footed rev. The engine shuddered protestingly into silence. Collins yanked open his door as if he meant to take it with him and, after O'Brien had sat still long enough for him to get the idea, he pulled open the back door in the same style. It might have been a subtle intimidation ploy but somehow I thought it was just that Collins didn't know any other way to behave.

We went up the steps and into the building. There was a different sergeant on the desk but he looked just as pissed-off with the job as his predecessor. I suppose the old lift was still running but I didn't get a chance to find out. We went down a set of steps following a sign which said Interrogation Rooms 1 to 6. Room 1 was long and narrow, painted cream and the only furniture was a table and two straight-backed chairs. There was a small shade over the light but not enough to make it comfortable and there was something very disconcerting about the washstand and towel in the far corner. It made the room feel like a fourth-rate hotel hole-up which you take when you're running low on money and aren't expecting any glamorous company. I sat down in one of the chairs and began feeling in my pockets for tobacco. O'Brien took the chair opposite, put a cigarette in his mouth, lit it and blew the smoke into my face.

"No smoking," he said.

I forced a laugh. "You aren't really going to pull all this interrogation stuff are you? Doing it in relays with your handsome mate, no smoking, no sleep?"

"Depends on you, Hardy, makes no difference to me. I can go out for a drink or a nap any time. You're on the spot."

"Well, that's a start. What have you got on me?"

O'Brien took a small notebook out and flipped over some pages.

"A whole stack of things, big or small according to how you want to play it. Failures to report felonies and such."

I leaned back and smiled. "Littering, loitering."

O'Brien still looked confident. He grinned and scratched his ear.

"Very droll," he said. "How about murder?"

"I haven't murdered anyone lately that I can recall."

"That so? Try Terrence Cattermole."

"Never heard of him."

"He heard of you, he said you killed him."

"Now how could that be?"

"I'm giving you a chance to do yourself a bit of good. Judges and juries go for voluntary admissions, they go easy on people."

"Judges and juries can laugh cases out of court too. I'd like to help you, O'Brien, but you've got me shot to bits. I don't even understand how a murdered man can name his murderer."

"Have it your way. It seems a Land Rover went over a cliff up the coast a bit. Seems there were two guys in it when it went over. One of them was tied up with wire. You tied him up, Cattermole his name was. He got thrown clear, see? Just before he died he told us about it. He said that he and the other guy had roughed up a woman you're interested in, you followed them, jumped them, knocked the other guy out and put the wire around Cattermole. You put the Land Rover over the cliff. All this happened about five hours ago, that means you've got an accomplice who did some of the driving. Like to tell us who it is?"

"Shit, have you got it screwed up!"

"Well, that's the way Inspector Mills put it to me and my guess is that's the way someone put it to him. Now that's the way we can leave it unless you have something to say."

"What about?"

"I hear the name Gutteridge is involved."

"That so?"

"Yeah. And I also hear that the name Gutteridge is of interest in certain quarters. Need I say more?"

"Blood oath you do. What about my phone call at this point?"

"Oh yes, well, we go by the book here. Let's see, we'll need an extension phone. Collins can get one somewhere, can't you, Colly?"

Collins was leaning against the wall near the door.

230

He'd been listening with a slightly puzzled, but relaxed grin on his face. He was enjoying himself. For a horrible second I thought he was going to say "Sure Boss", but he didn't.

"Must be one around somewhere," he said through the grin.

"That's right. Then Hardy could ring Simon Sackville and he'd come running down and get him out on habeus corpus or something. Right Hardy?"

He had me cold and he knew it, or someone had told him. Sy was out of the country, consulting on a constitutional case—independence for some group of islands off to hell and gone. He was the only lawyer whose confidence I'd ever gained. That wasn't surprising as I was a slow payer and lots of trouble.

"Sy's away," I said, more to myself than O'Brien.

"Aaw, that's too bad," O'Brien said, "maybe you could get one of his partners and explain it all to them?"

Sy's partners were as straight as he was strange—they only tolerated him because he was brilliant and almost always successful. They disapproved of me the way a saint disapproves of sin.

"No way," I said wearily, "and you know it."

O'Brien grinned. "How about legal aid?"

"You're holding all the cards, O'Brien," I said. "I wonder how that came about. You're not smart enough to figure all this out for yourself."

Collins levered himself off the wall and moved towards my chair.

"My turn, Paddy?" he said.

"Not yet." O'Brien waved him back and leaned forward towards me over the table.

"Look Hardy, you're a smart guy. You can add two and two. We know this Cattermole was a hood. No one's very worried about him. Maybe the whole thing was an accident. If you've got something to say about Mark Gutteridge I think we can work something out. I've got Inspector Mills' promise that he'll interview you in private himself and that you won't lose by it. He's standing by."

The penny dropped. The Gutteridge files were being used and some top cops were hurting. As long as they thought I knew something about the Gutteridge files I was worth keeping alive. My life wouldn't be worth two bob if I told them a thing, either way.

"How about Jackson?"

"What?" O'Brien was startled and dropped his suave mask for a second.

"Senior Detective Charles Jackson, the crooked cop, bent as buggery."

"He's on suspension," Collins said.

"Shut up Colly!" O'Brien rapped out. "What's Jackson to you Hardy?"

"He's shit to me," I said, "and your Inspector Mills sounds like double shit."

O'Brien slammed his notebook down on the table and banged his fist on top of it. He drew a deep breath and seemed to be internalising some deep moral struggle. Cop training won out. He scooped up the notebook, tucked it away in his pocket and got to his feet.

"OK, Colly," he said, "five minutes, nothing visible." He walked across to the door and went out of the room. Collins leaned across and snibbed the lock. He walked up behind me and took hold of the lobe of my right ear. He pinched it.

"Tell me," he said.

"Get stuffed, you don't even know what you're asking about, you dumb gorilla."

My vision and my breath and my hearing were all cut off by the kidney punch. It knocked me off the chair and left me hunched up on the floor fighting to keep control of my stomach and my bladder. Collins reached down into the waistband of my trousers and put his hand around my balls.

"Let's hear it."

Nothing had changed. I was dead if they found out that I knew nothing worth knowing about the files. I had to pretend that I knew and to take whatever they dished out.

"Get your hand off my balls, you faggot."

He squeezed and I screamed and writhed away from him. He came after me and I lashed out at him with a foot. It caught him on the thigh and made him beserk, he jumped on me and started pummelling me with his fists. Through the mist of red and black I was dimly aware of a hammering on the door. Collins let go of me and I saw the door open, then slid down into an ebbing and flowing sea of pain.

I woke up in a cell and my watch told me it was three hours later in my life. They'd taken my wallet and keys but left me the tobacco and matches. I struggled up to a sitting position on the bench and looked around. I suppose it would have been luxury in Mexico—sleeping bench, large enamel bucket, fairly clean washbasin and dry concrete floor—but I wasn't taken with it. My mouth tasted like a sewer and I rinsed some water around in it and tried to smoke a cigarette. The taste sent me running to the bucket for a monumental heave and I crawled back to the bench and pulled a thin grey blanket over me. My kidney and testicles competed for the major seat of pain award. I curled myself up under the blanket and became aware for the first time that my trousers were wet. I sniffed at my hand and got the unmistakable smell of urine from it.

By experimenting carefully I found a position in which everything didn't hurt at once. I held it until sleep hooked me and reeled me in and away from my bed of pain.

CHAPTER 20

Breakfast came at 6.30, a cup of instant coffee and two pieces of soggy toast. I got it down somehow and sat on the bench feeling miserable. A cop came in an hour later and emptied the bucket, the only diversion for the morning. I sat on the bench smoking cigarettes and longing for a drink. I thought of asking if I could telephone the hospital but there were disadvantages in bringing Ailsa's name to the cops' attention just then. Mostly I worried about whether they were going to try to hold me on the charges they could get together and whether I could get anyone to put up the bail. Sy usually arranged such things for me and he'd picked a great time to go off liberating the Third World. Fretting, and a disgusting mess that could just have passed as an omelette, took me into the early part of the afternoon. I'd reconciled myself to several weeks or more of Long Bay jail when Collins unlocked the door and beckoned me out of the cell. Just the sight of him made me ache in all the old familiar places. He didn't look as chipper as he had the night before though. He held the door open.

"Out."

"Where to?"

"It'd be a quick trip to the harbour if it was up to me, but it seems you got friends."

That sounded hopeful. I followed him out of the lock-up to a kind of lounge, a gentle version of the interrogation room. We went in and O'Brien was sitting at a desk talking to another man. I didn't know him and from the look he gave me I decided I didn't want to. I was unravelled and unshaven, he was shaved as smooth as an egg. He looked to be quite tall, a self-satisfied number. He wore a light grey suit that didn't come off the peg, handmade brogues, a pale blue shirt and a tie from one of the good schools or regiments. His hair was thick and dark although he must have been approaching fifty to judge from the tiny wrinkles etched into his suntanned face. His teeth were white and his eyes were blue, he was perfect. O'Brien waved me into a chair and Collins took up his usual position by the door. He'd have done the same in a Bedouin tent.

It was one of those occasions where nobody likes anybody else. I sat down and O'Brien broke the silence.

"This is Mr Urquhart," he said, "he's got a writ for your release Hardy and we're just working out the details."

I looked over at Mr Cool and he gave me a slight nod which would have cost a month's earnings if I'd been paying him.

"Good," I said, "don't let me disturb you, just pretend I'm not here."

"You don't seem surprised," O'Brien grated out angrily.

"Not at all."

When someone hurries in with a writ for your release you don't sit around discussing your good fortune with the cops, you just accept it graciously and hope he'll throw in a drink afterwards. Urquhart reached into his breast pocket, pulled out a wallet that looked as if it had cost more money than I'd ever had in one, and extracted an envelope. He put it on the table in front of O'Brien who prodded it and blinked.

"What's this for?" he said.

Urquhart smiled. "I understand this is how you like to do business, Mr O'Brien. My principal has no objection and I think Mr Hardy hasn't noticed anything untoward."

He inclined his head towards me and I smiled smoothly back. I pointed at the envelope lying alongside the legal document.

"Bit of betting money for you there Paddy," I said, "Collins can help you pick yesterday's winners."

"That will do Hardy," Urquhart snapped. "I'm sure the sergeant knows his business."

O'Brien looked again at the envelope and let out a breath slowly. He glanced up at Collins who had an idiot smile on his face.

"Very well, Mr Urquhart," O'Brien muttered, "all in order I think."

"I should think so," said Urquhart quietly, "I'll see you outside Mr Hardy. I assume you have possessions to collect?"

"Just the gold watch and lighter and the mad money. Lead the way Sergeant."

Collins opened the door and the lawyer walked out purposefully—he was the kind who memorised routes in and out and never got lost no matter how many times you turned him around. When he was gone O'Brien gave me a hard look.

"Don't put a foot wrong Hardy or you'll be back faster than you can fuck."

I shook my head disapprovingly and drew my finger across my throat.

"Cover your tracks, mate," I said, "heads are gonna roll." I walked out with Collins close behind me.

"What are you talking about?" he said anxiously.

"Don't worry Colly, you have a solid asset."

We got to the admission desk and I was given my things back in exchange for a signature in a ledger. I stuffed them into my pockets and headed for the door.

Collins padded after me. "What d'you mean solid asset?" he asked.

I tapped my forefinger against my temple and kept moving.

Urquhart was standing on the pavement propping up a gun-metal Celica that looked fresh from the showroom. When he saw me he went around to the driver's side and got in. He beckoned at me with an imperious forefinger and I got in beside him. He turned a key which apparently started the engine, not that you'd know from the noise level. I pulled the seat belt out slowly to show him that I knew how they worked and settled myself down into the leather.

He didn't smile, he didn't say anything until we were out into the traffic—he was gold plated and platinum tipped. He avoided a truck and rounded a bus with two easy movements.

"I am Miss Gutteridge's solicitor," he said at last.

"Oh yeah, lucky you."

"Don't try to upset me, Mr Hardy, you won't succeed. I'm not interested in you, and your tough guy act doesn't impress me. People who have to be bailed out of police lock-ups in the sort of condition you are in are obviously stupid and no amount of repartee can redeem them."

"Yeah. I have the same view of people who wear three hundred dollar suits and have to shave every day, so we're even. How did Susan know I was in the can and why did she tell you to get me out?"

"Miss Gutteridge called me late last night and asked me to contact you to discuss a matter she wishes you to pursue. Your telephone didn't answer, your answering service is hopelessly unsatisfactory, so I called at your address and made inquiries. I felt you couldn't do whatever is required of you in jail."

"Very true. Where's Susan, in hospital?"

"I haven't been instructed."

"Of course not, you're a messenger boy, not privy council."

He winced and pulled in to the kerb. "Your jokes are as terrible as your appearance, I think I'll ask you to get out." I opened the door and eased my aching body out slowly. "Here will do," I said. He reached over, closed the door and glided away into the traffic with the air of someone who had won the round. Maybe he had.

I hailed a taxi and got home in ten minutes. Nobody had broken in, nobody was waiting for me behind the door with a cosh. I called the hospital and was told that Mrs Sleeman was sleeping well and taking solid food. I left the message that I'd call that night if possible and the following morning if not. I didn't ask about Susan Gutteridge, but the receptionist sounded just a touch excited when I gave my name. She told me that Miss Gutteridge had a message for me which I was to collect at the hospital. I gripped the handpiece so hard my knuckles cracked.

"Miss Gutteridge is a patient in the hospital?"

"Yes." The receptionist sounded like a willing participant in a high drama.

"For stabilisation of diabetes, under Dr Pincus, right?"

"Yes, and . . ."

"And what?"

"For two broken legs and multiple broken ribs. She was run over just outside the hospital."

"When?"

"At ten o'clock this morning."

"How did she manage to write a message?"

"She insisted, she terrorised the emergency ward and wrote your message before she allowed the doctors to attend to her. She threatened them with lawsuits. She's sedated now. The message must be very urgent, Mr Hardy."

"Can't you give it to me over the phone?"

"No, it's in a sealed envelope. After what she said I daren't open it. You'll have to collect it yourself."

I told her I'd be there within half an hour. I hoped she wasn't going to be too disappointed when she saw me.

The hospital lobby was crowded with departing visitors when I arrived. Most of them looked in good health and glad to be on their way back to the land of the healthy. The receptionist didn't disappoint me. She was dark and fresh looking in crisply starched linen which was fashionably cut. It made her look like someone playing a part in a TV hospital drama. Perhaps she expected me to play with a hat and unlit cigarettes. I didn't, but she had the thrill of looking at my investigator's licence before handing over the envelope. I walked back to my car and got in before ripping the paper open. The writing was shaky as you'd expect and this reinforced the feeling of fright which the short note conveyed: "Mr Hardy—I was deliberately run down. The car was a red Volkswagen. Please help me. One of my solicitors will contact you, name your own fee. Please help."

There was a shaky, scrawled signature at the bottom. I rolled a cigarette and tapped my fingers on the steering wheel as an aid to thought. The Gutteridge Terroriser was still operating and his targets had been narrowed down by one. I wondered how much pressure from how many directions had been put on Bryn to make him crack the way he had, but I knew that the question would never be answered. Bryn had taken the brunt of the danger that lay in association with the files squarely on his chest and it had killed him indirectly. Now the two remaining targets were both asking for protection. Conflicts of interest would have to be sorted out and I intended to get onto that as soon as they were able to stand the strain of each other's company. Right now the straightforward move was to round off some unfinished work by checking on Walter Chalmers.

I drove across to his place via the flats where Naumeta Pali lived. Her place in this was one of the most puzzling aspects of the whole affair. There was no red Volkswagen parked under the building so I kept going. Chalmers' house was in what is called a garden suburb in England. It was a large brick bungalow, built soon after World War I by someone who had money to spend. There was a deep front porch with a low brick wall around it and two massive plaster cast water maidens on top of the porch pillars. The house had a high pitched roof with deep overhanging eaves and nicely carved woodwork around the windows and ventilation ducts. The block it sat on was larger than average for the area, getting on for half an acre and it was crowded with flowers, bushes and shrubs. I saw every kind of flower I can identify, which is four, and dozens of others. The lawn was meticulously cut. Someone spent many hours per week in that garden and knew what he was doing.

I took a run past the house, turned at the top of the quiet street and came back down on the other side. I stopped a few doors further on. There was no activity in the street. There wouldn't be—this was a both-people-working and children-at-creche-or-school zone. I got

243

out of my car after finding a clipboard and some paper amid the rubbish on the back seat. I riffled through the blank sheets of paper, adjusted the clip, tucked the board under my arm and marched up to the gate. I walked briskly to the front door and rang the bell. Behind all that shrubbery I was scarcely visible from the street or the flanking houses. If my entry hadn't attracted any adverse attention I was set. If someone had seen me go in and knew the house was empty I could be in trouble, but I probably had some time to work in before they'd get up the spirit to ring the cops. I gave it a minute. The air was warm and still and full of insect noises. I slipped a skeleton key into the old Yale lock and turned. The door came open as if I was the master returning from a hard day's work.

The door gave onto a hallway with wallpaper that reminded me of my aunt Joan's—men on horseback in pink coats, and dogs and foxes chasing each other from floor to ceiling. To the left were double glass doors which opened onto a large living room with a big handsome fireplace. On the other side of the house there were two large bedrooms and a bathroom and toilet. Behind this the kitchen ran the width of the house and behind that was a glassed-in sun porch with full length sliding doors. A very nice drinking area. The back garden was as well kept and well stocked flora-wise as the front. I went through the porch, down a cement path to the garage. All the usual carpenter's tools hung up above a bench against their silhouettes carefully painted in black on the fibro cement wall. A wide selection of gardening tools stood against the wall lined up like soldiers at attention. There were some oil stains on the concrete floor but no one's perfect.

Back in the house I began a systematic search of drawers and cupboards to see if I could turn up anything which might suggest involvement in Gutteridge affairs beyond what was normal for a loyal employee. Contrary to their image, accountants have a very high rate of criminality—their training and professional habits make them formidable schemers and planners. Chalmers, however, seemed as honest as Baden Powell. His kitchen drawers showed him to be a model of efficiency and tidiness. The household accounts were spiked and filed down to the last detail in the second bedroom which he used as a guest room and study. My keys got me into every drawer and cabinet and revealed a man pretty much as dull as Ailsa had portrayed him. He had plenty of money, from his salary and stock market investments which seemed to be cautious and consistently profitable. His income tax submissions were a joy to see. He practically deducted his shoe leather and they bought it every time.

The main bedroom presented a contrast to the rest of the house where the fittings were austere, almost plain. This room had a softer, sensuous feel. The double bed was low slung and springy, the sheets and pillow cases were black satin under a knotty Peruvian woollen cover. There was a large cedar wardrobe with two full length mirrors and a chest of the same wood which stood five feet high—both thousand dollar antiques. The right hand door on the wardrobe offered the first resistance I'd met with in the house. It had a double lock with the second mechanism low down and concealed by a movable panel. I had to work on it with two keys and a piece of stiff plastic to get it open. The hanging space inside was crammed with full length and street length dresses and nightgowns, they ranged from frilly, frothy affairs to sleek streamlined jobs. A set of shelves in the cupboard was occupied by layers of silk and satin underwear—panties, bras, petticoats, stockings and suspenders. A box on the bottom shelf was full of make-up—lipsticks, false eyelashes, brushes and pencils, eye shadow and other pots and tubes beyond my experience.

The bottom drawer of the set between the two full length doors also put up a struggle. I jiggled it open with a long key and a lot of quiet swearing. Ross Haines couldn't have been more wrong about Chalmers; he was a homosexual alright, but about as repressed as Nero. The drawer was full of photographs, loose and glued into several albums. Many of the pictures were heavy stuff even in these permissive times. They showed a man whom I took to be Chalmers, in woman's clothing, making love, sometimes in pairs, sometimes in threes and fours. Several of the pictures had been taken in the room I was in, some were outdoor shots, others were taken in what looked like motel rooms. One album contained photos of Chalmers taken over about twenty years. He was a medium sized man with a thin face and hair that time was harvesting. One picture was arresting: Chalmers stood, dressed in a suit cut in the style of twenty years before, alongside a woman with a fresh pretty face and a neat figure. From their accessories and the background it was clearly a wedding picture—Chalmers' smile was a death mask grimace. There were a few blank leaves in the album following this picture and signs that others had been torn out. Later leaves held snapshots of men, sitting around tables, standing in streets or sprawling on grass or sand. Chalmers wore white, open-necked shirts in most of the pictures and he looked like the photographs you see of Kim Philby in Russia—not quite relaxed in front of the camera, but obviously having a good time.

I muttered "Good luck to you" under my breath and returned the photographs to their original places as carefully as I could. I looked around to make sure I hadn't disturbed the room and left the house by the front door. Clipboard under my arm I walked to the car. I rolled a cigarette and smoked it down while staring through the windscreen. Walter Chalmers had his own deep secrets and I judged that this made him unlikely to trade in those of other people.

CHAPTER 21

I was back in the hospital by five o'clock. The same
crowd of visitors milled about in the lobby waiting to
catch lifts up to the wards. There was a different receptionist at the desk but the same smell in the corridors.
Ailsa was sitting up in her bed. She was wearing a little
make-up and a different nightgown. This one had a
loose tie around the neck, a sort of drawstring, and
she was fiddling with the strings when I walked into
the room. She looked outwardly better but inwardly
worse. The hands she held out tentatively to me were
trembling and cold. I held her hands for a minute and
broke the silence clumsily.

"What's wrong love, cigarette withdrawal or
morphine addiction?"

"Don't joke, Cliff," she said, "just look at that."
She nodded down at the newspaper which was lying

folded up on the bed. I picked it up and read the lead story. It said that Dr Ian Brave, who had been held in custody in connection with the sheltering of Rory Costello, had escaped from the hospital wing of the Long Bay jail. Tickener had the byline and he'd made the most of the meagre facts he'd had to work with. Brave had been taken ill with severe vomiting and internal pain and had been escorted to the hospital. He'd been sedated and an armed guard had been set up outside his room. The room was inspected hourly and Brave had vanished between eleven o'clock and noon. The guard denied leaving his post and said he'd heard nothing suspicious from inside the room. Tickener described Brave as a "consulting psychologist" and mentioned obliquely that he had an intimate knowledge of drugs and had used hypnotism in the treatment of his patients.

Ailsa was gnawing at her nails as I read and she dug a jagged one into my arm as I put the paper down.

"I heard about Bryn on the news this morning and now this. What's happening, Cliff? I'm scared, I don't understand it. I don't feel safe even in here with Brave out there somewhere."

I poured her some water and tried to calm her down, but she was close to hysteria. She brushed the glass aside.

"I don't want water. How could he escape from prison? How could he?"

"Easy love, you're safe here. It could have been fixed for him. He's had one cop in his pocket, why not more? The story doesn't say whether it was a police guard or a prison guard. I don't really think he could have used hypnotism on the guard, but it's possible. It gives the guard an out anyway."

"Jesus, it scares me," she said.

"Me too," I said, then mostly to myself, "I suppose he could have fixed it while he was inside."

She jumped at it. "Fixed what?"

She was so edgy that it seemed better to give her something real to bite on rather than let her fantasise herself into nervous collapse. I told her about the attempt to kill Susan Gutteridge and worked back from that through her abduction and my part in Bryn's death. I didn't tell her that Susan wanted to hire me. She listened attentively and reached up to touch my face when I was finished. She seemed calmer. We went into one of our silent communings, looking at each other with foolish smiles on our faces.

I broke the mood by getting up to look at the chart clipped to the end of the bed. It didn't make much sense to me but she told me that it meant that the intervals between them interfering with her were getting longer and that she was gaining strength. I nodded and smiled inanely and began to pace up and down in the narrow room. She let me make a few turns then she reached out for a paperback from the bedside table. It hit me on the chest.

"Will you stop that pacing. It's making me as nervous as hell."

"I'm sorry."

"Don't be sorry, be open, be frank. Talk to me about it."

I sat down on the bed again. "It's hard to talk about," I said, "there's loose ends all over the shop, there are hints of connections but I can't quite make them. Maybe I'm losing the touch."

"Don't be silly and don't be pretentious," she said, "and don't look at me as if you'd like to cosh me. You just need more information. For instance, what do you make of Ross and Chalmers?"

"Haines is Mr Anonymous, orphan. Got where he is by application and a ton of ability, night school and so on. Chalmers is as gay as a goose, do you want the details?"

"No, he does a terrific job for me, I don't care if he fucks sheep."

I grinned. "He doesn't. Do you know anyone who drives a red Volkswagen beetle?"

She thought about it. "Don't think so. I know a girl who drives a red Audi."

"No good, lower division."

"No, why?"

"There was one around the day your car was bombed, one followed me after that and Susan says the car that ran her down was a red VW."

She shook her head. I'd put it that way to see if the Pali girl was part of her world, or maybe I was just being nastily suspicious all down the line. There was no value in it anyway. I started to make a cigarette.

"Have you ever been to New Caledonia?" I asked abruptly.

"No, are you going to take me?"

"You'd have to take me, I can hardly afford the Manly ferry."

"New Caledonia is part of it?"

"Could be."

"You're not going to start pacing again?"

"No, I'm going to act, take control, be masterful."

"You can't be masterful with me for a few weeks, nothing to stop you taking control with someone else of course."

"I might just store it up a bit. I think Hemingway advises it somewhere. No, you're right about needing more information. I want to dig for it. I want to set up a session between you and Susan and sift through the circumstances of Mark Gutteridge's death down to the last grain. Will you be in it?"

She pulled a sour face and plucked at the sheet. "If you say so. I detest her, you know."

"That's no way to talk about someone who's in traction no more than fifty yards away."

"Say traction again."

252

"You're a bitch."

"You're so right. OK Cliff, I'll be in it. When?"

"I'll need your doctor's permission and hers, the sooner the better."

"You've got my man's permission as of now."

"I think it'll be much the same with her. Could be Monday then."

Bells starting ringing and we did a little gentle kissing. I promised her that I wouldn't go chasing off to New Caledonia and that I'd be in over the weekend. I joined the exodus of the sound in wind and limb.

For a day that had started in jail it hadn't turned out too badly. I bought a flagon of riesling and a few bottles of soda water on the drive home, put the car away with consummate ease and went cautiously into the house. I was pretty sure I hadn't been followed at any time in the day, but if I was wrong and O'Brien had observed my illegal entering then I was in the shit. It would be like him to pounce just as I got the top off the first bottle. But the house was empty. I took a quick look at the mail—bills and invitations to spend money I didn't have on things I didn't need. I was getting the proportions of ice, wine and soda just right when the phone rang. I jumped a mile and spilled the wine. The sudden movement put a shaft of pain through my kidneys and reminded me what a rough twenty-four hours I'd had. I sloshed a drink together and took a big gulp of it before moving creakily to the phone.

"Is that Cliff Hardy?"

"Yeah. Tickener?"

"Right. Did you see my stuff today?"

I grunted.

"What's wrong, you don't sound too good."

I grunted again and drank some more wine.

"Look, I was wondering if you had any ideas about where Brave might hide out."

"Sorry, no idea. I'm still on the same case though and I'll let you know if I turn up on Brave."

"Fair enough."

"What do you hear about the constabulary?"

"I hear that some very high people are very edgy. A retirement is foreshadowed and two guys have gone on their holidays. No sign of Jackson, he could be a lead to Brave. What do you think?"

"I think it's terrible that such a fine band of men should be subject to such morale-lowering pressures, but don't splash it all over the front page."

Tickener's sigh came whispering across the wire. "I suppose that's the price of fame, I get a private eye to wisecrack with over the phone."

"That's right, are they talking A grade yet?"

"Can't be long."

We agreed to stay in touch and rang off simultaneously. I made another drink and put some eggs on to boil. I wandered up into the room where I kept my books and looked through the four volumes of the

254

Naval Intelligence series on the Pacific Islands. I'd once met one of the professors who'd had a hand in writing them in a bar in Canberra. He was a tall, gaunt-faced character who told a good story and liked a drink. He'd told me about his work in intelligence when I told him what I did for a living and he told me where to get the books second-hand in Sydney. I bought them out of curiosity and I'd never been disappointed. The professor was dead now and I often regretted I'd never seen him again and got him to autograph the books. There was a long section on New Caledonia in volume III.

I mashed up the eggs, sprinkled curry powder on them and made them into a couple of bulging sandwiches. I took the food and another drink to the table and read about the islands while I was eating. New Caledonia had been something of a political football between France and the Australian colonies for a time, but it had come firmly under French military rule about the middle of the nineteenth century and had stayed that way for over fifty years. There'd been a couple of native rebellions but they'd been put down firmly in good French colonial fashion. In the end the French had managed to convince the majority of the islanders that the smart thing to do was to become black Frenchmen. The place had settled down, had a fair tourist trade, some extractive industry and was receptive to development capital. The Palis were chiefs in one of the settled areas close to Noumea. They'd seen the light in religion and politics pretty early and had done quite nicely all through. The information was very much out of date and I browsed around looking for something more current. I turned up a two year old copy of *Pacific Islands Monthly* that mentioned concern among New Caledonians at the behaviour of some Australian mining engineers who'd blundered in on a ceremony they shouldn't have seen. There was also a letter from a New Caledonian about the French nuclear tests in the Pacific.

I tidied up the kitchen and worked through a bit more of the wine and soda. Things didn't become any clearer and an hour of television didn't help, and a re-read of two chapters of Louis Golding's *The Bare Knuckle Breed* only reminded me of Cyn who'd bought it for me and made me wish I had someone to spend the night with. I wandered up to the dartboard, pulled out the darts and went round the board in twenty throws. Like hell I did. I went to bed.

CHAPTER 22

There was nothing useful to be done on Saturday or Sunday. I paid Bryn's cheque into my TAB account and drew out some money, half of which I lost on the horses within the next four hours. I bought some flowers and went in to see Ailsa in the afternoon. We agreed not to talk about the Gutteridge case and tried to get by on books and other subjects but it didn't work very well. I drank too much wine that night and stayed in bed with my head aching until late the next morning. At two o'clock, as I was thinking of getting up, the phone rang and the hospital informed me that Miss Sleeman wasn't feeling well and didn't want any visitors. Great. I got up and went for a long walk through Annandale and down into Balmain. The sky was low and grey and the discarded race tickets blowing along the pavement increased my bad temper. The water at the end of the peninsula looked like a dark, bottle green swamp, barely rising and falling, and the boats riding on it looked like they were stuck in the ooze. I tramped home, took the dead albino's Colt apart and oiled it. It was a little worn but a fine gun despite its owner. Guns are like that. I assumed it was untraceable, the serial number was filed away; a useful gun.

At 9 a.m. on Monday, wearing my best suit, the grey one again, I was in Dr Pincus' office being told that he wasn't in and that I couldn't see him when he did come in. Mrs Steiner was doing the telling and it was a pleasure to watch her at work. She was wearing a brightly printed kaftan and her hair was tied back in a glossy bun. With the slope of that forehead and nose she could have just stepped off a Phoenician oarship. I stood in front of her desk thinking that if Pincus was keeping his hands off her he must have a wonderful marriage.

"You're just saying that," I told her, "because you think you have to, and you do. But I know it isn't true. In the parking lot beside this building there's a space reserved for a car. The space is full of Rolls Royce and the guy who hoses down the lot and watches over the cars tells me it's Dr Pincus' car. He's in and my business is important."

"He has a patient with him."

"He hasn't. There's no talking going on in there," I pointed to the heavy oak door, "and your appointment book shows he kicks off at 10 o'clock. Half an hour is all I need."

Her eyebrows shot up and she bared her beautiful white teeth at me.

"Half an hour!"

"I know that's probably a couple of hundred dollars' worth of his time but I still need it. A quarter of an hour might do."

Like most people connected with the medical profession, she took umbrage at the mention of money.

"It's not that, he's terribly busy today, he's seeing patients all morning and going to the hospital this afternoon."

"Yeah," I said, "so am I."

That seemed to hold her for a minute and I walked past the desk and knocked on the door. She half rose from her chair but I had the door open and was part of the way through before she could do anything about it.

The television hadn't done him justice. He was of medium height and build and his smooth, olive-skinned face was alight with what you'd have to call piercing intelligence. His white coat was a thing of beauty and had certainly cost more than every stitch I had on. He was bald but he looked like he'd never given it a second's worry. He frowned when I came into the room.

"I'm sorry to intrude doctor, I know you're busy but this is important. My name's Hardy, a patient of yours is a client of mine—Miss Gutteridge."

That was stretching the facts but I wouldn't get time for the niceties.

"Ah yes," he said, "the detective. She mentioned you. She seems to trust you. Please sit down."

I sat. He had everything the top Macquarie Street man should have—voice, looks and a fitness and vitality to him that gave you something to aim for.

"I'll come straight to it, doctor," I said. "I want to arrange a meeting between Miss Gutteridge and her father's widow, a Miss Ailsa Sleeman. She is only a few years older than Susan Gutteridge."

"Why?" he said as I drew breath.

"To discuss the circumstances surrounding Mark Gutteridge's death four years ago. Both women have been threatened and assaulted, the reason why lies back at that point I believe. I think such a meeting would be productive and help me to pursue the case more effectively."

"Can you give me some more details, briefly?"

He wasn't fidgeting or looking at his watch. I had his whole attention and had to make the most of it.

"Not many. The police investigation of the death was less than exhaustive. Some facts are unclear, some things went missing, unexplained. There's blackmail involved and intimidation. Susan Gutteridge's insulin was tampered with for example."

He leaned back in his chair without taking his eyes off my face.

"Yes, she told me that. I find it intriguing, I must say."

"You'll authorise the meeting?"

"Susan Gutteridge is an unstable person. I tell you this in professional confidence of course."

I accepted the compliment.

"Her diabetes is in a mess from what she tells me, she needs a lot of rest and treatment. But a diabetic's condition is affected by the emotions to a great extent. Susan Gutteridge is very worried and frightened. Have you considered the possibility that she is guilty of some crime?"

I said I had and expressed the opinion that it might help if it all came out. He stroked his chin and let his eyes stray off to his bookshelf.

"So they say," he murmured, "so they say."

"There's an old enmity between Susan Gutteridge and Ailsa Sleeman, this meeting might resolve it. Ailsa is an intelligent woman and a strong one, she could become a friend to Susan."

"That's probably better psychology," he said. "Very well Mr Hardy, I'll authorise the meeting. Where and when? Susan Gutteridge is in hospital, you realise."

"I do, so is Ailsa, same place."

He raised an eyebrow. "What for?"

I told him and that seemed to clinch it. He said he was going to the hospital early in the afternoon and would leave messages supporting what I wanted to do.

I had no doubt that those messages would be treated like the order of the day. I thanked him and asked if he'd like to be present at the session. He looked ruefully down at his desk calendar.

"I would like to be," he said, "very much, but I simply haven't the time. You must let me know how it works out."

I said I would, we shook hands and I went out. A fat woman in a coat much too warm for the day that was shaping up was sitting in the waiting room. I gave her my hard-boiled look and she squirmed a bit. Mrs Steiner was looking flustered and she pressed the wrong button on the intercom when Pincus buzzed her. She got it right on the second try.

"Mrs Hamersley-Smith is here doctor."

Pincus said something inaudible to me and Mrs Steiner repressed a smile. She raised a finger which boasted a long, blood red fingernail. Mrs Hamersley-Smith waddled past me and reached the door just as Pincus opened it. Beautiful timing. I smiled at Mrs Steiner.

"Can you tell me when Dr Pincus is due at the hospital and how long he'll be there?"

The twenty minutes of the boss's time had done me a power of good in her eyes. She flicked at her desk calendar and ran the crimson nail down a page of the appointments book.

"He's there for an hour and a half," she said, "from two o'clock until 3.30."

I thanked her and left. I carried the image of her dark, bottomless eyes with me all the way back to the street.

I had a few hours to kill which isn't supposed to happen to a private detective busy on a case but sometimes does. I could have killed it by doing some banking and writing cheques for people who could legitimately expect them, or I could have gone to my dentist for a check-up or I could have put the car in for a service. I didn't. I walked across to the Public Library and ordered a batch of newspapers for the year 1972. They came on microfilm in fifteen minutes. I worked through the papers pretty fast looking at the business news mostly and checking the correspondence columns trying to get a feel for the shape of things as they were then.

Mark Gutteridge got a fair bit of coverage as a canny and successful land developer, but there was nothing out of the ordinary about it—no shady deals hinted at, no subsidiary companies collapsing and ruining shareholders. His death got a big spread and there were follow-up stories over the next few days. I read this stuff closely to brief myself for the meeting later in the day. The reporters were starved of facts from the start. The cops were close-mouthed about their investigations and the coverage soon tailed off into human interest material about Gutteridge and his family. There were a couple of good photos of Ailsa, an

263

indifferent one of Bryn and one of Susan that was so poor that it took imagination to relate it to the person I knew. There was no mention of robbery, no details on the gun or the wound, and the coroner's verdict came in as smooth as silk stockings on shaved legs—"Death by his own hand while of unsound mind". I made a few notes, tucked them away in my pocket and told the attendant that I'd finished with the papers.

I left the library looking for somewhere to have lunch. I approached a cafe in a new chrome, concrete and glass building and a name on a directory board jumped out at me. Sleeman Enterprises' office was on the fourth floor and I took the lift up just for the hell of it. The decor was all plastic, glass and middle-of-the-road wall to wall carpet. There were a few pot plants, not so many as to prevent the employees seeing each other, and a general air of work being done. A desk just outside the lift had a sign reading "Inquiries" hanging above it and a dark-haired girl looked up from her typing when she saw me peering keenly about. A good sign that, a receptionist who can type. She asked if she could help in a voice that suggested she was serious about the offer. I took out my wallet and extracted a card a little guy who'd come to my office a month ago had given me. He gave me the card but he knew I was a lost cause.

"My name is Riddout," I said, "Claude Riddout, I'm from Simon's Office Furniture and Decor."

"Yes Mr Riddout?"

"Well, I was just visiting a client on another floor and I thought I'd glance in on a few other establishments just to see if our services might be required."

"I don't think . . ."

I waved both hands in the air. "No, no, I can see that everything is very nice here, very tasteful indeed, I compliment you, it must be very pleasant to work in such surroundings, very pleasant indeed. You wouldn't believe the drabness I see in some places."

I'd succeeded in boring her silly in half a minute which is good going.

"Yes, it's fine, now uhmm . . . is there anything . . .?"

"No, no, if I could just look about a little, take a wander down a corridor or two? I promise I won't intrude on anyone. I'd hate to interrupt the workings of such a smooth running organisation. Just a peep, just a professional peep."

She grabbed the out although she had to cover herself. "Well, I really shouldn't allow you to, but if you make it brief I suppose it'll be all right. The stairs are at the end of that corridor."

She pointed, I ducked my head at her and set off down the passage. There were three offices off to the left along one passage, one on each side of a short connecting corridor and a further three or four on both sides of another passage. Some of the offices had names on the door, some didn't. Some were partitioned to permit a secretary to work away out of sight of her master but within beck and call. Along one wall was a large map of Australia and the Pacific islands. Little pins with red heads were stuck in at various points— all the mainland capital cities as well as places like Geelong and Wollongong, and here and there among the islands—Port Moresby, Suva, Noumea, Pago Pago.

The biggest office had Walter Chalmers' name on the door. The next biggest was occupied by Ross Haines, I opened the door to Haines' secretary's cubicle and said "Oh sorry" to a startled blonde. I did the same to Chalmers' secretary and got an ice cold look from a middle aged woman wearing violently dyed red hair and a Chanel suit. I went back to the lifts past the receptionist who saw me coming, put her head down and kept it there like Anne Boleyn on the block.

I grabbed some fruit from a street stand and made do with that for lunch.

At 3.45 I was at the hospital and as unpopular as a bikini in a nudist camp. I'd been shunted about from reception desk to waiting room and back again, but, given the size of the place, I'd made it fairly fast into the hospital director's office. He had a couple of medical degrees, Harvard business administration ticket, a hyphenated name and he didn't like me. He looked clean-cut like an American lawyer and he spoke in a clipped upper class voice like an English doctor.

"This is all extremely irregular, Mr Hardy. Hospital routines are delicate things, not to be tampered with lightly."

I didn't say anything, the fact that I was there meant that I was going to get what I wanted and if I had to take a little crap from him along the way I would. He ran his hand over his greying crewcut and riffled through some papers on his desk.

"However, the two ladies are not dangerously ill, private patients of course so no one will be disturbed."

What he meant was that the two ladies were rich and rich people who've been well treated in hospital sometimes remember that when they've got their chequebooks out. I nodded.

"Dr Pincus and Sir John concur in the matter," he went on, "so I think it can be arranged."

I don't know how hospital directors are fixed for status and prospects, but this one had elected to keep two medical heavies very firmly on side. That was fine with me. I grinned at him infuriatingly. He levelled up his papers and plonked a solid silver paperweight in the shape of a kidney on top of them. It was my day for making people glad to get me out of their sight. He flipped an intercom switch.

"Are we ready for Mr Hardy?"

He looked relieved at the reply and even more relieved when the door opened and a male nurse presented himself. The boss said, "Nurse Mahony will attend to you, Mr Hardy." I said, "Thank you" and he pretended not to hear me.

The nurse was tall and brawny; anyone who made jokes about him might very soon be attended by him in his professional capacity. I had trouble keeping up with him as he strode down the corridor. I broke into an undignified trot, then checked myself.

"Slow down nurse," I panted, "and tell me where we're going."

"Sorry sir," he slowed imperceptibly, but he called me sir. "We're going to the conference room on the fourth floor. It's a sort of VIP room. We get business executives and politicians in here from time to time. In for check-ups and so on. They sometimes need facilities like telex machines, computers and tape recorders. We've got them here, got a computer terminal and all."

"Great, what about the ones who have to stay in bed?"

"It's a big room, the beds can be wheeled in and arranged with writing tables and so on alongside. The room will hold ten beds. The hospital can provide a stenographer."

"I don't think I'll need that, but it sounds like a good set-up. You sound proud of it."

He gave me a sideways look and grinned. "It's interesting," he said. "One gentleman died in there when he got some bad news on the telex. Very wealthy gentleman he was."

"Serve him right," I said.

"That's what I say. Here we are."

The room was all he'd promised. It looked like a boardroom except for some of the chromium fittings and it smelled antiseptic instead of cigars and good booze. There was a long table with slots in for the beds. When in place the person in bed was within reach of a cassette tape recorder, a set of earphones, a telex keyboard, a fresh writing pad and a row of sharpened pencils. A chair was drawn up to one of the slots, two others were occupied. Ailsa sat propped up by pillows, her arms were bare and her hair was shining like a burnished helmet. She smiled at me as I came into the room in the shadow of Nurse Mahony, it looked as if all was forgiven. Susan was opposite her slumped down in her bed. There was a huge lump under the bedclothes from the waist down which made her look like a victim of Dr Moreau. She looked peeved and anxious.

It wasn't going to be easy.

CHAPTER 23

Susan started on me right away.

"Hello Hardy," she jeered. "What are we having here, a seminar? Professor Hardy is it?"

Her old self was showing as it always would. I knew I could expect to see a deal more of it before we'd done our business. It would abort the whole exercise if it got out of hand, so I had to be careful not to provoke her too early. I nodded to the nurse who gave a you-rather-than-me look and closed the door behind him. I checked my watch, sat down in the chair and tried hard not to be pompous.

"Hello Susan, Ailsa," I said calmly. "It's a bit much isn't it? We could probably go somewhere less formal, but they think they're doing the right thing. It's in deference to your millions I gather."

"Oh, it's all right," Susan snapped, "though God knows what good it'll do. Why aren't you out looking for whoever ran me down?" She jerked her head at Ailsa. "And bombed her."

At least she was acknowledging Ailsa's existence, that was encouraging for something coming of the session.

"I am in a way," I said quietly, "I'll be surprised if we don't work most of it right here."

"How, will we play charades? We're a bit disadvantaged."

I looked across at Ailsa who hadn't spoken.

"Ailsa's employing me. Maybe this is not such a good idea after all. She can call it off if she likes, or you can pull out, Susan."

She came to the hook like a hungry fish, the last thing she wanted in her starved, unhappy soul was to miss this show.

"No, no, you could be right Hardy. I'm sorry, I do have faith in you. I'm in pain, I feel so wretched . . ."

Ailsa had sat there looking interested in Susan's emotional swoops and amused at my role as MC. Now she displayed her tact.

"We're neither of us very well, Cliff," she said, "I tire very easily and I expect it's the same with Susan. Shouldn't we get on with it?"

"I think so," I said. "Susan?"

"Yes, I've been thinking back. I know what I know. The police weren't interested from the beginning."

271

I didn't want her to have it all down pat. It was time to stop being bland and agreeable.

"Yeah, so you told me. I want to cover a bit more ground than that. I've got a few questions for you both that could be uncomfortable, but first I've got to deliver a monologue of sorts. I'm sorry."

Ailsa winced at the pomposity of it, but nothing showed in Susan's face that I could interpret. She looked old and strained, the actual relationship between the two women could have been reversed to judge from their appearance.

"Neither of you has been quite frank with me," I began. "Perhaps you haven't been honest with yourselves. This affair has reached a crisis point, you've both put some trust in me and I know a lot more about you and your affairs than anyone else. But we've got to go a bit further. Bryn knew a lot about you but he's dead. Someone else knows a lot too and he, or she, is the person we have to identify. It could be Ian Brave, I don't think so, but he's a candidate. If we're going to pin this person down you're both going to have to come clean about some things. You know what I mean. It might be painful for you, but you're both under some sort of threat of death, so the pain is relative to that. I want undertakings from you that you'll be honest, to the limits of your knowledge."

"And sanity," said Susan. She was wrecking a fingernail with her teeth.

"Of course." I smiled at her trying to lighten the mood a bit. "I don't want either of you going back to Nanny and the wielded slipper, but short of that, can I have your word that you'll tell it like it is, or was?"

They both nodded, Susan slowly and painfully, Ailsa with a neutral, sceptical smile.

"Right, Ailsa you told me that you thought Mark Gutteridge had been hounded to death, if not exactly murdered."

"Yes, that's right."

"You believed Brave to be behind it. If it wasn't Brave, or if it wasn't *only* Brave, does that give you any other ideas? Is there anything else you remember as relevant? I mean about your husband's conduct, his state of mind, apart from what you knew Brave was doing to him?"

Ailsa massaged her temples and drew her palms down the side of her face.

"God, I wish I had a cigarette," she said, "but I'm giving them up. Yes, there is something. I didn't mention it before because I thought Brave was all that mattered." She looked across at the other woman. "It's going to be hard on her," she said.

"That's inevitable," I said, "let's hear it."

"Let me get the sequence right." She paused for a full minute. Susan kept her eyes on Ailsa's face and not a muscle moved in her own. Flesh seemed to be falling away from her bones, she wanted to hear it and at the same time she wanted to be far away.

273

"About a month before he died," Ailsa began slowly, "Mark found out that Bryn was queer. An anonymous letter gave him all the details, so he said. I never saw the letter. Bryn hadn't given Mark the slightest ground for suspicion, he acted very straight, macho even if you can imagine it. But he told Mark that he'd been queer since he was sixteen. Mark was devastated by it. He became impotent, at least he was with me and I don't think there was anyone else. He was distraught about it, it was total. He'd been pretty active before, not a stud or anything, but enthusiastic. Well, he started reading about impotence and he came across the Don Juan complex thing, latent homosexuality and so on, you know it?"

"Yes."

"Mark became convinced that he was tainted and responsible for Bryn being the way he is, was."

"Is that all? Did he see a doctor?" I knew the answer before I asked the question—he wouldn't, couldn't, not Mark Gutteridge.

"No, he didn't. I'm quite sure he only talked about it to me, and then only because he had to. But that isn't all, there's one thing more. About a week before he died Mark was involved in a fight, he had very badly skinned knuckles and he'd dislocated two fingers. He wasn't marked on the face. I think he must have hurt the other person very badly. Mark was a powerful man."

"You don't know who he fought with?"

"No, he wouldn't tell me. The way he said 'he' and 'him' made me think it was someone he knew, not a stranger. But that was just an impression, I could be wrong."

"You could be right. Is that all?"

"That's all. He couldn't make love for the last month of his life. But I never heard him sounding suicidal about it. If he did kill himself it could have contributed, but I still think Brave put the real pressure on."

"Maybe. No unusual letters found after his death?"

She considered it. "No, the executors took all the business correspondence of course. I looked through the personal letters, photographs and things. It all harked back a long way, before my time mostly. I turned it over to Bryn."

"Why?"

"Oh, you know, father and son and all that. It seemed like the right thing to do."

"Yeah, I suppose so. It all ties in with some of my ideas. Not easy stuff to talk about."

"It's not easy to listen to either." Susan spat her words out as if they had a bad taste. "God, what muck! It's probably true though, we're a degenerate lot."

"What do you mean, Susan?" I said softly.

"You're the detective, you work it out."

She was going to get full mileage from the situation, I was going to have to play her very carefully. She had to have an atmosphere of intrigue and trauma to work in if she wasn't going to hold back.

I made a cigarette and Ailsa asked me for one and I made another and gave it to her. I lit the cigarettes and pulled the heavy crystal ashtray over to within Ailsa's reach. Susan jeered again.

"Love is it? Scarcely young though."

"What would you know about it?" Ailsa said icily.

"You'll see. What are you going to ask me, Hardy? What's your first probing question?"

"I think we'll switch for a minute to the more straightforward stuff. I want to know who was living within the grounds of the Gutteridge house on the night he died. You were both there?"

"Yes, I was there," Susan said. "I'd come up to visit my father, Bryn was there too, I don't remember why. Anyway, we stayed for a meal and then I felt a bit ill. I stayed the night, so did Bryn."

"Why? Was that unusual?"

"No, we did it fairly often. Mark liked us to stay and see him at breakfast before he went to work. Plenty of room in the house of course."

"Bryn got drunk that night," said Ailsa.

I was surprised. "He seemed a pretty careful drinker to me."

"He was," Ailsa replied. She looked at Susan for confirmation and got a slight nod. "So was Mark, but they both went at it a bit that night. After dinner they got on the whisky. I don't drink so I went to bed."

"To read?" I asked.

"Yes."

"What, what did you read?"

She played with the ties on her nightgown. The cigarette had gone out, she hadn't enjoyed it so maybe she was on the way to beating them.

"I can't remember," she said.

"Good," I said. "Now, I want you to write down on the pads the names of all the people you recollect as being on the spot that night. Include yourselves."

"Oh Hardy," Susan said, "this is so corny."

"Just do it please, you'll be surprised."

"What are you paying him to set up this nonsense, Ailsa?" Susan asked. Ailsa smiled, stubbed out the half-smoked dead butt and took up her pencil. The two of them switched on their recall apparatus. I pulled my pad towards me and started doodling and writing words that had nothing to do with the matter in hand. I looked up at them a couple of times over the next couple of minutes. Susan looked relaxed, as if the writing exercise was therapeutic for her. Ailsa sucked on the pencil, substituting it for a cigarette. She probably hadn't written anything without smoking in the last twenty years. I wrote down my version of those present—I had only four names and one unnamed servant. I was going on the newspaper reports. The two women looked up more or less simultaneously.

"OK," I said, "let's have a look."

I got up and collected the leaves torn off their pads. Ailsa's sheet read: Ailsa G., Mark G., Susan G., Bryn G., Mrs Berry, Verna, Henry, Willis. Susan's read: Gutteridge—Mark, Bryn, Susan, Ailsa. Cook (Mrs Berry), maid (Verna), driver (Willis), gardener (Henry), assistant.

"Good," I said, "pretty close, one discrepancy. Susan says the assistant gardener was there, Ailsa doesn't list him. Was he or wasn't he, and what was his name?"

"He was around all right," Susan said, "I remember because he was sick, he lived in quarters behind the garage. The light was on there and Bryn mentioned it to Mark. He said the young gardener was sick."

"What else do you know about him?"

"He wasn't interviewed by the police in the house. I suppose they saw him in his room."

Ailsa nodded. "That would be why I didn't list him," she said. "I was going on the order of the police interviews."

"What was his name, Ailsa?" I asked.

"I don't know. Do you, Susan?"

The thing was drawing them together a bit which was good.

278

"No, he was fairly new, I don't think I ever heard his name."

"What did he look like? He was young?"

Susan thought about it. It was obviously difficult for her to think about servants other than in the abstract.

"He was young I think," she said, "hard to tell, he had a beard."

"That makes sense," said Ailsa. "All men with beards look the same to me, the driver had a beard."

"But Willis had a small beard, a gingery one, pepper and salt sort of. The gardener's beard was fuller and darker, like, like . . ." she giggled, "like Fidel Castro."

Finding Castro funny was just her style, it explained a lot about how the rich are able to carry on merrily being rich. But she'd hit the right note and things came together in my brain and clinched and paid off like a perfectly executed piece of football play. It must have showed in my face because they both straightened themselves up in their beds and took on expectant looks. Ailsa said it.

"He's important, isn't he Cliff, the gardener? And you know who he is. Come on, tell us."

I took a deep breath and pushed the things I'd been fiddling with away. It's a strange feeling when you've worked it out or got close enough, you become reluctant to surrender it. I went to a lecture once given by a guy who was an expert on the Tasmanian Aborigines;

his expertise was mostly a matter of word of mouth, he hadn't published very much. He said practically nothing in the lecture, he couldn't bear to yield it up. It's like that.

"I told you it'd get harder," I said. I looked at the woman with her lank hair, the bright eyes and the vast hump where her legs should be, "Where were you in May 1953, Susan?" I said.

CHAPTER 24

She took it pretty well, she didn't turn green or any other colour and she didn't scream. Her hands gripped the bed cover a bit harder, but the main expression on her face was that of relief. She'd lived with it a long time until it had become a part of her, but never a comfortable part, never something that augmented her. It was more like a demon to be exorcised except that the exorcism might be too painful, and the hole left by its departure might be too great to bear. There was probably an associated fear, a fear that didn't matter and had never really mattered to anyone but her. A fear that her innermost personal experience didn't matter a damn to the rest of the world. At least now, at whatever the cost, it looked as if it did matter somehow and she felt relief.

She looked at me and spoke through a smile so thin you could slip it through a bank vault door.

"You know where I was, don't you?"

"Yes, I think so."

"Then you tell it. I'd like to hear someone else talk about it. No one has ever referred to it but me for over twenty years and I talk to myself about it every day."

"You're sure you want me to say it? I might get something important wrong."

"That won't matter, go on."

"You were in Adelaide. You gave birth to a child, a boy. He was healthy. You were fifteen or sixteen. The baby went to an orphanage."

"No, he was adopted!"

"Maybe it didn't take, I don't know. He grew up in an orphanage though."

She was crying softly now and speaking through the sobs. "What could I do? What could I do? I couldn't keep him. They sent me away and arranged it all. I kept his birthday every year."

"What do you mean?" I said quickly, then something like an understanding hit me, "No, you don't have to explain, Susan."

"I want to, it's not much to tell. Every year I buy a birthday card and write something on it and seal it in a plain envelope. I post it, just like that."

"Oh Susan." Ailsa stretched out her arms to her, ten feet away across the table.

I got up and went round to her. Her shoulders were heaving and tears were streaming down her face.

I tried to touch her hands and put an arm around her but she rejected me with savage, jerky movements of her arms and head. Her mouth was working convulsively and she had her eyes shut tight as if she wanted to blind herself.

"She's had enough Cliff," Ailsa said softly. "Ring for the doctor."

I picked up one of the telephones in the room and got an immediate line to an action point of some kind. I spoke quickly describing Susan's condition, and a doctor and two nurses were in the room within seconds of my replacing the phone. Susan had calmed a little but this was no less disturbing; she stared straight in front of her and her lips moved silently. The doctor gave me a hard disapproving look and slid a needle into her arm. Almost immediately the stiffness went out of her and she relaxed back onto the pillows. Her eyes fluttered and closed. The nurses released the brakes on the bed and wheeled it out of the room. The doctor looked at Ailsa inquiringly but she shook her head.

"I'm all right doctor, I want to talk to Mr Hardy a little longer. I'll have him call when I want to go back to my room."

She said it firmly and that, along with the reminder that she was in a room of her own, was enough to send him off about his business.

I rolled two cigarettes, gave one to Ailsa and lit them. After a few puffs she butted it out.

"I'm going to stop smoking, really! Stop tempting me!"

"You never know how strong you are till you know how weak you are."

"Bullshit!"

"Yes, yes it is."

I sat down on the bed and ran my fingertips down her arm.

"I'm getting better," she said, "I won't break."

I leaned down and kissed her. After a minute she pushed me back. She smoothed down her cap of hair and gave me a look that reminded me that she was paying my hire.

"Well, you certainly broke her up," she said.

"I didn't mean to, but it was bound to happen."

"I suppose so, I've never had any children, you?"

"No."

"They make you vulnerable."

"You're vulnerable anyway."

"Oh, profound."

"That's me."

I meant it though and I was considering how to face her with her own little piece of vulnerability right then. I couldn't think of any subtle way and it probably wasn't necessary.

"Do you want to know who Susan's son is?"

"Yes of course, you've been detecting?"

"Just a little. He's the man you know as Ross

Haines." I went on to give her the whole thing in a piece. "I found some records that tie it up. Birth extract, picture of the orphanage. There's a picture of him taken a few years back wearing a dark beard. My guess is that those scars he's got are the result of the beating Mark Gutteridge gave him. They've changed his appearance enough to let him dispense with the beard."

"But why would Mark beat up Ross?"

"I don't know. My guess is that Ross confronted Mark in some way. I'm really guessing now, but I think he found out about Bryn and wrote the letter to Mark. Maybe he tried to blackmail Mark, I don't know."

"He must have hated him."

"He hates all of you."

She took this in painfully, some strain and tiredness was showing in her face and she had to think back over her relationship with a person she never really knew. It's a hard thing to do. I'd done it myself about Cyn a few times and it never failed to leave me feeling wretched and stupid. It's a consolation that you have to be very unlucky to make more than one of these complete misjudgments in your life, but Ailsa had the added problem that the person she now had to totally reconstruct was trying to destroy her.

"Just explain it to me as you see it now, Cliff." She lay back on her pillows and twined the drawstring of her bedgown in her fingers.

I picked up a pad and a pencil and drew a few squares, put names in them, scribbled a few dates and connected the bits and pieces up with arrows and dotted lines. I'm not much of an abstract thinker. I crossed pieces of the diagram out as I spoke.

"Ross Haines grew up in an orphanage. Maybe he was adopted out at first and that's how he got the surname, but something went wrong with the adoption, must have because I think he was in the orphanage for most of his young life. The adoptive parents could have been killed I suppose, I don't know. Maybe he was only fostered out. Anyway, he was bright and he had a lousy time. Orphans don't get any of the system's breaks. He did better than most by becoming a landscape gardener. He was pretty good at it. My guess is that he had no sort of a life at all as an adolescent. To judge from his possessions he had nothing from the time he wanted to remember with affection. OK, he's working away in Adelaide as a landscape gardener, working for rich people and that's important. He's wondering who the hell he is and what he's doing not being dead when somehow he finds out that he is a Gutteridge. I don't know how he does it, gets hold of his actual birth record somehow? Don't know. He has an old, faded photograph of her, you could say there's a resemblance. From that point on his course is straightforward, if insane. He comes to Sydney, gets a job as Mark's gardener, snoops out Bryn, puts the needle into Mark and goes on belting away at every Gutteridge he can find. The files are a bonus. He uses them to squeeze people for things, testimonials, money, God knows what else. He's bent on destroying the family that disowned him and he's doing pretty well. He might have had a hand in Mark's death, Bryn's gone as a result of events he set in train, you and Susan have both come pretty close. It all hangs together, but there are a few things that puzzle me."

"A lot of things puzzle me," Ailsa said. "He could have killed me twenty times, why didn't he?"

"I think the strategy is to do some other sort of damage first. He probably wanted to send you bankrupt."

"I see. What things puzzle you?"

"Quite a few. It's hard to believe that he isn't interested in the Gutteridge money, he's not that mad. But how could he get it after knocking off all the Gutteridges? He might be able to establish a legal claim if he can prove he's Susan's son. But suspicion would fall straight on him. It wouldn't work. Another thing, why didn't he just tell Mark that he was his grandson. He's a well set up lad, not a queer or anything and Bryn was out of favour. He could have done himself some good you'd think. Instead of that he goes sneaking about poisoning minds. Doesn't make sense."

Ailsa shrugged. "Something else," I said.

"What?"

"There's not a scrap of proof. It would take a serious, detailed investigation to establish Haines' movements and actions and there's no way of setting

287

one up. The police wouldn't look at it, and more than that, he's got the files and I think they could get him some high level police protection if he ever needs it. He's pretty safe."

"I'll fire him," she said.

"Let's mull that over for a while first. It might not be a good idea."

"What *would* be a good idea?"

"We need to know more about him, to get something on him if possible, maybe force him to make some mistakes or get within reach of the law in some way. At present all we have on our side is that he doesn't know we're on to him, that plus you and Susan being safe in here for a while."

Ailsa's concentration was fading. She was interested and involved but tired and drained emotionally. She was still on drugs, there was an artificial quality to her composure and it was starting to crack. She gathered up some strength to see it through for now, but it was obviously an effort.

"What do you want to do now, Cliff?"

"I want to meet this guy again to size him up. Also I think I should go over to Adelaide to check out his background as much as possible, try to get a line on him that will help to explain things. I especially want to know why he's used the search and destroy method lately instead of infiltration and sedition."

"He's done that?"

288

"Yes, the methods of attack have changed, some-one else could be involved of course, in a secondary way maybe."

"You sound like a military man."

"I was."

"You didn't tell me."

"That's true of a lot of things. You don't like military men?"

"Not especially, but I like you. And do you realise you haven't had a drink for two hours?"

"Yeah, I'll have to do something about that soon, my brain has almost seized. I need something from you love."

"What?"

"A note from you introducing me to Haines and instructing him to introduce me to whoever handles your executives' expense accounts, travel warrants and such. There is such a person?"

"Yes, it's a delicate job actually, taxes involved."

"Don't tell me. I think this could throw a scare into Haines as well as being useful for itself."

"It's all right with me, I hope he shits himself."

I gave her a pen and some instructions and she set to work on a pad that carried the hospital's letter-head. The result was a signed note that authoritatively introduced me to Haines, without any reference to our earlier meeting of course, and directed him to arrange an air ticket to any part of Australia and the Pacific and expenses of up to one hundred dollars a day.

"This will make Ross furious," Ailsa said.

"That's too bad, I'm weeping."

I took the note, folded it up and put it away in my breast pocket. The only advantage I've ever found to wearing suits is the number of pockets you get with them, but it still doesn't swing me in their favour. I sat with Ailsa for a while and we said the things you say early on in an affair when the words are new and the feelings are mint fresh and shining bright. She told me to be careful. I said I would be. I called for the nurses and they wheeled her back to her room. I gathered up the bits of paper in the conference room and stuffed them into my pocket. I was desert dry and wrung out from the afternoon's work.

CHAPTER 25

I was at the reception desk of Sleeman Enterprises at 9.30 the next morning. The same girl was behind the desk but at first she didn't associate my denims and shirt sleeves with Mr Riddout. When it dawned on her, her face took on a sickly look and she started to cast about her for help.

"Yes Mr Riddout?" she stumbled over the words. She'd giggled about Mr Riddout to her friends and now she was embarrassed to see him again in the flesh.

"Hardy's the name Miss, I want to see Mr Haines."

"But I'm sure you're the man I saw yesterday. You looked around . . . interior decorator."

I made a non-committal gesture and handed her Ailsa's note. She read it quickly despite her agitation and got up from her chair.

"I'll tell his secretary," she said.

I reached over, took the note and eased her back into her chair by the shoulder.

"Calm down," I said. "I'll tell her. I just let you see that so you'd let me go through. That's OK?"

"Oh yes, yes, the door you want is . . ."

"I know where it is."

I gave her a small salute and a grin and went down the passage. I knocked on the door and went in before the blonde answered. She didn't like it and got ready to high hat me. Her hair dominated her, it was fine and yellow and swept up into a beehive arrangement that defied belief. Her voice rasped slightly and I suspected that the hair would be harsh to touch from silicone spray.

"Can I help you? Sir."

The last word just got into the sentence and hung there looking as if it might lose its place. I took out the note, unfolded it and put it on the desk. I put my licence card down on top of it and gave her my strong, silent look. Her reaction to the name Sleeman nearly cracked the mask of make-up on her face and had the same effect as on the other girl. It brought her to her feet, sharp.

"I'll tell Mr Haines, he's in, you can see him . . ." She was practically stammering. God knows what would happen if Ailsa herself walked in. They'd probably start fainting and this one would spill her nail polish all over the copy.

"That's nice," I said, "I'm glad he's in, but couldn't you just buzz him?"

She looked down at the intercom as if she'd never seen one before and didn't know whether to talk into it or put a coin in it. She sucked in a breath and flipped the switch.

"Mr Haines, a gentleman to see you. It appears to be important, he has a letter from Miss Sleeman."

"Five minutes." Haines' voice had a nice timbre and pitch even over the furry intercom.

I collected my papers and walked across to the connecting door. The blonde jumped up and moved towards me with beckoning hands.

"You can't go in," she said breathlessly. "He said five minutes."

"I'm not afraid," I said and opened the door.

Haines got up looking surprised and I looked him over carefully. He wasn't as big as he'd seemed the first time I'd seen him, but he was taller than me and he was noticeably heavier. It was all wrapped up in an expensive linen shirt with epaulettes and the latest thing in gabardine slacks—a high-waisted production with narrow belt loops and deep cuffs. He had thick dark curly hair and even this early in the morning his beard was making his chin blue and shadowy. He looked a bit loud, a bit florid. My mind jumped about trying to register a firm impression of him before giving it up. He bore a close resemblance to a picture I'd seen in the

293

papers of Mark Gutteridge, twenty years back, accepting a racing cup after one of his horses had carried off a major event. Others might have missed the similarity but Mark Gutteridge, who was probably a two shaves a day man like this one, could not have.

It seemed to be everybody's day for getting up abruptly from their chairs. Haines was nearly clear of his when he checked himself and moved back to its padded leather comfort. He was sharp, he'd recognised me immediately I'd stuck my face in and he didn't like it a bit.

"Don't get up," I said, "this won't take long. Your boss has a little chore for you."

I handed him the note, he read while trying to work a big chunk of flesh out of his lower lip. When he finished he put the paper down on the blotter and slid one of its edges under the leather envelope corner that held the blotter in place. I went up to the desk and repossessed the note. He didn't object and I was beginning to wonder if you had to spit in his face to make him act as aggressive as he looked. He made himself comfortable in his chair without looking at me: I thought he might feel he had an edge sitting down so I perched on the end of the desk. That still left quite a space between us. He reached out for a cigarette from the open box in front of him. He flicked one out and lit it with a gold desk lighter.

"What's the nature of your business with Miss Sleeman?"

I was listening for a South Australian accent. I didn't pick any up but maybe there's no such thing.

"Sorry," I said, "didn't catch it."

"What is your business with Miss Sleeman?"

I paused while he blew smoke around and tried to think of something to do with his left hand.

"I don't think you're too bad," I said. "Just much too young for what you're doing and a bit out of your depth. You'll get the hang of it."

"I don't know what you're talking about. I asked you a question."

"It doesn't deserve an answer. The business is private, confidential, that's all you have to know. Now do as you're told."

He opened his mouth to speak but I cut him off. "And don't say 'You can't talk to me like that' because I just did."

"I wasn't going to say that."

"What *were* you going to say?"

"Never mind." His voice was firmer and he seemed to think he was making up some ground. "I can see that you're trying to push me around as much as you can short of hitting me again. I wonder why?"

He *was* making up ground. He let go a smile that crinkled up the fine white scars around his eyes and mouth in a way that was probably very attractive to women.

"How is Ailsa?" he said suddenly. He'd dropped the hurt look and the probing look, now he was mild and charming. He was a chameleon.

"She's OK," I said gruffly. It seemed inadequate.

"Bloody awful business," he said, "I got the gist of it from Sir John Guilford, and I read about Bryn. Dreadful. A chapter of accidents."

"Maybe," I said. "I don't want to sit here exchanging chummy gossip with you, Haines. I don't like you, you don't like me. But since we're at it, did you hear about Susan Gutteridge? She's in hospital too."

He looked and sounded surprised. We were talking about his mother although he didn't know that I knew it. Nothing like filial concern showed in his face but there was no way it would—his feelings about his own flesh and blood were unique to him.

"God, no. What's the matter with her?"

"Hit and run."

"How bad?"

"Broken legs, she'll live."

He shook his head. It was a bad moment for me because, despite myself, I believed what I saw—a man who apparently didn't know a thing about events he was supposed to have engineered. It was time to get on with it before I found myself giving away too much for this stage of the game. I got off the desk and made impatient movements with my feet. He looked at me curiously for a second and then flicked the intercom button. He told the secretary he'd be with Mr Kent for a few minutes and we went out of the office.

Mr Kent looked like just the sort of man for tax dodges, he faded into the background without a trace. He had wispy hair, a grey suit and a general air of not being there at all. Like everyone in the place he was smart and efficient. He read Ailsa's note, reached into his desk for a manila folder and wrote my name on the top of it. He went to pin the note inside the folder but I stopped him and told him I wanted to keep it. He smiled knowingly. "Very wise," he said. He pressed a button and a girl appeared in the open doorway about two seconds later. "Photocopy please," Kent said extending the note to her, "and arrange credit cards for Mr Hardy. The usual things." The secretary nodded a sleekly groomed head and whispered away. Kent busied himself with a ruled form on which he wrote my name and made some entries in a tight, cribbed hand. There was no love lost between him and Haines who straightened his cuffs and looked more or less in my direction.

"Satisfied Hardy?" he said.

"Very. Thank you Mr Haines. Don't fall in any swimming pools."

Kent looked up bemused but Haines' face was a bored, non-reacting mask. He inclined his head to Kent and went out, leaving the door open. Kent got up and shut it. I couldn't think of anything to say to him and he seemed to feel the same way about me. We lingered in silence until the girl came back with the papers. She handed them to Kent who dismissed her with the economical nod that seemed to be his speciality before slipping the photostat into the file. He handed the original back to me.

"A credit card valid for the standard airlines for six months will be ready for you at the desk, Mr Hardy," he said. "And now, a Cashcard?"

"What's that?"

He unleashed what appeared to be the whole of his personality in the form of a tight, self-satisfied smile. "It's at the desk, you can use it to draw a hundred dollars a day for the next calendar month."

"Wonderful," I said, "what about taxis, call girls and squaring cops?"

"Your problem, Mr Hardy. To me you are a miscellaneous expense."

He scribbled the day's date on the outside of the folder and pulled a bulging, loose leaf file towards him like a long lost lover. I was dismissed, I know a perfectionist when I see one.

The girl at the front desk was having a bad day. She held out two cards, one of them similar to a bankcard, the other plainer with a gold edge.

"Please sign these, Mr Hardy."

I signed them. She slipped them into plastic holders and handed them to me.

"Don't worry," I said, "capitalism is doomed."

She gave me a brilliant smile. She'd solved it, I was a madman.

I went home, packed a few things into an overnight bag and phone booked an afternoon flight to Adelaide. The credit card worked like a charm at the first bank I came to. I caught a taxi out to the airport and called the hospital half an hour before my plane was due for boarding. I left messages for Ailsa and Susan telling them not to see anyone except their doctors. After buying the Sydney afternoon and the Adelaide morning papers I went through the ticket collection and seat allocation routines and got on the plane. It was half empty which felt strange until I remembered that it was nearly always that way in first class, I just hadn't had much experience of it.

The plane boomed along for two hours damaging the ozone. I had a couple of gins and tonic because I like the miniature bottles.

Adelaide doesn't rate too highly with me. It's flat and there's no water to speak of. The celebrated hills are too close to the city. It feels as if you could kick a football from the city stadium up into the hills without really trying. When I go there it's always raining and I'm never dressed for it. The plane slewed about a bit on the wet runway and we all scampered for cover in our lightweight ensembles. The rain was more a spit than a shower, but the only happy-looking people at the terminal were those who were flying the hell out of the place.

I went to the Avis desk and hired a Ford Escort for two days after proving beyond all doubt that I was Clifford Hardy, licensed to drive, and handing over enough money to make it not worth my while to steal it. My luggage came down the chute, I slung it into the back of the car and drove in to what they call the city. I tried to cheer myself with the thought that the Athens of the South is a great place for cheap food and drink, but I only half-succeeded. The buildings were dribbling water down their grey faces and those damn hills were still much too close. I checked in at the Colonial Hotel across the road from the University and ordered a bottle of Scotch with ice and a soda syphon. I settled down with a tall glass, a map and the telephone directory. The orphanage was listed and I called it. I might as well have saved my breath and money. The woman I spoke to wouldn't confirm that Haines had been an inmate, wouldn't give out information about past directors of the place and wouldn't arrange an interview for me with the present boss. She wasn't interested in sarcasm either, she hung up as I was thanking her. But that was all right. The first dead end in an investigation is a challenge to me, it's only after one or two more that I feel hurt and start sulking.

They couldn't conceal the address of the place from me. I located it on the map, poured out and drank

300

a quick neat one, and tucked the ice and soda away in the miniature fridge. I got the car out of the hotel parking lot and drove off towards the hills. The rain had stopped.

It took me nearly an hour to reach the orphanage which put the time at close to five o'clock. The photographs I'd seen of the place hadn't done it justice. It was straight out of Dickens or maybe even Mervyn Peake; every angle and corner suggested order and discipline. It had no charm; I like old buildings, but I wouldn't have minded if they pulled this one down. It looked in pretty good shape however, and the grounds were well cared for which suggested a groundsman. Groundsmen and caretakers tend to be long-term employees and I was counting on that now. I parked back up the road from the main gates and set off on a circumnavigation of the grounds which covered about ten acres. The main building stood on a rise more or less in the middle of the land which was enclosed by a high fence of cast iron spears. A paved drive ran from the main gates up to the front of the building and down to a smaller set of gates on the other side. There was a football oval and a fair bit of lawn and garden but too much asphalt and government issue cream paint.

I scouted around the fence until I found what I was looking for—a small cottage in the northeast corner of the grounds. It would have been a city trendy's dream, sandstock bricks, double fronted and without obvious signs of later improvements. A man was standing in front of the cottage doing nothing in particular. At that distance he looked old, bent over a bit, and there was a pipe smoking gently in his face. He had his hands and a good part of his arms deep in the pockets of a pair of old khaki overalls. I stuck my head up over the spears.

"Gidday," I shouted.

He stood like stone. I shouted again with the same result. He might have been deep in reverie, but it seemed more likely that he was hard of hearing. I looked around for something to throw and found a piece of rotten branch. I heaved it over the fence and it landed a bit off to one side of him. He took the pipe out of his mouth and looked at it. Then he put the pipe back and looked at it again. I reached down for another piece of wood to throw when he made a slow turn in my direction. I stood there with the wood in my hand feeling foolish. I gave him another hail and he ambled over to the fence, scuffling his feet in the damp leaves. He made it to the fence in pretty good time given that he wasn't in a hurry.

"Didn't mean to startle you," I said.

"You didn't startle me, mate." His voice was the old Australian voice, slow and a bit harsh from rough tobacco and a lifelong habit of barely opening his mouth when he spoke. I handed him one of my cards through the fence and brought a five dollar note out into the light of day.

"I'd like to ask you a few questions if you've got the time. There's a quid in it."

He stuck the pipe back in his mouth. The hair was classical, a brutal short back and sides and his ragged moustache, yellow from tobacco had nothing in common with the modish Zapata model. He was one of the old style of tie-less Australians, one without a collar to his shirt so how could he wear a tie? He inclined one ear towards me, but his faded blue eyes were sceptical.

"How long have you worked here, Mr . . .?" I bellowed.

He shuffled back. "Don't have to shout mate," he said, "I can hear orright. My name's Jenkins, Albie Jenkins and I been here since the war."

He didn't mean Korea.

"Since 1945?"

"Forty-six. I got demobbed at the end of forty-five and this's the first job I took, been here ever since. I went through all of it, unnerstand? Middle East, New Guinea and that."

"I see, like this job do you?"

He appeared to be thinking about it for the first time. He took the pipe out, looked at it and put it back again.

"Dunno," he said slowly. "S'orright, crook pay but a place to live, they leave ya alone. You weren't old enough to be in it, were you?"

"No, I was in Malaya though."

"Where?"

"Malaya."

"Oh yeah, against the Japs?"

"No, later, against the communists."

He shook his head. "Never heard of it." He wasn't interested, the only real wars had been those with the Germans and the Japanese. I asked him if he remembered a dark boy who would have been at the institution in the 1960s, but he didn't have a clue. He explained that he didn't have much to do with the kids. He said that they'd be able to help me up at the office and when I told him they wouldn't he shrugged as if that settled it. I handed him the five dollar note to unsettle it.

"Who's in charge here now?"

"Bloke named Horsfield, soft bugger if you ask me."

"He's new is he? Wasn't here when you came?"

He sparked up and drew hard on the pipe, the smoke surged up into the trees that grew along the fence. Then the pipe died abruptly. He took a pull, found it dead and knocked the ashes out against the fence. He waved it about for a minute to cool it, re-packed it from a leather pouch and got it going again. I waited while he did it.

"No," he chuckled through the spittle, "when I came it was the Brig, tough joker, ex-army, kept everyone in line and they bloody loved him."

"When did Horsfield take over?"

"Five, six years ago."

The big question. "Is the Brig still alive?"

"Yeah, course he is. He'll bloody live for ever, he was out here for something or other last week. Had a yarn with him, 'bout the war."

"What's his full name?"

He scratched his chin. "Jesus, I'm not sure, just think of him as the Brig. Easy find out though." He jerked his thumb back at the cottage. I pulled out another five and it went through the fence. He tucked it along with the other one into the bib pocket of his overall and shuffled off to the cottage. I stood at the fence gripping the iron until it occurred to me that I must look like one of our primate cousins who didn't quite make it to civilisation, suicide and the bomb. I let go the fence and dusted off my hands and tried to think of something else to do with them. As usual, a cigarette seemed the only answer and I rolled one and had it going by the time Albie came back. He looked down at the sheet of paper he was holding and read off it very carefully: "Brigadier Sir Leonard St James Cavendish."

I couldn't see much problem about finding that in the phone book. I reached through the fence to shake his hand, he obliged but he was very out of practice.

"Thanks, Mr Jenkins, you've been a great help."

"Orright, so've you. I'll be able to have a decent drink for change."

He shambled off through the leaves. I finished my cigarette and ground the butt out into the concrete in which the iron spears were embedded.

I stopped at the first phone booth I saw and called the Brig. He lived in Blackwood, not far away, but you don't just drop in on Brigs. A gentle female voice answered and confirmed that I had the right residence. I gave my name as Dr Hardy from the Australian National University and told her I wanted to consult the old soldier on a point of military history. She said she'd ask her husband and I stood with the silent phone in my hand for about five minutes feeling guilty and exposed. She came back and told me that Sir Leonard would be delighted to see me and would ten o'clock the following morning suit. I said it would, got my tongue around "Lady Cavendish", hoping that was right, and thanked her. I drove back to the hotel. The rain had started again. I had a Scotch and wasted the time watching the news on television and watching the rain pissing down on the churches.

I had a shower and went out at 7.30 to look for the laminex cafe where I'd eaten a brilliant steak on my last visit to Adelaide three years ago. I could still taste the steak and the carafe of house red had been like Mouton Rothschild compared with the swill we buy in the east. I found it at the end of one of Adelaide's narrow, quiet, wet main streets. I ordered the same food and drink and experienced that feeling when eating alone—that everyone is looking at you with pity whereas in fact no one gives a damn. I combated the feeling by reading Forsyth's *The Dogs of War* which I'd bought at a news-stand opposite the hotel, and I learned all there is to know about equipping a mercenary force while I worked through the meal. It was better than spreads I'd paid three times as much for in Sydney, but when I got outside the cafe that cool drizzle reminded me that I was a long way from home. I walked fast back to the Colonial and worked on the Forsyth a little more. I went to sleep and had a long, involved dream about Uncle Ted and his two-up games at Tobruk.

CHAPTER 26

I skipped breakfast in the hotel's lounge-dining room in favour of a quick research job in the Barr Smith library at the University of Adelaide. Cavendish got a mention in Lean's *Official History of Australia in World War II*. He'd been in on Wavell's North African offensive in 1941, with the Ninth Division at El Alamein and he was there at the capture of Wewak in May 1945. There was one obvious question—why didn't he go on to Borneo? But there was plenty to ask him about the New Guinea campaign and his assessment of MacArthur whose reputation is a bit on the decline at present I gather. The morning drizzle had cleared when I left the library and the traffic was moving quickly along the roads which were drying out by the minute. It took me three quarters of an hour to get to Blackwood.

He either had a private income, or Brigadiers' pensions can't be too bad, or he'd done all right out of flogging off army jeeps for scrap metal, because Sir Leonard St James Cavendish wasn't feeling the pinch. He lived in one of the better houses in a neighbourhood which comprised mostly hundred foot frontages and tennis courts in the back yard. Adelaide doesn't have the same amount of old, gilt-edged money as Melbourne or the new, flashy stuff of Sydney, but there are plenty of people in the city of churches who've put it together at some time and are watching it grow. Cavendish's house stood on a corner block with frontages on three streets so the high, white painted brick wall was enclosing a tidy parcel of prime residential land. The house was a mock Tudor job with lots of stained wood strips, sitting well back from the road in a leafy setting. The whole effect made me wonder why the Brig had taken on the directorship of an orphanage—a multinational oil exploration corporation seemed more the style.

I parked the car on the street outside the house. That still left room for two buses to drive side by side down the middle of the road and not scrape the Jaguars cruising along on either side of them. A high iron gate was hinged to brick pillars with plaster crests on them. Bands and blobs of colour were bright against the faded white background and there was a Latin inscription under the crest. I saluted it all with the manila folder full of blank paper I was carrying. A stroll from the house down to collect the milk and papers at the gate would set you up nicely for breakfast. The house had a long, low verandah in front of it with some sort of thatch on top. I pushed the bell beside the heavy oak door and it opened almost immediately. A small wisp of a woman held the door open. She couldn't have been more than five feet tall and she seemed to be having some trouble keeping control of the door in the draught. Her hair was white and her face was wrinkled and beautiful like an old parchment. Her voice was the one I'd heard on the phone.

"Dr Hardy?"

"Yes."

"Please come in, my husband is on the back terrace reading the newspaper. He's looking forward to your visit. Would you like some tea?"

I thought it might be in character to accept even though I detest the stuff. She showed me down a long passage hung about with paintings which looked pretty good and some interesting Melanesian weapons. We went through a big sun porch lined with books and she opened a wire door out to a flagstoned terrace. A man was sitting on a garden chair positioned so he could get some sun through the tips of the trees. He had the *Advertiser* spread out on the table in front of him and he folded it up and got to his feet as I approached.

"Good morning, Sir Leonard, it's good of you to see me."

310

We shook hands.

"How do you do, Mr Hardy. Please sit down."

He pointed to a chair on the other side of the table and I took it. He was a bit blimpish, clipped moustache and plenty of colour in his face. His voice was quiet and soothing to judge from the few words he'd spoken, not the snarl a lot of army officers acquire or affect. He had on a white shirt, open at the neck, grey trousers and an old corduroy jacket. He wore slippers but had none of the appurtenances of old age—hearing aid, glasses, walking stick; he looked about sixty although he was actually seventy-one.

"Well sir," he said, "so you're a military historian?"

"No, I'm a private investigator."

"I see."

"You don't sound surprised."

He smiled. "I'm not, except at your coming clean so quickly."

"I had an idea I couldn't fool you."

He smiled again and nodded. "I'm flattered, you were quite right, you didn't fool me. There is no Dr Hardy in History at the ANU. My son's a Fellow there you see, and I have the current calendar in there among my books."

He pointed to the sun room. As he did his wife came out carrying a tray with tea things on it. She put it down on the table, poured milk into three heavy enamel jugs and swilled the stuff about in the pot.

311

"I'm sorry Dr Hardy, I should have asked, do you take milk?"

I nodded and forced a smile while fighting down nausea.

"And sugar?"

I shook my head.

"You've lost your tongue," she said, "I hope you two haven't fallen out."

The Brig reached across for his tea and cupped his hands around the mug. 'No, no. Thank you my dear. No, we haven't fallen out. Mr Hardy isn't a military historian as I told you. It turns out he's a private investigator. Now he's going to drink his tea and tell me all about it."

"How interesting. Drink your tea, Mr Hardy." She pulled a pencil from her apron pocket and reached for the paper. "I think I'll do the crossword while you sort it out. Don't mind me."

She'd known me for a fake before she'd opened the door and she'd played it as cool as Greta Garbo. I sipped the tea. It all tastes the same to me whether you make it in muslin tea bags or boil it up in a five gallon drum. I swallowed a minute amount and kept my hands around the mug as if I might possibly go back for more.

"I'm sorry about the deception," I began. "It was very important that I see you and I wanted to make sure you'd give me a hearing. I thought the military history device would get me in."

"I don't mind about the deception young man, lived with it all my life, in the army and after. I'm mildly interested in military history, not a fanatic though. War's uncivilised. Trouble is, a lot of people enjoy it. I like that remark by the man who *would* be a colleague of yours if you were an historian. 'War is hell, and army life is purgatory to a civilised man'. Good, that. Where did you get the idea I'd take the military history bait?"

"From Mr Jenkins out at the orphanage."

"Talked to Albie did you? Well you got the wrong end of the stick. I yarn to him about the war for his sake, not mine."

"I can see it now. You would have seen me anyway?"

"Probably. See anyone who wants to see me, might be interesting. Which brings us to your business."

He'd handled it pretty well as I guessed he'd handle most situations in his life. The woman worked away at the crossword, the cryptic, making good progress. They looked like a comfortable couple with affection flowing strongly between them. The incongruity between the house and the job he'd held for twenty-five years still puzzled me though.

"Yes, I hope you can help me," I began. "I'm investigating a family matter in Sydney. It's very confidential and complicated. There's at least one murder involved, possibly more. A lot of money too and the happiness of several people who've done nothing wrong. I believe that a young man who grew up in the orphanage here is at the centre of it. I've come over to get more information about him, to help me get on with the case in the best way."

"What sort of information?" There was still no military bark to the voice, but some of the gentleness had gone out of it. He was looking intently at me. I had his attention, his co-operation was still to be won.

"I'm not sure, almost anything, your impressions of his character for one thing. What I really want to understand is how he came to do the things he did."

"You will have a choice about how you proceed in the matter? Your subject didn't actually commit murder?"

"I believe I will have a choice. No, I'm pretty sure he didn't kill anyone and isn't directly responsible for a death."

"Very well, so far so good. You'll understand that I'm reluctant to talk loosely about the St Christopher boys. It's hard for anyone who hasn't spent a lot of time in such a place to understand what a handicap most orphans start out with. First, who are we talking about?"

"I'm sure you're right, Sir Leonard," I said. "The man I'm referring to is named Ross Haines. He's twenty-three and he spent his first fifteen or so years in the orphanage. He found out who his mother was and he's been operating at close quarters to her and her

314

family for the past few years. His grandfather, his uncle and a friend of his uncle are all dead and Haines' activities are some sort of key to their deaths, the causes. His grandfather's widow and his own mother have been harassed and assaulted, attempts have been made on their lives. Haines' motive appears to be revenge on the family that disowned him at birth, or before birth even. The family money may be a consideration, there's a lot of it, but that's a cloudy part of the affair. I'm retained by a Miss Sleeman, Haines' grandfather's widow, a second wife. I have the backing of Haines' mother, but she doesn't know about her son's involvement. It's very delicate as I said. A lot of people have been hurt and some more will be, that's inevitable. My client is in hospital, she was assaulted and tortured. I can show you a letter which establishes my standing with my client. Apart from that and my professional documents, you'll have to take me on faith."

I handed the letter and my licence across to him and he studied them closely for a minute or so. His wife had finished the crossword and was listening intently. Cavendish looked up.

"Don't you like tea?" he said.

"No, I hate it."

He smiled and handed back the papers. "You should have said so. But never mind, you're direct enough and your eyes don't slide around all over the place. Been in the army ever?"

"Malaya."

His nod might have been approving, but remembering the quote he'd spouted before I couldn't be certain.

"I'll help you as far as I can," he said. "Have you any more to add at this point?"

"No. I'll be grateful for all you can tell me about Ross Haines. If you remember him at all."

He leaned back in his chair and let the sun strike his face. The veins were intact and the high colour was healthy. I decided that it probably came from gardening and walking rather than the bottle. He crinkled his eyes a little with the effort of memory. "I do, very well indeed," he said. "And there's a good deal to tell. Haines was in the orphanage for fifteen years or so as you say. He'd been adopted after birth but the parents parted within a year of taking him and he came to us. He also had a slight deformity of the shoulder. It was corrected by an operation when he was three or four, but parents want perfect children so he stayed in the orphanage. He was fostered once but the people returned him after a couple of months. He was uncontrollable. This was when he was about six or seven. He wouldn't go to school and played merry hell when he was dragged there—wild tantrums, totally negative and destructive attitudes. The couple who took him on were pretty rough, they knocked him about a bit, but I expect he gave as good as he got. After he got back to us he was changed, quiet, cooperative, worked well at school. He was very bright. A bit unnerving really, he was glad to be back at the institution."

"Did he ever give you trouble after that?"

"Yes, he did. In two ways. He was very mild and amiable, some of the others would tease him, run him ragged for days. He'd let this go on longer than you'd think flesh and blood could stand then he'd turn on them and thrash hell out of them. He was big for his age and strong. Then he'd go back into his shell."

"How often did this happen?"

"Oh, I suppose half a dozen times. He put one boy in hospital but he'd been unmercifully teased, persecuted really and had shown great restraint. It was impossible to discipline him for it. He was in the right."

"What was the other way he gave trouble?"

"It was strange. Haines was very able in his studies and he excelled in a variety of sports—beautiful cricketer, natural talent. The sporting ability is very important with these lads, get them into teams, have them travel, meet people. Builds up their confidence."

"But Haines wouldn't be in it?"

"That's so, he wouldn't play in teams outside the orphanage grounds. In home matches of football and cricket he'd score goals and runs all over the place, but he wouldn't play the away matches. Dropped him from the teams as discipline, all that, made no difference. He hated stepping outside the place, excursions were a nightmare to him, eventually we stopped taking him. He'd stay behind and read or train for some sport or other. Probably haven't made it clear: he was a great reader, read everything and he retained it. They wanted him for a television children's panel game, brains trust sort of thing, you know?"

"Yes, I think they're ghastly."

"Just so, but some children thrive on them in a way. Haines went white when it was put to him, he refused to consider it. He was violent."

"How did the suggestion come up in the first place?"

"Haines had been entering competitions in newspapers, puzzles and general knowledge things. He was an omnivorous newspaper and magazine reader, devoured the things. Won prizes all the time."

"What sort of prizes?"

"Book vouchers mostly, money too, small sums. It was banked for him. The newspaper people must have talked to the television people, same crowd I expect, and they approached us about him. Well, he reacted as I told you, he threw things, went into one of those rages that he used to display in fights. And he stopped entering competitions, never touched them again. He seemed to ease back on everything, he'd pass his subjects at school and do respectable things with the bat, but all the brilliance was gone. Sometimes it would flash out, so would the ungovernable temper,

318

it was all still there but he kept it completely under control. He could probably have got a scholarship to go on studying but he had a horror of competing. He opted to go to work at fifteen or so, gardening I think it was?"

"That's right."

"He left us when he was sixteen, he was earning a wage, boarding with a respectable family, time to go."

"Did you ever see him after he left, or hear from him?"

"Never."

"What was your relationship with him like?"

"Quite good, as far as he'd let it be. I used to nag him a bit about not trying his best, but I gave that up. He was his own man from a very early age."

"At some time he discovered who his mother was, or became convinced he knew. Could you pin-point a time when that might have happened?"

Cavendish looked across at his wife. "You remember Haines dear," he said, "can you help with this?"

She took off her gold rimmed spectacles and polished them on the sleeve of her cardigan. "Yes," she said quietly, "I believe I can." She replaced the glasses precisely. "Haines was involved in the office incident, wasn't he? About the same time as the television idea came up. He was in a state over that and his part in the affair was never clear."

I sat up, this sounded like it. "Could you please explain, office breaking . . .?"

"There was what I believe is called a sit-in at the orphanage," said Cavendish. "Some of the boys were protesting about being denied access to their personal records. They aren't permitted to see them, that's the law. Right or wrong, that's the law. Some of the older boys broke into the office, barricaded themselves in there and ransacked the filing cabinets."

"Haines was one of them?"

"No, his part in it was curious. He volunteered to act as negotiator. The boys were on hunger strike in the office. Haines went in and talked to them and they came out. He was in there for about an hour. It wasn't a popular act."

"Why not?"

"There was some talk that Haines had put the others up to it. He denied it and it was never confirmed, the accusation was put down to spite. But there were whispers. Some of the boys were eager for a fight, and the intermediary was seen as something of a spoil-sport."

"Haines could have seen a file on him when he was in the office?"

"Yes."

"What information would that carry?"

"Date and place of birth, parents' name or names if available, medical details."

"Haines' file, did that have his mother's name on it?"

"I don't know but almost certainly it would. Such records are very precise and very private."

"And a marked change in Haines' behaviour dates from this time?"

Cavendish spread his hands out on the table, there were fine white hairs across the backs and the nails were broad and strong, no nicotine stains, no tremors.

"It does, Mr Hardy. We put it down to the idea of going on television. The impact of that on him seemed more dramatic than the other affair which only lasted a couple of hours. But it could have been due to the discovery of his mother's name." Cavendish paused, then he rapped his knuckles against the table. "No, no, how stupid of me. Those records were all computer coded in the late sixties. Haines couldn't have got a name from his file, just a number. Still, that might have been enough to set him off, certainly the psychologists said he was obsessed with the parentage problem."

I leaned forward grasping at it. "Just a minute sir, two things. How could a number set him off?"

"Some of the files would have had a multiple zero number—parents unknown."

"I see. Now, Haines was examined by psychologists?"

"Yes, several times. A team from the University was working on a study of orphaned children, their

321

psychological problems and so on. They were very interested in Haines and examined him at some length. I can't remember the details, I recall one of the team telling me that Haines was positive that his people were wealthy, substantial citizens, but that's a very common complex I gather."

"Was this examination done before or after the office sit-in?"

He raised his eyes to the sky, then glanced at his wife.

"Dear?"

"After, I think," she said, "soon after."

"I really can't remember, Mr Hardy. I'd trust my wife's recollection though, steel trap mind she has."

I smiled. "I can see that," I said glancing at the blocked in crossword. "It's interesting, and fills in a lot of gaps."

"I don't know whether it will help you much though. Haines was a very complicated boy, an unusual individual in every way. I'm sorry to hear he's in trouble, but I can't say I'm surprised."

I was only half-listening now. "Oh, why's that?"

"Colossal determination combined with a very passive, yielding streak. Very odd combination, unstable elements I'd say. No, I shouldn't say that, that's what the psychologist said."

I nodded. "Were the results of this study ever published?"

"Yes," he said, "in something called *The Canadian Journal of Psychology.* I understand it's a periodical of repute. I've never read the paper, should have I suppose, but it was a full-time job running that place."

"Will you have some coffee, Mr Hardy, or a drink, it's after eleven?" Lady Cavendish obviously thought it was time to wind the show up.

"No thank you, I've taken up enough time and you've been very helpful."

There must have been an inconclusive note in my voice because Cavendish leaned forward with a quiet smile on his face.

"But you haven't finished?"

"No. You might think this impertinent, but I must ask you something else."

"Let me guess," he said. He got up and took a few springy steps across to where the lawn began, he bent down, picked up a pebble and juggled it up and down in his palm. "When we live in such style why did I spend twenty-five years running an orphanage?"

"Right," I said.

"Easy," he looked at his wife and they exchanged smiles, "we've only had this place for a couple of years and we'll only have it a couple more the way the rates are going. I inherited it from an uncle, title too, the old boy lived to ninety-six, still thought of Australia as a colony. When I left the army, Mr Hardy, the deferred pay was negligible and I had a large, bright gaggle of a family to educate. The orphanage directorship was the best thing offering. I tried to do it in an intelligent fashion, it wasn't always easy."

"I'm sure you did," I said. I got up and shook hands with them.

Cavendish flicked the pebble away, he looked sad. "You might drop me a line to let me know how it works out," he said quietly.

I said I would. They walked with me down an overgrown path beside the house and we said our goodbyes near the front verandah. I went down the path to the gate and looked around before I opened it; they'd half-turned and he had his arm down across her thin straight shoulders.

CHAPTER 27

I drove back into town and checked out of the Colonial. The Avis people took their car back and gave me enough refund money to pay for a bottle of beer and a sandwich in the airport bar. I killed the waiting time there, pouring the Cooper's ale carefully so as not to get the sediment, and pushing the crumbs of the sandwich around on my plate. I watched the sediment settle in the bottle thinking that the bits and pieces of this case were starting to settle into place, but not satisfactorily. The whole thing needed a violent shake if it was going to be resolved in the Gutteridge woman's favour. I might have to give that shake myself, but I had a feeling that it might be done for me and pretty soon.

I finished the Forsyth book just before we landed at Mascot. I settled back into a taxi seat and almost fell asleep on the ride to Glebe. I kicked an old clothes appeal and several monster sale leaflets out of the doorway and stomped through the kitchen to make some coffee. I dumped the overnight bag under the table knowing that it'd stay there for days and hating myself for it. A newsboy yelled out in the street and I went out to the gate and bought a paper. I read it while I drank the coffee—the election was still in doubt, there was an earthquake in Greece, a cricketer had his shoulder packed in ice and Dr Ian Brave was still being hunted by the police. I finished the coffee and the telephone rang. I grabbed it and got Ailsa's voice, panicky and barely coherent over the wire.

"Cliff, Cliff, thank Christ, I've been ringing for hours and minutes . . . no . . ."

"Hold it, Ailsa, hold it. Where are you?"

"Hospital. I've seen Brave."

"What!" I shouted. "Where?"

"Here, right here. I saw him when I was going to the toilet. He didn't see me, but Jesus I went cold all over. It took me a while to calm down and ring you and you weren't there!" Her voice went up to the panic level again.

"I'm just back from Adelaide. Look, when was this?"

"I don't know, I didn't know the time. Half an hour ago?"

"What was Brave doing?"

"He was leaving, but I know what he *had* been doing."

"What?"

"Seeing Susan."

I let out a breath and my mind went blank.

"Cliff, Cliff!"

I came back and muttered something into the phone. She almost screamed the thing apart.

"What are you going to do?" Her anger and fear pulled me together. I got some control into my voice, told her I was getting a gun and lots of help and that everything would be all right. She wasn't happy but she rang off after I promised to call her as soon as anything happened.

I got the Colt out of the oilskin cloth I'd wrapped it in and pushed the cloth back behind the bookshelf. I grabbed an old army jacket with deep zipped pockets and headed for the back courtyard. Before I reached the door the phone rang again.

"Sweet suffering Jesus," I shouted into it, "what?"

"Hardy, it's Tickener. I've just seen Brave."

"Shit, not again, where? No, don't tell me, at the hospital."

"Right, how did you know?"

"Never mind, how did you get on to him?"

"I've been following that black girl, you know, Pali?"

"Yeah, and . . .?"

"She came streaking out of her flat, first time she's been there in days. I picked her up in Redfern, spotted

327

the car. Then she drove to the hospital and picked up Brave. I've got them both in sight but they're going to split. He's hiring a car. Who should I stay with?"

"What else have they done?"

"She went to a bank."

"Who's holding the money?"

"He is, she handed it over to him."

"Stay with him, he's going for a fix. I know where she's going. See you." I hung up and belted out to the car. In the rear vision mirror I saw a drawn, yellowish face that looked tired and frightened.

A different black kid was playing ball against the same wall when I pulled into Haines' street. I drove around the back and saw that his car slot was occupied by a white Mini. I parked up near the end of the street beside a set of sandstone steps which led up an embankment and ended with an iron railed landing a good thirty feet up from street level. I got the jacket from the back seat of the car and the Colt from under the dashboard. I put the gun in a pocket, slung the jacket over my shoulder and went up the steps. The landing was overhung with shrubs that had rooted in the thin soil of the embankment. It was after six o'clock and the sun was just starting to sneak down to the high points of the building line. I hung the jacket on the railing, rolled and lit a cigarette and waited.

Half an hour and two cigarettes later, a red Volkswagen turned into the street. It did a circuit of the block the way I had and stopped opposite Haines' house. A girl got out. She was wearing pink slacks and shoes and had a lacey, fringed poncho affair over her shoulders. From where I was crouched I could see that her skin was the colour of polished teak and the inky frizz of her wig stood out a foot from her head. I started down the steps as she went through the front gate. I stumbled on a step and my jacket hit the metal rail with a terrific clang. I swore and crouched down but the sound hadn't carried far enough to alarm Naumeta Pali. I crossed the street and went up the side of the house to the back stairs that led up to Haines' door. I heard the door close above me and climbed the stairs quietly taking two at a time. I heard the sound of voices in the flat and then the ringing click of a telephone being lifted. The girl spoke again but what she said was inaudible. I pressed up close to the wall beside the door and tucked my ear into the doorframe. The receiver banged down and I heard the girl speak in her smoky, French accented voice.

"Come on, Rossy," she purred, "we're going to the mountains."

I took the steps four at a time on the way down.

I was down behind a car parked twenty feet away from the Volkswagen when they came out. Haines was walking a little ahead of the girl with his hands in the front pockets of a windcheater jacket. Pali had her arms under her cloak but from the way it bulged out about waist high it was obvious that she was holding a gun on him.

There were a few people in the street but she ignored them. She walked Haines to the driver's door and said something to him, emphasising the words by moving her hands under the poncho. Haines opened the door and got in, another gesture from the girl and he buckled on the seat belt. She moved around the front of the car with the gun held up chest high and levelled at Haines' head through the windscreen. She'd handled a gun before. She opened the passenger door and got in. She sat slightly swivelled round. I heard the engine kick and saw a puff of smoke from the exhaust. The car started off in a series of kangaroo hops. Haines was nervous and who could blame him? I kept low and under the protection of other cars as much as possible and ducked and swerved my way back to the Falcon. I slung the jacket into the front seat, started the engine and was moving up the alley in time to see the VW making a right turn out of the street into the main road.

The mountains were probably the Blue Mountains which meant that we had a couple of hours driving ahead of us. The route the VW took along the roads in this part of the city seemed to confirm that destination. I had plenty of gas and plenty of gun, I should have felt reasonably confident but I didn't. Pali's phone call from Haines' flat nagged at me like a hangnail. I supposed it was to Brave and it was reasonable to assume that he was coming to the party too. I was covered there to some extent, by Tickener, but I couldn't be sure that the reporter would be able to control the junkie psychologist in a tight spot. Then again, Brave and Pali could have agreed on the meeting beforehand and the phone call could have been to a third party who I didn't have covered at all. I couldn't call for police help unless the VW stopped and even then my story was thin and only Grant Evans could help me. I didn't even know if he was back from his enforced leave.

This potentially dangerous loose end kept worrying and distracting me as I drove so that I almost lost the Volkswagen at a three way junction. I pulled myself together and concentrated on keeping back and varying my lanes and position among the other cars in the traffic stream. Haines was driving better now, quite fast and tight and making good use of the gears. We hit the Katoomba road as the last flickers of daylight died in the trees beside the highway.

The easy time to tail cars is at dusk and later. There's not much possibility of them spotting you or of you losing them if you stay alert, but there is a kind of lulling feeling about it which introduces the chance that you might ram your subject up the back number plate while in a hypnotic trance. I fought this feeling as I trailed up the hills and coasted down the "use low gear" grades. The traffic thinned after Penrith but there

331

was enough of it to provide cover and the winding road and glaring oncoming headlights demanded concentration. We passed through Katoomba after eight o'clock; the real estate agents had closed so half of the town's business was under wraps, only the usual pinball places and take-away-food shops kept the neon going in the streets. The pubs emitted a soft, alluring light through the lead-glass windows which reminded me that I hadn't had a drink in hours and was heading away from sources of it fast.

After Katoomba it got harder. There was a little chopping and changing on the highway as cars peeled off to houses in the hills whence their occupants commuted to Sydney at the risk of their sanity. I'd taken a fix on the peculiarity of the VW's tail light which was a bit brighter on the right side than on the left and I clung to it like a mariner to a beacon. I had my doubts about it twice, once after oncoming lights on high beam dazzled me, and again when a lighter coloured Volkswagen surged up in the right hand lane to pass everything in sight and I started to go with it. A truck coming round a bend lit it up as a grey or light blue job and I slipped back and picked up Haines and Pali who weren't doing anything so fancy.

They pottered uncertainly along in the left lane for a while and I had no choice but to dribble along behind them. Cars sped past us and I was starting to feel conspicuous when the VW's left indicator flashed and the car shot off up a steep road that left the highway at a forty-five degree angle. I looked quickly in the rear vision mirror. There was no one behind me so I didn't touch the indicator arm, I just slammed the Falcon down into second, killed the lights and took the turn praying that the road didn't fork three ways or end in a ditch. The lights ahead bobbed and danced in front of me; the road was rutted and lumpy and the Falcon's springs and shockers took a beating as I ground along in second. At one point the road moved back close to the highway except that we were now above it. Cars scuttled along below like phosphorescent ants beating a path to and from their nest.

We were driving through thickly timbered country, still climbing steeply and following wide, looping bends to left and right. The nearly full moon sailed clear of the clouds and illuminated the classic Blue Mountains landscape—tall, arrow-like gums and sheer-faced ridges that had defeated a score of explorers until Blaxland, Lawson and Wentworth had brought a little imagination to the job. The moonlight gave me a look at the road and allowed me to give the other car a bit more leeway. It also increased the risk of being spotted because moonlight can gleam on chrome like sunlight on a steel mirror. Fortunately, the Falcon's chrome was rusted and dull. Then the Volkswagen disappeared. I hit my brakes and pulled up well back from where I'd last seen the lights. If I'd spotted someone tailing me up there in the mountains I'd kill my lights and engine and coast down a bit waiting for the bastard to come blundering through. I had to assume something like that was happening now, at least until I proved otherwise. I turned off the interior light switch that operates when the door is opened, slipped my arms into the service jacket and eased open the driver's door. I dropped out and rolled under the car. Nothing happened so I worked my way back to the wheels, got my feet under me and scooted across to the other side of the road.

People expect other people to get carefully out of cars on the non-traffic side and keep to that side of the road, sometimes people have to break that rule or they get dead. I hunkered down in the grass and scrub beside the road and peered into the blackness ahead of me. Nothing to be seen, but that didn't mean a thing. I took the pistol out and crept forward with it held stiffly in front of me; still nothing visible and not a sound except my breathing and soft scuffling in the bush where some species were doing their best to exterminate others. Very sensitive stuff, I thought, totally in tune with the environment, Hardy. But a waste of talent. Where I'd seen the last flash of the car's lights was a dirt track running off into the scrub. The grass in the middle had been scythed down between the wheel ruts by the underside of cars and back from the road was a tree with the word HAINES painted vertically down it in white.

My flashlight was at home, corroded to blazes, and the moon had decided to play it coy among the clouds. It was close to pitch black when I started up the track to what was evidently Haines' weekender. Judging by the distance from the road to the shack and trying to remember when I'd last seen a house light, it was a fair sized block. The house wasn't much, a fibro and galvanised iron structure with decking around it on three sides. It looked self-built, but Haines had put his main stamp on the place in the garden. When my eyes got used to the dark I could see terraced vegetable beds and trellises with tendrils twining through them. Almost outside the door, hanging over the decking was a huge clump of bamboo, the leaf tips tall and waving just slightly in the night breeze. Water from the roof, a few chickens and a still out the back and the place would be self-sufficient.

I picked my way carefully through the vegetable beds and staked plants and did a circuit of the shack. It had a door in front, one at the back and a single window in each side. The track from the road came up and looped around the house, the Volkswagen was parked on this path at the back. A brick path from the back door led to a fibro dunny and there was a lean-to shed holding what felt like garden tools. An axe was embedded in a chopping block outside the shed. The wood pile was healthy, a big stack of the kind you use in a stove or sealed heater. I crept up to the decking out

335

from the left side window and tested it with my foot. It was solidly built and didn't creak. I eased the Colt back out of my pocket and moved over the boards to the window which was about chest height from the deck level, too low to stand, too high to kneel. I crouched and inched my head up to get half an eyeball's worth of look-in.

CHAPTER 28

The room I saw was the whole of the shack. It had a sink at one end flanked by a refrigerator and a small stove. There was seagrass matting on the floor. The girl was sitting in one of the two Chinese saucer chairs and Haines was sitting on the bed which looked like a pile of mattresses, maybe three, with a tartan blanket over them. I couldn't see a telephone so Pali hadn't set anything up here. The girl was nervous and Haines was frightened, they sat like figures in a painting that couldn't move a muscle until the end of time. Haines' mouth moved but I couldn't catch what he said. The girl got up and moved smoothly across the room like a classy featherweight. She slammed Haines in the face with the gun and hit him again across the hands when he brought them up to shield his eyes. Haines collapsed on the bed and the girl moved back and half-turned away from him. From where I was I could see Haines fumbling behind the mattresses. There seemed like a good chance he was going for a gun and it was time to move if I wanted anybody left to talk to. I smashed the window in with the Colt barrel and made it to the door in two strides. I kicked it in and was inside the room while Haines and the girl were still interested in the broken glass. Haines had a gun in his hands but it was still tangled in the blanket. He'd never have made it. I pointed the Colt at the bridge of the girl's broad, flaring nose.

"Put the guns down," I said harshly.

Haines gave up the struggle with the blanket but the girl held on to her gun. She held it loosely, pointed nowhere in particular. She looked dazed, out of touch with what was happening, but dangerous. I raised my gun to send a bullet over her head and pulled the trigger. It stuck like a wrong key in a lock and I remembered the clang my jacket had made when it hit the iron railing. I threw the gun at her but I was way too slow, she ducked slightly and brought her pistol up so that the bullet would hit me in the throat.

A thin, high voice shouted my name. I swayed out of Pali's line of fire and she snapped at the trigger as a man appeared in the doorway. The bullet hit him in the eye and he screamed, blood welling out over his face. His hands scrabbled at the broken door jamb but couldn't get hold, he staggered back over the deck and there was a thrashing, snapping noise as he collapsed into the stand of bamboo. The girl stood still, in shock, with her eyes staring, seeing nothing. I took the gun from her and pushed her down into a chair. Haines had blood dribbling down the side of his face from where Pali had hit him and he didn't look like giving trouble. I heard a rustling outside.

"Tickener?"

"Yeah, you all right Hardy?'

"I'm fine, come in."

He came in cautiously through the shattered door. He was even paler than when I'd first seen him and he was shaking as if he needed a drink, a cigarette and a cup of coffee all at the same time. Me standing there with my hands full of guns didn't help his nerves.

"Couldn't you put them down?" he said.

"I will, just for you." I put the pistols on a ledge above the window. I bent down and retrieved my Colt, I freed the action and put it in my pocket. "Thanks Harry, this one was going to shoot me when you sang out." I pointed at the girl who was sitting stiffly in the chair with her knees drawn up.

"So was Brave," Tickener said, "there's some kind of pistol out on the boards. Shit, you can't move for guns around here."

"Is Brave dead?"

"Very."

"You had no trouble keeping up with him?"

339

"Not much, he went for a fix like you said, then straight up here."

"It was quite a procession," I said.

"I know a bit about the girl," Tickener said. "Who's he?"

"Name's Haines—bomber, gunman, hit and run merchant."

Haines snapped out of it and looked across at me.

"What the hell are you talking about? I'm none of those things."

"What about sending anonymous letters, that more in your line? Harassing women?"

He answered slowly, taking the difference in tone and content of my words seriously. "Yes, I've done those things. I had reasons."

"I know you did. What about blackmail? What about Mark Gutteridge's files?"

He looked away and clamped his lips and jaw as if trying to give himself strength of character.

"Look boy," I said sharply, "you've lost control of this. You must be able to see that. This bitch was going to kill you, or at least she wasn't going to cry if it worked out that way."

Haines looked across at Pali, she was still striving for the foetal position and not making it. Her hands were twisted in the strings of the poncho and she was looking intently at the knots and poking her fingers through the holes. I handed Haines a tissue from a box

340

on the floor which had been heavily trampled in the last few minutes. He dabbed at the cut on his face.

"I've got the files," he said slowly. "I didn't use them much, I got some money and I kept my word."

"Who did you squeeze?" Tickener asked.

"Who're you?" said Haines.

"Keep quiet, Harry," I said. "It's all right, Haines, this is all between us, it doesn't go any further. My job is to protect Ailsa and your mother, that's what I'm interested in. I'm not playing God."

"You know." His head jerked up. "How could you?"

"I put it together. You tell me if I'm right. You were hung up on the idea of your family background, you couldn't accept that you were a pleb. You read all the papers and the magazines, you saw pictures of Mark Gutteridge and saw the resemblance. You found out that Gutteridge had a daughter and that she was in Adelaide when you were born, I don't know how you did that, but you concluded that she was your mother and you decided to destroy the Gutteridges."

"That's pretty close," Haines said softly. "I got a picture of her and showed it around the hospitals. I didn't get a positive identification but a few people were pretty sure."

"You got something out of the orphanage file then?"

He looked surprised. "You know a lot don't you? Yes, I worked out that I was born at a hospital, I cracked that code, the rest was easy. You're wrong when you say I wanted to destroy them though. Not at first, I wanted them to, to . . ."

"Accept you?"

"Yes. I tried, he refused to listen. I found out things about his son. I told him."

"Did you kill him?"

"No, I didn't! He killed himself I think, I don't know. I still don't know why he treated me like that. He beat me up." He lifted his hands to the fine scars on his face and fingered his off-centre nose. "I found him dead. I got the files though."

"I don't like to interrupt," Tickener said nervously, "but I don't understand any of this, and there's a dead man outside."

"That's all right, Harry," I said. "You should stick around and learn something and he's not going anywhere."

"I suppose not." Tickener dropped into a saucer chair and I sat on the bed beside Haines. "Is there anything to drink?" he asked. I looked at Haines who nodded at a cupboard over the sink. Tickener went across, opened it and pulled down a bottle of Cutty Sark. He took four glasses from the draining rack on the sink and poured solid slugs into them. He brought them over, I accepted one, so did Haines and in one smooth, snakey movement Pali knocked the one he held out to her to the floor. Tickener shrugged.

"Your loss, Miss," he said.

I took a pull at the whisky. It was good but it burned my dry throat and didn't help a slight headache that was ticking away inside my skull. It was a bad way to feel when there were some sharp distinctions to be made. I rolled a cigarette and accepted a light from Tickener who lit up one of his stinking tailor-mades. Haines refused his offer of a cigarette and Pali didn't even acknowledge it. She was starting to take an interest in proceedings again though. I drew a breath and started in again.

"What happened after Mark Gutteridge died?"

"I hid the files." Haines took a sip of the whisky and nearly choked on it. He coughed and snorted into a tissue. Pali gave him a look of contempt and reached out her hand to Tickener.

"Cigarette please."

Her voice startled him but he obliged her fairly smoothly. She leaned back in the chair and crossed her legs, the pink denim stretched tight over her thighs and her breasts lifted under the cloak as she lifted the ciga-rette to her lips.

"Go on, boy," she said, "this is damn interesting."

Haines made a better job of his next go at the Scotch. "I sat it out for a while. I hid the files, I could see what they were worth. I did some night classes,

343

I got a job at Sleeman's. I formed a relationship with Ailsa. I thought I could bankrupt her without any trouble. I used to watch Susan Gutteridge, I hated her and I wanted her dead. She looked very ill most of the time anyway."

"Yeah, that was Bryn's work, Brave's too maybe. You remember Brave, from Adelaide?"

"No."

"You should. He was the psychologist you spilled the beans to in the orphanage. He's been working the other side of the street."

He got that genuine puzzled look again. "What do you mean?"

"Never mind, go on."

"I got some money from the politicians and lawyers, and a couple of policemen; I bought this place. I kept on at Susan Gutteridge, but I wasn't sure what I wanted to do anymore."

"I was!" Pali's voice was like snakeskin rippling through your fingers, beautiful and repellent.

"Shut up you!" I snapped. "You'll get your turn." I looked at Haines. "Do you see it?" I said. "You told Ian Brave about your suspicions that you were a Gutteridge. You did some work on it and squeezed Mark Gutteridge. Brave also had something else on him that concerns you. He had information from Ailsa as well. Maybe he killed Gutteridge, maybe not, we'll never know. That is, if you're telling the truth and you didn't kill him."

344

"I didn't," said Haines, "I wanted to but I didn't."

"I believe you, well, anyway, Brave misses out on the files. He doesn't know you're around, you've got a beard and keep a low profile. Ailsa he can't approach because he's lost an old hold he had on her but she doesn't seem to fit the bill. He suspects Susan, so does Bryn and they go to work on her. Brave turns up with this one." I nodded at Pali. "She's got political axes to grind, Ailsa and Susan have business interests in her country and Australia didn't do much about the French atom tests. Right?"

Pali sneered at me and blew smoke at the ceiling.

"OK," I went on, "I put it together this way: Bryn didn't know about you Pali, and you started going it alone, making the heavy phone calls and so on. You fell out with Brave and he fell out with Bryn. Bryn panicked a bit, people Haines was squeezing started putting pressure on him. He called me in. Brave went right off, he killed Bryn's boyfriend. Pali blows the whistle on Brave when she finds out he's into mad sidelines like sheltering escaped crims. We raid Brave and he's out of the picture for a while. Bryn goes on the rampage and finishes up dead. Then Brave gets a real line on Haines and the files and he and Pali get back again for one last fling. That brings us all here folks."

"What was all that stuff about bombing?" asked Tickener.

"Ailsa Sleeman's car got bombed and Susan Gutteridge was run down," I replied. "At first I thought it had to be someone working in with Haines or Brave, now it looks as if it was his bird on her own hook. That right?"

There was no getting under her skin. She turned to look at me, her face was beautifully boned and every fold and curve of her skin added up to the sort of beauty you don't often see. She knew it too and her cool smile infuriated me.

"Listen you savage," I said violently, "you might think you're Angela Davis, but you're just another homicidal mess to me." I ticked off the points with a forefinger across the palm of my hand. "One, I've got a gun with your fingerprints on it, that gun killed a man here tonight; two, your car will have signs on it of your running down Susan Gutteridge; three, I've traced where you got the materials for the bomb. You're gone a million girlie, you're in prison or deported if I tell what I know. You might leave Australia under your own steam if you co-operate now."

It didn't touch her, she was a fanatic. She blew more smoke.

"Since this is all so civilised among you nice white people," she said evenly, "could I have that drink now?"

Tickener picked up the glass and poured a generous dose, at a gesture from me he passed the bottle over

346

and we had a little more all round. The girl tossed the whisky off and held out her glass for more, Tickener poured and she sipped a toothful. She looked at me and her mouth split open in a wide, bitter grin.

"If it does your ego any good Hardy, you're pretty right in what you've said. Australian capital is screwing New Caledonia and those bitches you're protecting are up to their twats in it." She let the grin down into the glass for a second and when she looked up her face was a mask, vaguely triumphant and hard as flint. "Australia doesn't care about the nuclear tests as long as the shit comes down on our dirty black hides and not yours."

"Spare us the rave. You're a killer, you can't criticise anyone."

It was a pathetic response, she knew it and I knew it.

"But you'll let me go Hardy," she said softly. "You're a liberal, soft as butter, you haven't got the guts to do anything else. You probably half agree with me."

"You might be right," I said wearily. "Anyway you're not important. It suits me to have you on a plane to New Caledonia tomorrow and that suits you too. You're on your way."

"Jesus, Hardy!" Tickener was up out of his chair spilling his drink down his shirt. "You can't just turn her loose. She killed a man tonight. I don't have a bloody clue what's going on. Look at her, I'm not sure she should be allowed out on her own, she looks like she'd cut off your feet and eat them."

I laughed. "She'll go like a lamb Harry." I picked the bottle up and poured him another drink. "You've got all you need, you can break the Brave story once and for all, final chapter, in about two hours. I'll phone the cops and your story only needs a few touches to it."

"Yeah, like who killed Brave?"

"That's easy, we don't know. I'll phone in that he's dead, I won't identify myself, the cops will think it's a spin-off from the Costello thing. That's easily fixed. You get an anonymous tip. It's simple."

Tickener scratched his chin. "That puts you and me in very deep. Three people know what really happened. You're clean, why not let it all come out the way it really was?"

"I'm protecting my client," I said. "This way no one gets hurt, no injustice is perpetrated. Do you really think most situations like this get properly aired and resolved down to the last detail? Come on, Harry."

"I guess not. OK, have it your way. What about them?" He pointed to Haines and the girl.

"She's leaving the country tomorrow."

All eyes swung to Haines. He was finishing his drink, his face was white and his big body looked light and fragile. I was reminded of Cavendish's description

348

of him as passive, given to violent outbursts. There didn't seem to be an outburst left in him.

"What about him?" said Tickener.

I looked at Haines again and something clicked in my mind and I felt sorrier for him than I've ever felt for anyone in my life, except myself.

"No worries there," I said softly, "I've just worked the last little piece into place. He'll do whatever I say because I can tell him what he's needed to know all his life."

Haines looked up at me with complete under-standing. He'd lived for twenty-odd years for just the moment that was coming and nothing was ever going to be the same for him after it had passed. It was going to be a kind of death.

CHAPTER 29

I washed up the glasses and put the liquor away, then I went around retrieving things like used tissues and cigarette ends. I got Haines to drive the VW around the track a few times and had Tickener bring up my car, his, and the hire car Brave had arrived in. We drove them round and by the time we'd finished the track was criss-crossed with tyre marks and skids that no one could make any sense of. I wiped the hire car, a Valiant, clean and left it parked halfway up the track from the road. Pali and Haines did most of the watching, Tickener and I did most of the work. When we'd finished we all congregated, by chance, around the body of Dr Ian Brave. He lay on his back, fully stretched out, with broken bamboo stems jutting up all around him and pushing through his clothes. He was inelegant and lumpy in death, he looked like an old, collapsed scarecrow. One eye looked sightlessly up to the clouds, the other was a dark horror; one half of his face was a smooth, chalky white, the other was crumpled and stained dark—it was a map of heaven and hell. Pali looked down at him and I thought I saw a nerve jump in her ebony mask.

"How did you fall in with him?" I asked gently. She responded to the tone of the question by making a keening movement of her head. She ran her right palm down the inside of her left forearm.

"Drugs," she said.

I nodded and turned away. I didn't touch Brave and cautioned the others to keep well clear. I left the gun where it was. A few footprints wouldn't matter. The cops would figure it the easiest way for them, but there was no point in leaving clues about which might set them doubting. Haines was off in some private world of his own. He sat on the edge of the deck picking at his fingers and only came to life when Tickener suggested firing the shack.

"Why would you want to do that?" he asked nervously.

"To confuse things, cover the tracks a bit more," Tickener said.

"You're ruthless," Haines said shaking his head, "ruthless."

I laughed. "Don't listen to him, Ross," I said, "he'd just like to have a fire to spice up his story a bit."

Tickener grinned and lit a cigarette. "It's not a bad idea," he said. "And speaking of stories, how do I write it just from an anonymous tip-off? Where's the journalistic thoroughness of investigation, not to mention integrity?"

"Where it usually is," I said. "Listen Harry, you're learning fast but you've got a long way to go. You listen to the police radio, they'll send a car, the car will call for an ambulance, you'll get some details that way, not many. Your story is that this confirmed the tip-off, you took the plunge—journalistic flair and derring-do."

"It sounds shaky," he said doubtfully.

"It'll do," I said, "happens all the time. By the way, how's Joe Barrett these days?"

"Not so good," he said happily.

I went back into the shack for a last look around. I collected the guns and took a minute to examine Haines' little .32.

"Have you got a licence for this?" I asked him.

"Yes."

"How come?"

"Company executives who sometimes carry large sums of money can get pistol licences."

I tossed it to him and he caught it. "You shouldn't have it up here though," I said, "better shift it. It might get some cop's mind working, miracles do happen."

He put the gun in the pocket of his windcheater, he was as docile as an old, pampered dog.

352

"OK Ross," I said, "you've been a good boy so far, let's see if you can keep it up. Where are the files?"

He hesitated for just a second, he looked at Tickener who had on his bloodhound face and Pali who was immobile, uninterested. He raised his eyes to mine and if I looked as old and empty and comfortless as I felt it must have been like the last gaze into the mirror before you cut your throat.

"I'll show you." His voice was a hoarse, thin whisper. He went across to the food storing and cooking end of the room and knelt down. He peeled up the sea-grass and prised up three lengths of floorboard with his fingernails. It was a hiding place that an experienced man would have located within five minutes, but Ross was one of life's amateurs and nothing I'd seen of him so far suggested that he'd ever become a pro. He reached into the gap and pulled out a medium sized executive briefcase. It was black with lots of shiny metal trim.

"Let's have it," I said. "And put the boards and mat back."

I snapped open the lid, it wasn't even locked, and took a quick look at the contents. The case was full of letters, bank statements and sheets of paper with what looked like bank note serial numbers written on them. Some of the material was in original, some in photostat. There were half a dozen cassette tapes and an envelope full of photographs. I rifled through the

353

stuff. It was a complete blackmailer's kit with applications for development permits neatly stapled to notes about sums of money and times and places of delivery. There were different versions of subdivision plans with names of surveyors and others entered on the back along with information about money paid. There were several newspaper extracts from court proceedings with the names of police witnesses underlined and code numbers entered in the margins; typed lists of the names of municipal councillors had similar entries alongside as many names as not. The numbers bore some relation to digits written on the faces of the cassettes. Handled right it was a meal ticket for life and the only thing that surprised me was the relatively small bulk of it. Mark Gutteridge had been in business a long time and if this was his game he should have collected more dope than was here.

"Is this all?" I asked Haines.

"Yes, I gave the people I contacted the material that affected them. There must originally have been about this much again."

"How much money did you raise?"

"About twenty-five thousand dollars."

I groaned and sat down on the bed. "You must have driven them crazy," I said, "you said you marked some of the cops?"

"Yes, three, the really bad ones, they . . ."

"Spare me. You hit them for a thousand or so?"

"That's right, roughly."

"A fortnight's takings, a month when things are slack. No wonder there was flurry from on high, they wouldn't understand it. You were dead safe in a way. No copies?"

"No."

"Of course not, wouldn't be fair would it?"

"No."

"You're an idiot." I snapped the case shut and got to my feet.

"Hey can I have a look?" said Tickener.

I fended him off. "Harry this is too hot to handle, I can't let you have it."

"What are you going to do with it?" There was pain in his voice and I remembered that he'd saved my life.

"Tell you what I'll do mate, I'll look through it, get out a crumb that won't be traceable necessarily to this little box of goodies and give it to you. You can use it one quiet Wednesday when nothing's happening."

"What about the rest of it?"

"Burn it and let the bastards sweat."

We went out to the cars. I got in the Falcon and motioned for Pali to sit alongside me. She did it, like a sleepwalker. Haines drove the VW. I locked the briefcase into a compartment under the driver's seat. Tickener followed us along the track in his ancient Holden and we bumped down the road back to the highway. We drove to Katoomba like beads on a string with a set gap between us. I signalled a stop and went into a telephone booth for four minutes. It wasn't a NIDA performance but it was good enough to set the wheels in motion. I walked back to Tickener's car to check a few details of the story with him. We shook hands and agreed to meet soon for a drink. He pulled the Holden out and set off for his typewriter and coffee. It was midnight. We drove back to Sydney; Haines and the girl changed places at Central Railway and she drove off without a word.

I drove to Glebe, took Haines into the house and made some coffee. We talked around it a bit and confusion was the keystone of his attitude. He was a bit in love with Ailsa but too screwed up to know it. Any mention of his mother was like drawing a toenail. He was like a man with every layer of skin off except the last, tender to the touch at a hundred points, bleeding here and there where his obsession obtruded and teetering on a terrible abyss of pain. What I had to tell him pushed him over the edge and he fell, screaming silently inside his lonely, alien shell.

After that we sat quietly for a while drinking the last of the coffee. I called a taxi and he went back to what he had to call home.

CHAPTER 30

I crawled out of bed around 10 am. It was one of those bright, cool summer mornings that Sydney specialises in. I made coffee, got the paper in and read it out in the courtyard. Tickener had made the front page again with his account of the discovery of Brave's body. There were no pictures. Haines was mentioned as the owner of the property and I spared him a thought for the yarn he'd have to spin to the police, but we'd worked out an alibi—a phone conversation with his employer which I'd have to confirm with Ailsa today—in case he needed one. My guess was that he wouldn't. The cops had no reason to disbelieve that Haines' place had been picked at random for the revenge killing of Brave and no reason to connect Brave to Haines beyond the Gutteridge connection. I didn't think they'd be very interested in probing that.

I went inside and phoned Ailsa. She sounded well and I told her I'd be in that afternoon.

"Is it over Cliff?" she said.

"It's over."

"Is it all right?"

"It's all right for you."

"And Susan?"

"It'll never be all right for her. I'll tell you all about it this afternoon love, be patient."

"Not my strong suit as they say in the books."

I asked her if the police had approached her and she said they hadn't. I asked her to confirm Haines' alibi and she said she would, but she never had to. I rang off and went back to the paper and another cup of coffee.

Tickener shared the front page with the latest cricket win. That seemed to call for a modest salutation. I hauled the wine and soda and ice out of the fridge, made a bacon sandwich and set myself up out in the yard. The biscuit factory was just tingeing the air with butterscotch.

I got the briefcase out of the car. I scrabbled about for some kindling and paper and stuffed it into the barbecue I'd built out of bricks pinched from here and there at dead of night. I poured a glass of wine and opened the case. After thumbing through the papers for a while I selected and set aside a newspaper clipping, a typed sheet and a photostat of a land title deed. The remainder of the papers I fed into the fire. I put the cassettes across the top of the grill and watched them melt like chocolate. The smell in the air was of plastic, laminated paper and corruption. I drank some wine, ate the sandwich and watched the thin, dark smoke from the fire threaten the unsullied purity of Soames' whitewashed wall. The Gutteridge files were a heap of fine ashes interspersed with blobs of molten plastic when the fire died down. I pushed them about to make sure of the completeness of the destruction and slung the briefcase back into the car.

After a shave and a shower I went out and drew another hundred dollars with the credit card. I drove over to Paddington and rambled through the shops, eventually coming out with a djellaba in blue and white vertical stripes with a hood and drawstrings at the cuffs. I had lunch in a pub and drove over to the hospital.

Ailsa was sitting in a chair beside the bed. She was wearing a long, off-white calico nightgown cut square around the neck. I went up and kissed her on the mouth and then in each of the hollows of her shoulder bones. She smelled of roses.

"You look good, you smell good, you feel good."

She put her arms up around my neck.

"More," she said.

"You're the queen of the world."

I gave her the parcel, she unwrapped it and smoothed the robe out on the bed. She immediately began fiddling with the drawstrings.

She looked up at me. "It's lovely," she said. "Now tell me about it."

I gave her all the details, it took a long time and she listened quietly, tracing patterns in the raised nap of the robe on the bed.

"What was the black girl's motive?" she asked when I finished.

"Partly political. She's some kind of nationalist, anti-British, anti-French, anti-Australian. Anti just about every bloody thing. You have interests in Noumea?"

She nodded.

"So has Susan I suspect. Your people must be stepping on toes over there, maybe it's a genuine grievance, I don't know. Anyway, she was here for a little private terrorism. But Brave got hold of her, something to do with drugs. Brave was an addict. Did you know that?"

"No. I'll have to look into that."

"The Noumea operation?"

"Yes." She drew a deep breath and expelled it slowly. "Well, Mark started it all I suppose by keeping the files. There are a lot of casualties. What about the survivors? What did you mean about Susan never being right again?"

"That connects back to Ross," I said.

"Obviously, what about him?"

I got up off the bed and moved around the room.

360

I picked up one of her books and smiled at the dog ears at fifty page intervals.

"Don't start pacing again Cliff or I'll bloody kill you. No, I just won't pay you. Just tell me about it."

I sat down again. "I was on the wrong track about him for a long time. I thought he was obsessed by his mother, he wasn't. I was misled by the photographs he had. He was hung up about his father. Natural I suppose."

"Yes, yes," she said impatiently, "well, do you know who his father is?"

"Was. Yes, I worked it out eventually."

"How? Who?"

"How first. It was the only thing that fitted. Mark Gutteridge sent Susan away to Adelaide to have her child. OK, he wanted to spare her and everyone else the teenage pregnancy trauma. Fair enough. But a tremendous change in the nervous pattern of the Gutteridges dates from then. It manifests itself in different ways and they never get over it. That's the first point. Secondly, Mark Gutteridge wasn't a conventional man. He shouldn't have been horrified when his illegitimate grandson turned up with proof of his identity. He'd be more likely to be intrigued, inclined to do something for the boy, like a Renaissance prince, right?"

"Yes, I think so."

"But he doesn't. He flips. He can't handle it and that sets Ross off."

361

"All right, that's a lot of how. Now, *who* was Ross' father?"

"Bryn," I said.

I sat on the bed and Ailsa rested her head against my thigh and we watched the day dying slowly outside the open window. An ascending jet littered the sky with dirty brown smoke, its boom drowned out something Ailsa murmured and I stroked her hair in reply. Maybe she was thinking about Mark Gutteridge, maybe about the children she'd never have. I was thinking about raw, haunted people who twanged the nerves of everyone they touched—like Bryn, like Haines, like Cyn. They couldn't sloop along in the shallows where the water was warm and the breeze soft, they had to jut up into spray and icy winds with their secrets for sails and the rocks dead ahead.

Text Classics

For reading group notes visit textclassics.com.au